GW00372337

Fran O'Brien and Arthur McGuinness
established McGuinness Books
to publish Fran's novels to raise funds
for LauraLynn Children's Hospice.

Fran's fourteen novels, *The Married Woman,*
The Liberated Woman, The Passionate Woman,
Odds on Love, Who is Faye? The Red Carpet,
Fairfields, The Pact, 1916, Love of her Life,
Rose Cottage Years, Ballystrand, Vorlane Hall,
and *The Big Red Velvet Couch* have raised over
€650,000.00 in sales and donations
for LauraLynn House.

Fran and Arthur hope that *A Spanish Family*
will raise even more funds for LauraLynn.

www.franobrien.net

Also by Fran O'Brien

The Married Woman
The Liberated Woman
The Passionate Woman
Odds on Love
Who is Faye?
The Red Carpet
Fairfields
The Pact
1916
Love of her Life
Rose Cottage Years
Ballystrand
Vorlane Hall
The Big Red Velvet Couch

Buy now online www.franobrien.net

A SPANISH FAMILY

FRAN O'BRIEN

McGuinness Books

McGuinness Books

A SPANISH FAMILY

Published by McGuinness Books,
15 Glenvara Park, Ballycullen Road,
Templeogue, Dublin 16 RR71.

A catalogue record for this book
is available from the British Library.

ISBN 978-0-9954698-8-4

Typeset by Martone Design & Print,
Celbridge Industrial Estate, Celbridge, Co. Kildare.

Printed and bound in Great Britain by
CPI Group (UK) Ltd, Croydon, CR04YY.

www.franobrien.net

This novel is dedicated to Jane and Brendan McKenna
and in memory of their daughters Laura and Lynn.
And for all our family and friends who support our
efforts to raise funds for LauraLynn Children's Hospice,
Leopardstown Road, Dublin 18.

Jane and Brendan have been through every parent's worst
nightmare – the tragic loss of their only daughters.

Laura died, just four years old, following surgery to repair a
heart defect. Her big sister, Lynn, died aged fifteen, less than
two years later, having lost her battle against Leukaemia –
diagnosed on the day of Laura's surgery.

Having dealt personally with such serious illness, Jane and
Brendan's one wish was to establish a children's
hospice in memory of their girls.

Now LauraLynn House has become a reality,
and their dream has come true.

LauraLynn Children's Hospice offers community
Based paediatric palliative, respite, end-of-life care,
and the LauraLynn@home Programme.

At LauraLynn House there is an eight-bed unit, a residential
unit for families, support and comfort for parents and siblings
for whom life can be extremely difficult.

Putting Life into a Child's Day
Not Days into a Child's Life.

Chapter One

Jerez de la Frontera – the sign flashed into view. Alva stood among the crowd of other passengers waiting close to the door of the train. Here at last, she thought. She was tired after the flight from Dublin to Spain and then having had to stand for the journey from Seville as the train was packed with a mix of people, mostly Spanish, with occasional American, Asian, and other foreign voices, everyone lugging very large oversized suitcases. She held tight on to her own trolley bag hoping that it wouldn't slide along the floor as the train began to slow down. She could see the sun shining and was looking forward to feeling its warmth when she stepped outside. While it was still the end of February, she had checked the weather forecast and it had shown that for the next couple of weeks it looked very promising with day after day of sunshine. Coming from Ireland at this time of the year it was lovely to escape the damp and cold she had left behind.

Now there was a mad rush to climb down the steep steps of the train and Alva made her way through the crowd hurrying along the platform. She was exhilarated. Looking forward to spending time in this city. The railway station was beautiful, built with Moorish red brick and blue ceramic tiles in a design of archways in the Mudejar style.

Usually, her brother David handled their clients in Spain, but as he was exceptionally busy in the office, she had come to Jerez to discuss the business of Purtell Vintners, the wine company their family had run in Ireland for many years. They were a company expert in the buying and distribution of wines and sherries from Andalusia in Spain and French wines as well. She made her way into the railway station and walked through the sliding doors, down the ramp to where taxis were parked. But to her disappointment, the last one had just been loaded with someone else's bags, driven up to a roundabout and disappeared. She wondered how long it would be before another arrived, sat on a wall and waited. But it wasn't long before a car drew up and the driver took her bag, put it in the boot and opened the door for her. She sat in, and he asked her where she was going.

'La Casa Hotel, *por favor,*' she said, not really sure how far it was from the station. But the young man seemed to know where he was going, and drove through the narrow streets at a very fast pace. Alva's heart beat erratically as she was swung from side to side in the back of the car until at last he pulled up, jumped out and put her bag on the rather uneven cobbled pavement. '*Cinco* euro,' he said, and she paid him, and added an extra few euro as a tip. Lifting her case, she climbed up the steps. She needed to be in the centre of the city so that it was easy to get around and see the various wine and sherry producers she had contacted before leaving Ireland. She rang the bell. The door clicked and she pushed it open. The foyer was in the typical style of an Andalusian home. A very large mahogany table in the centre, surrounded by leather couches, and various doors leading to other rooms. She walked over to the reception desk and a very pleasant woman came out to meet her.

'My name is Purtell,' she said.

'You are welcome to La Casa Hotel.'

'It's lovely.' Alva glanced around.

'This is your first visit to Jerez?'

'Yes.'

'You are here for the festival?'

'No, it's business. But there were a lot of people on the train, so I assumed something is happening.'

'It is the Festival de Jerez – and there are flamenco concerts on in various venues for about two weeks.'

'I'd love to see Flamenco,' Alva was excited.

'You should go to some of the shows.'

'When does the festival start?'

'The first show was on last night.'

'Do you have a programme?' Alva asked.

'Here it is.' The woman handed it to her.

'Thank you …*gracias,*' she said, remembering to speak a little Spanish. Not that she had very much really, only a smattering. But she had been relieved to know that all the business people she would meet spoke English.

'The main theatre is the Teatro Villamarta in the centre. Here is a map.' She took one out and spread it on the desk. 'We are here.' She marked the street, and the direction Alva should go.

She took the lift up to the third floor. La Casa was a beautiful old building. With black wrought iron balconies on each floor. Exquisite blue and white azulejos, which were pictures on tiles which commemorate historical events, and magnificent richly coloured stained-glass windows on the stairwell and the roof. She stood by the balcony, and looked over. Blown away by the wonder of the space which stretched down to the patio below. As she had taken the lift up, cleverly hidden in a corner of the foyer, she hadn't seen the white marble fountain. A cherub sprayed water up towards her, the accumulation of water gathering below in a large circular pool.

Her room was spacious. Simply furnished in the Spanish style with teak furniture. She drew back the white voile curtains, opened the heavy shutters and stepped outside. Now she was able to see over the rooftops of the city. The reddish hue of tiles glowed. She could see the many church spires and old buildings with wrought-iron balconies and immediately she wanted to go out into the streets and explore. She heard the sound of someone playing the guitar, the soft chords echoing in the air. And then, the tempo increased as dancers drummed their feet on a hard floor in time to the music. She tapped her fingers on the balustrade with a sense of excitement. She leaned over to see the people strolling in the streets below. Sitting at tables outside cafes. Enjoying the warm evening sunshine.

After a shower and change she felt more refreshed and decided to go down. She took a seat at a corner table in a small bar and ordered a glass of red wine which was served with a tasty bowl of olives and sliced garlic potatoes. The tapas took the edge off her appetite and she stayed there, watching the people of Jerez passing by. She picked up her phone, and clicked the number of her partner, Darren, who should be at home. It rang out. There was no answer except his voice suggesting that she leave a message after the beep. 'Hi love, I've just checked into the hotel. Wish you were here.' She waited a moment, almost expecting him to pick up and longing to hear his voice. She could always be enticed by him, but she was disappointed now and cut off. Where are you, Darren? She whispered. Lately, he never seemed to answer her calls, and she felt it was odd. It grew dark. Alva sipped the last of her wine, and paid the bill. Then she examined the map and found her way to the theatre.

She wandered along the main street which was lined with restaurants and bars. It was quite wide and some shops were still open and she stopped to look in the windows, but didn't go in. She turned a corner and ahead of her she could see the large theatre. Two long queues wound across the courtyard and she joined the end of one until she reached the top and asked the man checking tickets could she buy one. But he sent her off around the corner of the building and she was annoyed with herself for

4

not having realised where the box office was. She hurried inside but was told there were no tickets available for the performance tonight. Disappointed, she left the office and walking through the door could see a man waving a piece of paper in his hand.

'*Un boleto*?' he called out, looking around.

'Yes please,' she said excitedly, and then corrected herself. '*Si, si ...por favor.*'

'*Veinticinco.*'

She nodded, glad she could understand that in Spanish that meant twenty-five.

She rooted in her bag, pulled out the notes and handed them to him. He pushed the ticket into her hand, and she quickly examined it hoping that it actually was for tonight and that he wasn't a chancer selling tickets for last week.

'*Gracias,*' she nodded, but he had already disappeared. She glanced at her phone to see the time and realising she only had a couple of minutes to get to the theatre entrance she hurried back. By now, the queue had diminished and she was relieved when the ticket was accepted by the man at the door. He waved her towards the stairs and she ran up the red plush carpet quickly, going into the first door she saw and handing the ticket to the usher. He glanced at it and indicated that she should climb even further up to the next floor until eventually she was finally seated.

The lights in the enormous chandelier which hung from the ceiling dimmed and the theatre darkened, and there was an air of expectation as the chattering of the people ceased. The long curtains swished back each side to reveal a dark stage, and in a single spotlight, a guitarist sat on a chair and began to play a haunting melody which echoed throughout the auditorium. She stared down, captivated. She sighed, a long soft exhalation and her shoulders relaxed. Just a little. But in that movement, the tension which had built up as she tried to contact Darren eased.

There was a loud burst of applause when the guitarist bowed, and then, a group of flamenco dancers appeared, and began to dance to the music of musicians seated behind. The girls' dark hair caught up and held with coloured combs and flowers which matched their bright dresses. Frills swirled around as they tapped their feet in time to the music and rhythm created by a singer. A group of men joined them. Tall. Straight. Wearing narrow black trousers, short red jackets, and broad-brimmed black hats. They danced in unison until another woman appeared from the wings to centre stage. She wore a most wonderful white dress with a long frilled train which she kicked back as she twirled and then picked up in her hand and moved across the stage. Her arm movements were so graceful Alva was enthralled.

After that it was a series of different performances by the group, with costume changes, each one more beautiful than the one before. Alva was disappointed when the company took their final bows, and everyone in the audience stood up and applauded. The noise resonated in the theatre, and the clapping of the hands of the audience took on an unusual rhythm. One beat. Then three very fast beats. One beat. And another three beats. Alva joined in, strangely excited. Drowned in the sound. She didn't want tonight to end.

She wandered downstairs among the crowd into the foyer and noticed a man serving sherry which spouted into small glasses he was handing to patrons. Alva joined the queue and before long was sipping an ice-cold manzanilla with enjoyment. She glanced around at the people there. She heard mostly Spanish accents but there were quite a few other voices to be heard as well. She finished her drink and walked out through the people who were gathered in the foyer and outside the theatre too. She wandered along and turned off on to a side street and walked through the tables in front of a restaurant and in the doors, grabbing a stool at the end of the bar which was packed with people eating. She picked up the menu, ordered a glass of wine, and just chose something from the menu at random. She didn't even know exactly what it was. *Chistorras con huevos frito.* But when the man behind the bar pushed it towards her, it was a delicious plate of small mini sausages with a fried egg on top, and a basket of warm freshly made chunky bread. When she had finished, she ordered another dish, *puntillitos,* which were small fried squid, and also really appetizing.

She enjoyed the atmosphere of the place, the laughter, the chat, but eventually had to force herself to leave and make her way back to the hotel. She had an early start tomorrow.

The following morning, she took a taxi to the Bodega Los Vinos in the old part of the town. Hidden behind thick medieval walls, the bodega was surrounded by lush gardens and fountains, the water sparkling in the sunlight. The main courtyard was in shadow, and she was brought through to an office by the doorman, who announced her as he held the heavy door open.

'Senorita Purtell?' A tall man appeared with his hand outstretched. 'I'm Antonio Sanchez.'

She took his hand and he welcomed her in.

'Please take a seat,' he pulled out a heavy ornate chair. 'It's good to see you, normally it is David we meet.'

'I'm sorry, but he couldn't make this trip,' she explained. 'We are very busy at the moment.'

'No problem, we are delighted to meet you, Senorita Purtell.'

'Call me Alva,' she said.

He smiled and nodded. 'Alva, a beautiful name.'

'I'm looking forward to tasting some of your exceptional sherries and placing our orders for the winter season.'

'I am very glad about that. Now let us go ahead and taste some sherries.'

He led the way into the bodega, and she stared up into the

dimness of the dark wooden beams in the ceiling and the archways which drifted away into the distance.

'The solera is the construction of stacked barrels,' Antonio explained as they walked along one of the aisles surrounded by what seemed like thousands of barrels. 'And the main arch is almost sixteen metres high.' He pointed upwards.

'It's an amazing place,' Alva whispered, duly impressed.

'Another important aspect are the very thick walls, which help to keep the temperature of the wines at the same level both day and night.'

He went on to talk about the history of the bodega and then suggested they taste some sherry.

They sat at a table, and he chose a bottle.

'This is a light manzanilla,' he said. 'It is produced in Sanlucar de Barrameda and is made from the Palomino grape.' He poured some into her glass.

She tasted it. 'A little dry,' she murmured, and made a note of it.

'Next a fino,' he said and picked up another bottle and poured for the two of them.

'I prefer the fino.' She noted the name.

They continued on tasting various sherries until they came to the sweet Oloroso which was a rich dark colour, very different from the manzanilla.

'That is so rich.' She swirled the liquid in her mouth and because it was the last taste, she allowed herself the pleasure of swallowing it.

Afterwards, a waiter brought plates of tapas, and she enjoyed the flavours of olives and cured meat, which relieved the heaviness of the lingering taste of the sherries.

'I will call you later when I have decided what to order,' she explained to Antonio.

She returned to the hotel to calculate the quantities and called Darren again. But there was still no reply. She called her father.

'Hi Dad, how are you?'

'Not so bad,' he replied.

'I've just checked out some really good sherry at Bodega Los Vinos.'

There was silence.

'Dad?'

'The bank called us in this morning.'

'What did they say?'

'They wanted to discuss our financial position. We're overdrawn on our accounts.'

'Hugh can go through all the details of the accounts with them.'

'He was with me today and David too but the bank insist we clear the overdrafts immediately.'

'Surely they can extend? We've been a long time in business,' she argued. 'And we've done quite well in spite of the pandemic.'

'Apparently not.'

She was surprised. They had a facility which they used, but to be over that was very unusual.

He sounded defeated. She was suddenly worried about him. Her Dad, Frank, was Chairman of the company, and in his late sixties now. This was the first time she had heard him sound so down. And it wasn't fair on him to be burdened in this way. He had put so much into the business, and his father before him. When Frank took over after his death, he had given every inch of himself. Every beat of his heart. Every breath he took. The business was him. And for some nameless group of bankers to threaten him, was criminal.

'I'm coming back,' she said immediately, and could almost hear the relieved sigh of his breath as he heard that.

'Thanks, love, I really appreciate it. I'm worried about the situation.'

'I'll just have to arrange another flight, and cancel my appointments. Let you know when I'll be arriving.'

'I won't do anything until you get here.'

'Have you seen Darren? I've tried to get him on the phone but there's no answer. I've left a voice mail but he hasn't come back to me.' She tried to hide the panic in her heart which caused her voice to quiver.

'No, can't say I have.'

'See you soon. Take care.'

Alva emailed her brother, David, straight away. More worried about her Dad than the business. Then she went online but found that the next flight from Seville was two days later, and couldn't find another which would get her home any earlier. If she took a connection to Madrid or London and onwards, it would take her as long.

She booked a seat on the train from Jerez. It was much quieter now and she missed the buzz of her earlier journey and regretted that she hadn't managed to see more of the city, but now it wasn't possible, and she was anxious to get home as quickly as she could. But Seville beckoned and as soon as she had booked into a hotel, she decided to explore the wonder of this ancient city. Narrow streets curved this way and that, and she made her way to the Royal Palace and was glad to find that the queue to enter wasn't as long as she expected and decided to join. It moved slowly, but she didn't mind. Anxious to linger and enjoy her last hours here in Spain. Breathing in the aromas of this city, listening to the voices, those excited cadences of the language, the lilting musicality of a singer accompanied by a guitarist she could hear in the distance.

She enjoyed the wait and was enthralled when she was eventually ushered inside. She put on headphones and listened to the audio guide telling her about the stories and the history of this ancient place. The buildings of the tenth century palace were a mixture of Moorish and Christian cultures. She wandered under overhanging sweet-smelling flowers which covered archways and stood by sparkling fountains which were scattered throughout the area, a maze of pathways and patios. She found herself in the Baths of Lady María de Padilla. Staring into the huge rainwater tanks named after the mistress of Peter the Cruel. The balconies above were reflected in the still water of the baths. Next was the breath-taking red-tiled Courtyard of the Maidens, and the Patio of the Dolls, her eyes following the exquisite ceiling above. She went through the patios and took a rest on a stone seat in a sheltered corner just to breathe in the wonder of this place. Then she entered the Ambassador's Hall, astonished by the circular gold ceiling. Her eyes feasted on this feature until she had to drag herself away, no longer listening to the disembodied voice on the headphones. She didn't need to be told any more. She just loved the wonder of this place. There was something enchanting about it and she could have stayed here for the whole day.

She had continued to call Darren on her phone, but without success. Later, she went back to the hotel, showered and lay on the bed. Closed her eyes and drifted. She didn't know what was ahead of her. If the company collapsed what would she do? She had spent the past ten years since leaving university working full time in Purtell Vintners. And all of her earlier years helping her father in the office. Her mother had left home when Alva was just five and her father had heard nothing from her since, and told Alva and her two brothers that he didn't know where she was. So Alva was the mainstay for her father and younger brothers, David and Cian, as Frank worked every hour of every day. It was only recently that Alva had managed to persuade her father to cut back to a five-day week. But he could still be found at work on occasional Saturdays and Sundays and he ignored anything she said.

After she arrived at Dublin airport, Alva went straight into the office. Anxious to talk to her father, and brothers.

'Dad,' she embraced him as soon as she saw him. 'How are you?'

'Not too bad, love.' He managed a weak smile. 'And you?'

'I'm fine, don't worry about me,' she smiled at him, reluctant to give him the impression that she was overly worried.

'The auditors are coming in this afternoon at four,' he said.

'Is there a particular agenda?'

'No, they want to discuss the figures we submitted for last year's accounts.'

'I'm sure they're fine.'

'I hope so.'

She looked at her watch. 'I'll just have time to slip home to change. I'll call into David, I presume he's in today?'

'Yeah, he is, I was talking to him a while ago.'

'Did Darren come in?'

'No, I didn't see him.'

'I still can't contact him.'

'That's odd.'

'Maybe he's out of coverage, wherever he is.' She dropped a kiss on his forehead and hurried out of his office, knocked lightly on David's door and waited to hear his voice call her in. But she heard nothing, waited a moment and then opened the door herself.

'I'm back.'

He was sitting at his desk, his head in his hands.

She walked across the room.

'You don't look good, are you feeling alright?' She peered at him.

He raised his head.

'Something wrong?'

'No, no …' He straightened up.

'What's this meeting with the auditors about?' she asked. 'I didn't want to put Dad under pressure.'

'They have some queries about the figures.'

'I'm sure they will be easily answered.'

'Hope so.'

Alva drove home to her apartment in Stillorgan, took a quick shower and changed, and then hurried back to the office.

Chapter Two

When Alva went into the boardroom her father, and brother David and younger brother Cian, who was responsible for IT. were already there, as well as Hugh, their accountant, and the auditors. Three of them in attendance today. She opened the proceedings. 'Why have you called this meeting today?' she asked. 'And requested that all of us should be in attendance here?'

'We have discovered there are certain irregularities in the accounts.'

She stared at the man, her eyes wide open. 'What do you mean by irregularities?'

'Yes, what do you mean?' Frank repeated.

'Your balance sheet is showing a loss.'

'But we've been showing a profit for the past number of years.' Alva pointed out.

'It must be because of the pandemic?' David said confidently.

She turned to the accountant. 'Hugh, why didn't someone in your department spot these anomalies? It seems amazing. What are they doing?'

He shrugged.

'It looks like you haven't been doing your job. What do you discuss at your meetings every Monday morning?' Frank demanded.

'I'll need to see the accounts.' Alva stretched out her hand. 'And I'll have to go over them in detail.'

'They're not final.' The auditor picked up a sheaf of papers and handed them to her.

She stared at the figures in front of her. 'There's at least a thirty per cent reduction in profit from 2020 to 2021.'

'It has to be the pandemic,' David said again. 'That must be the reason. Over the next while it should improve. We've defeated Covid now.'

'That's if the bank will support us,' her father rapped angrily.

'They're not going to let us go under,' David said. 'It's all bluff.'

'How do you know that?' Alva rounded on him.

'I could sense it from their manner.'

'We'll have to arrange another meeting with the bank tomorrow,' Alva said firmly. 'And we must go through the accounts this evening and be prepared.'

The meeting ended.

'I'm not free this evening,' her brother David said. 'I've to do stuff with the kids, there's a concert so I have to go.'

'We need to discuss the accounts,' Alva reminded.

'It will have to be in the morning.'

'O.K. see you then at nine.'

David left the room. Her eyes followed him. He was very tense, she thought.

'I'll be there as well,' her other brother Cian said.

'Maybe the bank will listen, now that we have the figures from the auditors,' Frank said.

'Hope so.'

'Let's have dinner together,' Alva suggested to her father. 'Although I don't know what food I have at home, Darren has been away as well obviously, so I'll have to shop.'

'Come home with me, I have some food from Marks and Spencer, we'll just have to heat it up in the oven,' her Dad offered.

'We haven't had a chance to sit down together for a while, and now we have this problem to deal with.'

'It will be good to talk about this whole thing, just the two of us,' Alva agreed.

After dinner, she opened up the accounts and they both sat looking through the pages. They were silent at first, concentrating on the figures.

'Look there, the purchases are very high, much higher than the previous year. I wonder why that is?' Alva mused.

'If the turnover is similar then why are the purchases so high?' Frank wondered.

'We'll have to look at that in more detail. I'll call Hugh.'

She did that, regretting that it was so late, although felt that it was sufficiently important.

'I need to have to look at the accounts, purchases in particular. Every month. Every invoice.'

'What?' Hugh sounded irritated.

'I need every detail. And I want it before we meet with the bank.'

'It will take some time.'

'Make sure the department start working on it first thing.'

'Look, is this really necessary?' he asked, tiredly. 'Looking for all that detail? You won't even understand, accounts are not your forte.'

'I may not be a fully qualified accountant, but I can understand figures.'

'We're very busy at the moment and this will hold us up.'

'Look Hugh, I need information at my fingertips when we meet with the bank. What time is the meeting?'

'Three o'clock. And I'll make sure to have all the data needed.'

'Just do as I ask and I'll see you in the morning, and I'd appreciate if you could be in as early as possible.'

Alva went home just after ten, hoping that Darren would be there. He worked in their company as well and was responsible for sales on the Irish market, although he wasn't on the board, but she would need him to attend the meeting in the morning. Before that she wanted to talk with him. To explain what was happening and ask his advice.

When she drove in, she was delighted to see his car in the carpark. He was home. A sense of relief flowed through her. She went in quietly, hoping to surprise him. He wouldn't be expecting her, thinking she was still in Spain. The hall lights were on, but the living room was in darkness. He must be in bed, she surmised, took off her shoes, put down her bag, slipped out of her jacket and tiptoed along the corridor, anticipating the moment when she would leap on to the big queen-sized bed and fling her arms around him.

She turned the brass handle, and pushed the door open. The room was softly lit, the cream lamps illuminated. She smiled and looked towards the bed. And froze.

Darren was lying on his usual side of the bed, his arm across the naked body of a woman. Both were heavily asleep.

For a few seconds she didn't know what to do. But Darren seemed to sense her presence and suddenly raised his head, a look of shock on his face. 'Alva?'

'What are you doing in my bed with that ...' she screamed.

'Alva, I'm sorry, it's not the way you think. Come on, get up.' He pushed the woman beside him. 'Wake up,' he shouted loudly.

The woman grabbed the sheet, covered herself, and stared at Alva with a blank expression on her face. Then she climbed awkwardly out of the bed, bent to pick up her dress and underwear which had been scattered on the floor, and ran into the bathroom.

'Get out of here,' Alva shouted after her.

She wanted to drag her by the hair and push her out into the corridor as naked as she was.

Darren stepped into his boxer shorts with a sense of calmness which aggravated her even more.

Alva just about managed to keep her patience and paced up and down the room while the woman dressed in the bathroom and Darren dragged on his clothes.

'Right, get out and take that one with you,' she ordered him.

'This is my apartment. I'm not leaving,' he objected.

'You will if you know what's good for you.' She lifted a heavy blue ceramic ornament which was on a side table, and threatened him with it.

'All right.' He went into the bathroom, and came out with the blonde-haired woman by the hand, and the two of them hurried past her, the scent of her perfume drifting.

'Don't come back,' she yelled after him. 'I never want to see you again.' She followed them into the hallway.

He glared at her, and then carefully took the woman's jacket and slipped it over her shoulders. Then he dropped a kiss on her lips, opened the door, and the two of them disappeared.

Alva was unable to believe what had just happened. She couldn't understand how she hadn't noticed the jacket which was hanging on the armchair. If she had, it might have prepared her for what she discovered in the bedroom. She walked into the living room, sat on the couch and burst into tears, her heart breaking. How could he do something like this to her? No wonder he didn't answer his phone. Bastard. She muttered out loud. Using every expletive she could think of. He had told her he loved her just the other morning before she left for Spain. There had been no sign of any hesitancy there. Although he didn't answer his phone lately, she had never thought he might be with another woman. Why had she trusted him so much? They had been living together for over four years. And they had been four wonderful years. And now everything had come crashing down. And she had never expected that. Why had she been such a fool?

She pushed herself up. And didn't even know how long she had been sitting there. Walking into the kitchen, she made a cup of strong coffee, and leaned against the counter sipping it. The tears drifted down her face again and she felt helpless. Wondering how she was going to face into the office tomorrow. Be controlled. Hide her feelings. Reluctant to even mention Darren's name.

Her phone rang. She went over to her bag, took it out and stared at the read-out. It was Darren. She turned her phone off. That night she didn't go into her bedroom and lay on the bed in the spare room. She turned off the light and stared into the darkness. The hours crawled, and when eventually she pushed herself out of bed at five in the morning, she felt she hadn't slept in days. She checked her phone. There were a number of missed calls from Darren. She was glad she had turned it off.

After having a shower she didn't feel any better, and couldn't imagine how she was going to work through the day. Her emotions were all over the place. Her love for Darren had seemed so strong, she had been sure he felt the same way. And now to find out that he was playing around with another woman hit her like a train. And to know that he was sleeping with her in their own bed was simply disgusting. How long was this affair going on, she wondered. Anger swept through her. The picture of the two of them lying in her bed kept flashing in front of her. The woman was beautiful. Tall and skinny. With that long blonde curly hair. She wasn't surprised that he'd go for that type, she thought bitterly, and almost threw up.

In the office, she tried to concentrate on the files awaiting attention until Hugh came in. It was difficult for her to hide her emotions, but as soon as he appeared, they got down to work and he pulled up the particular files on the computer that she had requested. She began to trawl through the invoices, going through month after month and noting down the various companies with whom they did business. It was tiring work, and although Hugh offered to do some of it, she refused. This was something she had to do herself.

Her father, Frank, arrived. 'How's it going?'

'It will take some time, but even then, there will be nothing new to tell the bank. Could you pull up the bank statements as of today? See have they changed much overnight,' she asked.

He did that.

'We are overdrawn on all of them?' She stared at the screen.

'The main current account is overdrawn by five hundred thousand.'

'That's right,' he agreed with her.

'While we have an overdraft facility the bank should have been on to us before this. It's really strange. If we look back to last year.' She scrolled up. 'We have almost the same amount in credit generally. What caused that reverse? Sales are mostly online, but still we've kept up with previous levels. I was so relieved about that right through the pandemic,' Alva said.

'I'm very worried,' her father said.

'So am I, but I'm sure we'll be able to convince the bank that they should give us a further facility.'

'But they'll look for collateral.'

'There is a mortgage on this building already.'

'They'll want more.'

'That's the worst part of it.'

The meeting with the bank officials wasn't promising. David and Cian were there as well as Hugh, her father and herself. The bank pushed them. Threatened that they would repossess their homes. Cars. Jewellery. Anything they had which could go towards repayment of the money they owed the bank.

'This is the first time we have been overdrawn on any of our accounts. You will have to give us some leeway,' she said.

'Otherwise the company will collapse,' her father protested.

'You have been overdrawn for almost a year, and have ignored any of our demands for the accounts to be put into credit. Now we will need a considerable amount of money to be lodged,' the bank official said.

'But that will take time,' Alva protested.

'We have given you time.'

'But ...'

'Give us a date,' Frank asked.

'You have a few days at most. Otherwise, we will have to take decisive action.'

The meeting at the bank ended. They went back to the office.

'I want to talk now,' Alva said bluntly as they swung through the doors. As soon as they entered the board room, she turned on Hugh, David and Cian.

'Why wasn't I informed about all of this?' she demanded. 'I'm the CEO of this company.'

'We were hoping that it would sort itself out,' David stuttered.

'For God's sake, that's so childish,' she snapped. 'Hugh, this is your responsibility. Do you realise that?'

'Yes.'

'Well, explain it to me. Why are there such anomalies in the accounts?'

'I don't know, but I'm going to find out.' He wasn't able to answer her question.

'I want you to stop all other work, and concentrate your time on finding out what has caused this situation.'

'But Alva, finding out why this has happened won't help. The bank could still push us into liquidation unless we can inject money into the company.'

'And where do you think we're going to get it?' she asked.

Hugh looked at her blankly.

'In the meantime, make no payments. Our payroll will have to go ahead as usual on Friday, and we will have to meet with the bank before that so we have sufficient funds in the account to pay the salaries. And Hugh, I want a list of all monies which are due.'

Trying to force her thoughts about Darren's woman to the back of her mind, Alva took out the files and began to trawl through them. Every account. Every client. Every invoice paid. Pages and pages of printout. She stared at the list, but was aware that she didn't know every client. Some her father handled, others David handled, and she dealt with the rest. But now she was looking for something unusual. A company which drew her attention. Someone she didn't know. But yet wanted to know.

She succeeded in searching through the listings until suddenly an unfamiliar name jumped out at her. Tichanko Inc. She searched for the address, Outlining the name with a yellow marker. She checked it out and discovered it was in the city of Bordeaux in the south-west of France. There were quite a few purchases. Very large amounts which increased regularly. She examined the list, and then pulled up the detailed orders on the computer screen. Nothing unusual there. She looked for a phone number, but there was none listed. Then she googled the name. But there was no detail at all for the company. No email. No website. It was odd. All she had was the company name and address.

She went into her brother's office. 'Do you know this company, David?' she asked, pushing the printout in front of him.

He stared at it for a moment. 'Yes, of course I do. It's one of my clients.'

'How long are we dealing with them?' she snapped, trying to be patient.

'Years.'

'It's strange, I don't know the name at all. What type of wine do they supply?'

'It's that very nice Merlot, you know the one. And others as well.'

'What's the name?'

'Saint Rochas is the main one.'

'I can't say I've ever tasted it.'

'We've a very wide range of wines, even I couldn't remember all of them.'

'Do you know the owner of the winery?'

'Not offhand.'

'I'm surprised that you don't know his or her name. I know the names of many of our clients.'

'Maybe you've a better memory than I have,' he smirked.

'That isn't funny, David. We're in a very serious position here.'

'I realise that.'

'I'll ask Hugh to get me the details.'

'No, I'll do that.'

'Can you look it up now?'

He placed his fingers on the keys and tapped.

She watched the screen.

'It's not coming up. I may have it filed under another name. I haven't time to look for it now, I must see Hugh before this meeting with the bank.'

'I don't understand how you haven't got any information about the company. How do you make contact with them?'

He kept looking at the screen.

'I need the information, and I need it soon,' she insisted.

'Leave it with me.'

She watched him for a moment, an uncomfortable feeling in her stomach. She went through the rest of the printouts, and found she was familiar with most of the names of the other companies they dealt with. The only odd one out was Tichanko.

They got together before they went to the meeting and discussed what possibilities there were which would appease the bank.

'You have compromised the company,' she accused Hugh

angrily.

He didn't answer.

'And David, it was so immature to ignore the bank's letters. It's like someone with their first mortgage. Ignore them and they'll go away. How could you?' she demanded. She wanted a clear answer but didn't expect she would get one from either of them.

'There's no point going on and on about it. That's past tense. We are where we are,' he interrupted.

'As we don't have enough funds we will be forced to liquidate.'

'Should we try other banks?' he suggested.

'And take out another mortgage?'

'Yeah.'

'We can't afford to repay two mortgages. Our figures are pathetic, we don't know when they're going to return to normal levels if ever.' She couldn't believe she was hearing such a suggestion from David.

'I will liquidate some of my investments,' her father said, 'And support the company. That will sort us out. I'll talk to my own accountant about that, and my solicitor.'

'That would be great, Dad, and it would get us out of this hole,' David said enthusiastically.

'I'm sorry you feel you must do that.' Alva reached across the desk and covered her father's hand.

'I put everything I had into this company.' His eyes were sad.

'I'm so sorry, I wish I knew what had caused this,' Alva said, almost on the verge of tears.

'It's not your fault.' Frank held her hand.

'It's nobody's fault.' David waved his hands in the air in a vague manner.

'I still want it investigated,' Alva insisted. 'Hugh, are you listening to me?'

'Certainly, Alva, I'll do my best.'

'And it must be uncovered. Something happened. I know

something happened.'

'We'll be sorted out in the meantime with my money, so you don't have to worry,' her father said.

'I want to thank you Dad for your generosity. You're fantastic.' Alva was really grateful to her father.

Chapter Three

Alva was still trawling through the information on purchases and payments which Hugh had given her when Darren burst into her office. He rushed across the room and kissed her. 'I'm so sorry, love, that woman meant nothing, I don't know what I was thinking. Please forgive me?'

She stared at him. And simply didn't know what to say.

'Do you understand what I'm saying?' he asked.

She nodded.

'I still love you, Alva.'

'How is that possible, and you with that …' She was unable to say the words she wanted.

'It meant nothing.'

'Nothing?' she exploded.

'It was just sex.'

'Such a betrayal of everything,' she whispered, feeling so hurt.

'It isn't a betrayal, she was just there, and I suppose I took advantage. You were going to be away and I needed a bit of company.'

'You mean to say you only met her a couple of nights ago for the first time?'

'Yeah, I barely know her name.'

'Ridiculous.'

'Well, OK, I know her a bit longer than that. We've just met occasionally.'

'And is she the first?'

'Of course, it was just a weak moment.'

'Be honest with me, Darren, I don't want lies.'

'I'd never tell you a lie, Alva, you know how I feel about you.'

'Perhaps she's better in bed than me,' she said sarcastically.

'Never.'

'Maybe she doesn't work as hard as I do.'

'Well, there's something in that.'

'What does she do?'

'She's a model.'

'I'm not surprised.'

'Alva, let's forget about this.'

'Are you going to see her again?'

'No, it's finished.'

'How could it be finished when it's supposed to be meaningless.'

'Well, you know what I mean, I won't see her again, I promise, believe me.'

Tears filled her eyes. 'You've hurt me deeply.'

'I didn't mean to.'

'You don't have a clue how I feel.'

'Course I do. I know you so well.'

'I wonder.'

'It's been so many years. What's it been? Five, six?'

'Four, you bastard. You can't even remember how long we are together.'

'What does that matter?'

She felt she was being railroaded by Darren as he tried to persuade her to ignore what happened last night.

'Let's go out to dinner tonight.'

'I can't, there's too much going on.'

'What do you mean?'

'There are problems in the company.'

'Problems?'

'The auditors have found anomalies in the accounts.'

He looked at her, shocked.

'We're seeing the bank later, we could be forced to liquidate, and the company might collapse.'

He stared at her. His face white.

'There has to be a simple explanation, Are they certain?'

'I haven't got the details yet.'

'What has Hugh to say.'

'Not much yet. He's going through the accounts.'

'I'll have to see him,' he said vaguely, and turned to leave the room.

'I want to talk to you this evening about this business with that woman, but I don't want to go out. We need privacy,' Alva said.

'Why can't you just forget about it. I told you it was just a once off.'

'I trusted you, Darren,' Alva was angry, but at the same time she tried to keep her voice quiet. The walls in the office weren't exactly thick, and she didn't want everyone to hear her private life being discussed so publicly.

'I'm sorry …' He was sheepish.

'If the trust is gone out of our relationship, then what's left?' she asked.

'Everything, Alva, all the love we've shared since we first met. And I don't want to lose you.'

'You're going the wrong way about that.'

'Give me a chance,' he begged.

'I can't.'

'I think you're putting the business before us,' he accused.

'No, of course I'm not.'

'Stupid bitch.'

'Our relationship is the most important thing in my life.'

'Well then, just let it go and we'll continue on.'

'You're asking an awful lot,' said Alva.

'Don't let a few little mistakes destroy everything, Alva. This is the only time I've ever done such a thing. And I feel so ashamed. The first time I just had one too many drinks and didn't know what I was doing. She came on to me, all persuasive, I hardly remember what happened.'

'You weren't drunk when you got out of bed last night. You were perfectly sober. You knew exactly what you were doing with ...that woman.'

'Alva,' he leaned closer. 'How many times do I have to tell you I've finished with her. She's only a tramp.'

Her phone rang. She put her hand on it. 'I'll have to take this.'

'Yeah, go on, business comes first as usual.' He was sarcastic.

'I'll talk to you later.'

'Dad, I wish you hadn't put everything you have as collateral into the company. It's too much.'

'What difference does it make to me. I have everything I need,' he smiled.

'You're so generous,' Alva said. 'Supporting us all. Although I'm still worried about why this situation happened. I think there was something underhand, it didn't happen accidentally.'

'That's your logical mind.'

'I vow that I'll get to the bottom of it,' Alva said vehemently.

'But that means someone is going to be blamed for wrongdoing.'

'If they did something then they have to stand up and be counted. Why should you have to bear the brunt?'

'But who is it?'

'It's someone in the company.'

'You're sure?'

'It's hardly someone outside. Some stranger?'

'No, I suppose not. But how are you going to find out who it is?'

'I'm determined, Dad. Why should someone put you in this position after all you've done?'

'I can't believe someone who has worked for us would be capable of doing such a thing. Most of our staff have been in the company for years.'

'Circumstances change for people, perhaps they needed money.' Frank could always see things from someone else's point of view.

'That doesn't give them the right to embezzle or do side-deals from the person who was more than generous to them over the years.'

'Steal?' He looked shocked.

'Well, that's what it is. Don't cover it up, Dad, we have to face it.'

'There has to be some logical reason for it all. I hate the thought of hearing these sordid details connected with someone's name. The person who did this will have really hurt me. I can't bear the very thought that someone hated me that much to steal from me.' He grimaced.

'People have two sides. A good side and a bad side. And clever people only show their good side.'

'So it has to be someone very clever?'

'Fraudsters are always like that.'

'It's a horrible thought that they would be prepared to do it.' He seemed very upset.

She hadn't wanted to meet Darren for dinner, thinking that it would be very difficult to have a conversation in a restaurant in earshot of the other diners. But she wanted to talk. They had to talk. Should she forgive him and just dismiss it as a mistake on his part? But next time another chance presented would he grab it with both hands again and forget her?

Darren put his head around her office door just after five. 'Hi love?' he smiled and came in. 'Are we on for dinner?'

'I don't know,' she said, hesitantly.

'Come on, I've made a booking at Naxos.'

'I prefer to talk at home, we can get a take away.'

He put out his hand and took hold of hers. 'Give me a chance, Alva, just this once.'

'All right then.' She sighed. Feeling that she was trapped. But how would she ever find out what was behind his guile?

The cork popped out of the bottle of champagne, and the waiter poured the fizzy drink into their glasses. They picked them up, and Darren clinked hers. 'To you, my darling,' he said.

She didn't say anything, just sipped her champagne and gazed around the interior of the restaurant. They always liked the atmosphere of the small intimate place. Candle-lit tables were always positioned a good distance from each other, and it meant you could easily chat privately and not have to worry about being overheard. The décor was Mediterranean. White walls hung with pictures of the Greek islands. Blue furniture. Greek music playing softly in the background. Meals were served on blue plates, table linen crisp white with matching napkins.

They chose various dishes. Among them Souvlaki. Taramasalata. Dolmades. Tzatziki and others. The food was always good but tonight she had to force herself to enjoy it. She didn't bother with dessert, and just sipped a coffee at the end of the meal.

'Alva, I hope you have forgiven me. I want you to ignore what happened with ...' he hesitated. 'I should never have done such a thing. I'm so sorry.'

'And so you should be.'

He lowered his head.

'Can I believe you?'

'Of course, you can.'

She wondered if she could forgive him and continue to live with him. And was it worth the effort which undoubtedly would be needed to get back to where they were before this thing happened?

'Will you forgive me?' he begged.

'That will take some time.'

'Not too long, I hope. Let's have another glass of champers to celebrate.' He took the bottle out of the ice bucket and poured. 'Cheers.'

They went home. She felt strange about that. An instinctive reluctance to go into their bedroom because of what had happened the night before. 'I'm sleeping in the spare room,' she said. 'You can sleep in our bedroom.'

He didn't object. 'Nightcap?'

'No thanks. I've had enough alcohol.'

He followed her into the bedroom.

'I want to sleep, Darren.'

'What's wrong with you, my love? I can sleep with you in here, can't I?'

'I need time, Darren. I can't …not yet,' she murmured. 'It's too difficult for me.'

'Don't think about her.'

'I can't help myself.'

'She's nothing.'

'So you say, but I just need a little time to put the thoughts of what happened out of my head.'

'Sure, I understand.'

'I'm tired, I need to sleep.'

'Yeah, sleep.' He marched into the bedroom.

Alva was first up, and Darren joined her a few minutes later. 'How are you, my love?' he asked, embracing her.

'I'm fine thanks,' she said, still feeling awkward.

'Glad to hear it. What have you got on today?' he asked.

'Still working on the accounts, I'm determined to find out what happened.'

'But surely that is a waste of time?'

'I don't agree.'

'I'm off to Galway, but I'll try not to be too late, I promise.'

'I will probably be working, so don't worry.'

'Call you.' He kissed her.

A hurried movement, she thought.

Chapter Four

Alva poured herself a cup of coffee, and although she wasn't in the slightest bit hungry, she took a bite of a croissant just to have something in her stomach. There was always coffee percolating in the canteen, and it was company practice to have croissants and rolls from a local bakery delivered each morning.

She continued her work of the previous day. Meticulously going through the accounts until the day began in earnest and she could hear the company come to life with the sounds of footsteps, and voices. She glanced at her watch and realising it was almost ten o'clock wondered where her father was. He was late. It was unusual for him.

As she pondered on the accounts, that company name, Tichanco Inc. pushed its way into her mind again. But she had found no explanation as to what or who that company was. She went to see Hugh.

'What do you know of this company?'

He looked at the name printed on the sheet of paper. 'It's one of our regular clients.'

'But I can't get in touch. No email. No phone number. What does that mean?' She tried to remain calm.

'Maybe it's mislaid. Could happen.'

'I can find the details of every other client but not this one. And we purchase a lot of wine from them. But mostly it's a Merlot at the medium price range. I'm suspicious, Hugh, and I need to find out who this company is.'

'Why are you suspicious?'

'I expect you to tell me what's gone wrong in our company. You've been looking for an explanation and I hope you'll be able to find it. The auditors will find out what it is but I'd prefer to find out ourselves. Only Dad has used his assets as collateral into the company we would collapse.'

'We are very lucky he has done that.'

'You keep working on the accounts and I want to see results soon,' She emphasised.

'Sure Alva, leave it with me.'

'If you want me, I'll be with Dad.' She left Hugh's office, and walked down to Frank's door. She knocked on it, but there was no reply. She opened it and looked in. But he hadn't come in yet. She spoke with his secretary, but when she checked the diary, she didn't see any appointments entered until the afternoon.

'I'm sorry, Alva, he may have made an appointment himself and didn't tell me.'

'I'll call him.' She picked up her mobile phone. His number rang. But it went on to voice mail and she left a message. Then she sent a text as well.

By lunch time, she had heard nothing from her Dad. But she decided to call over to the house and see if he was all right. To her surprise, his car was still parked in the driveway. She opened the front door and called him. But he didn't respond.

'Dad?' she called again, going through the downstairs rooms. But there was no sound in the house, so she ran up to his bedroom and burst in.

'Dad?' she rushed across to his bed. He lay there. Looking very pale. 'What's wrong, Dad?' She touched his hand. His skin was cold. She screamed and patted his face. Placed her fingers on his neck but couldn't detect a pulse. 'Dad, Dad?' she cried, unable to believe what she was seeing. She took out her phone and dialled

999, nervously asking for an ambulance. She could hardly speak, and stuttered as she gave the person at the other end of the line the address.

'The paramedics will be with you soon. Do they have access to the house?' he asked.

'When will they be here?' she asked him, in a panic.

'Is there access to the house?' he asked again.

She suddenly realised that they couldn't get in. She hurried then, slipping down the carpeted stairs and as she reached the wooden floor of the hallway she ran across and wrenched open the door. Leaping back up the stairs to her Dad's bedroom, she was anxious to call David and Cian and let them know about her Dad but couldn't do that as she was on to the man in the emergency services.

'The front door is open,' she told the man. 'Are you coming soon?' she asked again.

'As soon as we can,' he said.

She wasn't reassured. Lately she had heard more than once that the waiting time for an ambulance could be anything from a few minutes to a few hours.

'Hurry please.' She begged.

'Calm down,' he said. 'I'll talk you through helping your father. Can you do CPR?'

'Yes,' she said.

'Put your phone on speaker,' he told her, and then instructed her to clear her Dad's airways, and then check for breathing.

'He's not breathing,' she shouted, and knelt down. Pushing aside her Dad's dark blue pyjamas, she placed her hands on his chest, and began the compressions. Thirty times. The man counted her through it. And then told her to breathe into her Dad's mouth, turn her head, and breathe again. But she began to panic as there was no response from her Dad. He just lay there.

She had no idea how long it was before the paramedics appeared in the room. She kept on doing compressions until one of them took over. And then she stood up and watched as they placed two pads on her Dad's chest and began defibrillation. They motioned to her to stand back, and she found it very difficult to watch the procedure. It was so invasive and aggressive she gripped her hands together and prayed to God to help him.

It was only then that her eyes strayed beyond him. And she noticed some containers of tablets had fallen over on the bedside locker. She reached down and picked one up. There was nothing in it. Not even one pill. She looked at the name of the medication. She knew he took some blood pressure pills, but didn't know exactly which type of medication it was. She picked up the others, and found they were also empty. Shock seared through her. Had he taken an overdose?

As they worked on her father, she called David, but as there was no reply she phoned the office but he had gone out to a meeting. She left a voicemail and a text. Next she tried Cian, and to her relief she heard his voice. Quickly, she explained what was happening and he said he was on his way. She called David again and listened to his voice but didn't leave another message. She would have to continue calling. He had to know. No one else must know beforehand. She thought of calling Darren, but didn't. She would tell him afterwards, once David knew.

The paramedics continued working on her dad and then two Gardai arrived, followed by Cian. In tears she threw her arms around him, so glad to see someone she loved.

'How is he?' he asked.

She shook her head, as she watched one of the paramedics talk with the Gardai.

'Oh my God. What happened?'

She looked around for the bottles of medication but couldn't see them now.

'It could have been an accidental overdose.'

Cian was horrified.

The Gardai walked across the room and asked them a few questions. But both of them denied any knowledge of what happened to their father.

The paramedics took their father into the ambulance, and Alva and Cian followed them to the hospital. Sadly, Frank had been pronounced dead shortly after he arrived there, and it was only then that David rang and she could tell him what had happened.

Alva, David and Cian went back to the house and then had the task of telling the family about their father. And later David and Cian went to see the undertaker and left Alva on her own. She couldn't deal with the organisation of the funeral. It was too much.

She felt in shock. Paralysed. And couldn't believe what had happened. Her darling father had died. And the possibility that he had taken his own life was just too difficult to accept. She prayed that the post mortem would reveal a more natural reason for his death. Although the paramedics had not told her anything, it was just her own mind taking her down that unwelcome road. She wanted to bang a door closed on the world, but that wasn't possible. She had to face it.

She called Darren who was still in Galway and told him. He was equally shocked, and pulled off the motorway as soon as he could and rang her back. 'I'll be home as soon as I can my love.'

She felt a sense of relief, so looking forward to seeing him. While the last twenty-four hours were horrendous since she discovered Darren with that woman, the tragedy of her father's death was a million times worse. She looked around the room at her father's possessions and tears welled up in her eyes.

But then the questions began. Although she tried not to let them in and persuade herself that there were no answers yet. And there wouldn't be for some time. And until then she had to wait to face that truth. She stayed in the house for another couple of hours, just wanting to be there on her own.

Her phone rang. It was Darren.

'I'm home, love, where are you?'

'I'm still at the house.'

'Have you eaten?'

'No …I'm not hungry.'

'I ordered a takeaway, oh, there he is now. See you soon.'

Although she found it very hard to leave the house, she went home then to the apartment. Pressed the remote and drove into their parking space. By the time she had taken her stuff out of the car, Darren had rushed to meet her, his arms around her, holding her close. She dropped the briefcase and the bag and hugged him tight. Just loving the feeling of his body close to hers. Needing his love so much tonight.

'I'm so sorry about your Dad, Alva, it's terrible, such a shock for you, for all of us. I love you, and thanks so much for giving me another chance,' he whispered.

She was suddenly aware of what his words meant. But said nothing.

'Come on in, the food will be cold.' He put his arm around her shoulders and they took the lift up to the apartment.

'You sit down now, and have a glass of wine. It'll help you relax.' He poured a glass and handed it to her. She sipped it. Letting him plate up the Chinese meal, and as he did that, she stared into the distance of their large living room. This apartment had been the place of their dreams. And now it had been contaminated by that woman Darren brought here.

'Here we are, sliced roast duck with green pepper and black bean sauce, just a little ginger on the side, and no chillies at all.' Darren brought the plates to the table. 'Do you feel like

39

something to eat now?' he asked.

'Yes, a little.' She hadn't the energy to refuse.

'It's your favourite,' he reminded.

'Yeah, my favourite,' she grimaced.

'Come on, try some.'

She took a couple of forkfuls of the duck and swallowed it but after a few minutes she couldn't eat any more.

'I'll make some coffee,' Darren offered.

She sat silently as he did that and brought it over. She took a sip. The heat of the liquid warmed her insides, and provided refreshment.

'Can I do anything to help,' Darren asked.

'David and Cian are talking to the undertakers, they are arranging everything.'

'I'm so sorry for you. I was fond of Frank. It's a shock to me as well.'

'I can't believe that he might have done such a thing.'

'The police won't know exactly how he died until after the post mortem.'

'The thought of it is terrible. If he had just slipped away in his sleep then maybe I could accept that, but the other alternative is too awful.' Tears filled her eyes.

'Don't worry, darling.' He took her hand in his.

She didn't take it away but left it sit quietly, accepting his sympathy. The anger she felt the day before had diminished, and she felt a numbness sweep through her.

'I think I'll go to bed,' she murmured.

'Let me clear up.' He took the dishes into the kitchen.

She pushed herself out of the armchair and stumbled along the corridor, automatically pushing open their own bedroom door. But she stopped then, forcing herself towards the spare room.

'Alva?' She could hear Darren's footsteps behind her. 'Where are you going?'

She turned to meet his questioning eyes.

'I'm sleeping here.'

'But why?'

'Because ...' she said.

'Because what?'

'I don't want to sleep with you, not after ...'

'But I told you she means nothing to me.'

'Look, I'm still here, just leave it at that. I want to have a decent sleep if I can, although I probably won't be able to close my eyes.'

'Please, Alva, don't leave me alone in that big bed.'

'You'll be out like a light, Darren, you won't even notice I'm not there.' She opened the door, walked through and closed it behind her.

Chapter Five

The next few days passed in a blur. Alva's heart was broken. But she was relieved to some extent when she was informed that her father had died from a stroke probably caused by the fact that he hadn't been taking his medication at all lately.

She would have liked to keep the funeral simple knowing well that it was the way Frank wanted, but didn't succeed. David and Cian insisted on having their own way. It was a large funeral. People crowded into the church. The altar was festooned with white lilies. The music was provided by a singer accompanied by a classical group of musicians. The eulogy by the priest was full of praise for the man that Frank had been, followed by David and Cian who spoke about him. She would have liked to speak about her Dad but didn't think she could hold her composure for very long and decided against it.

For her the burial was the worst part of the day. She stayed a while at the grave. A slim figure dressed in black. Just standing there thinking of him, after the rest of the family had left. She had asked Darren to go on to the hotel with David and Cian and welcome family and friends. She eventually left a while later glad of the time she had spent with her Dad.

Lunch had been arranged at The Merrion Hotel and even though she arrived late, no-one seemed to notice her absence. Everyone enjoying a drink before they would sit down to lunch. As she walked into the private room of the hotel, she focused now on getting through the rest of the day. Shaking hands and hugging friends and relatives who had no opportunity to sympathise with her earlier. Bill, her father's only brother living in Ireland, appeared. 'When will we meet with the solicitors?' he asked.

'What do you mean?' she asked, puzzled.

'For the reading of the will?'

'It's on Tuesday next, at ten o'clock,' she said.

'The usual solicitors?' he asked.

She nodded.

'I'll go along,' he said.

She wondered how many other family members would be there, and people who thought they might be included in Frank's will. While she hadn't mentioned the meeting had been arranged to anyone other than her brothers, she couldn't rely on them to keep their mouths shut. A waiter appeared at her side with a tray of drinks and she took a glass of water. The last thing she wanted was to drink, needing to keep her head clear. She met some cousins and Darren joined them and stayed chatting with the group she was with now. She thought that it was unusual. Generally, at any social setting they both attended he was never to be found close by. Always somewhere else. Talking animatedly with other people.

The afternoon crawled by, and she wished it would end. The talking grew tiring. Finding herself saying the same words. Shaking hands. Accepting hugs and air-kisses. And returning them. The mood of the people grew more jocular. The effect of a free bar. She began to feel worried. A lot of people were driving and she couldn't see how they would be in a position to safely make their way home. She excused herself from the people with whom she was talking and made her way through the crowd to find her brother.

'David?'

He turned to her, and smiled. 'Alva?'

Immediately, she was drawn into the group he was chatting with, and once again, she had to go through the ritual of their condolences. She thought she might have already talked with them earlier, but didn't remember.

Eventually, the group broke up and she managed to talk to David on his own, and voiced her worries. 'Let's close the bar, it's almost seven.'

'I can't do that.'

'Why not, no-one has an unending free bar at a funeral. How long did you book the room for?'

'Twelve o'clock.'

'That's ridiculous. Look at the condition of most of the people who are drinking. They'll have to get taxis home.'

'They're my friends and colleagues. We owe them this much.'

'But what about the cost?'

'There's plenty of money to cover it.'

'Not in the company.'

'Dad's estate will easily cover any expenses.'

'We hope. And we haven't read the will yet.'

'Anyway, he was going to invest all his money into the company but that won't happen now.'

'We can't just throw it away like this.'

'We will inherit. He always said he would divide his estate between the three of us, you, me and Cian.'

'That money will have to be put into his company, as he wanted to do.'

'To prop up a company which is on its knees?'

'Dad worked hard in the company.'

'Well, I'm taking my share, I'm putting nothing into it, no matter what you do.'

'We don't even know what we'll receive. You have to wait until we meet with the solicitor. By the way, did you mention the meeting to many people?'

He looked at her, quizzically.

'Because Bill is coming, and I didn't tell him about it.'

She didn't sleep well that night, and got up about five o'clock. She glanced into her own bedroom but it was empty. She checked her phone relieved to see a text from Darren saying that they had all stayed at the Merrion. In a way she was glad to hear that, but at the same time an uncomfortable thought reminded that perhaps he had spent the night with that woman. Jealousy swept through her and she wondered whether this feeling of insecurity would continue to dominate her days?

She went into the office. Another day had to be faced and as she walked along the corridor, she approached her father's office and stopped outside the door. Hesitantly, she reached out and touched the brass handle. Her eyes caught sight of the name plate with a horrible feeling of loss. She went in.

The heavy mahogany desk was positioned in front of the window, the brown leather chair turned to one side in exactly the same position her father had left it that last night they had both been in the office together. Suddenly she could see him moving around the desk as he had done only a few days ago. She whirled around.

'Alva?'

She heard his voice call her name.

'Dad?' she asked. 'Where are you?' She was convinced he was there. That he hadn't gone home. That he hadn't died. That he hadn't been buried yesterday. That he hadn't left her.

She sat down on her father's chair, and swung gently left and right. There was something comforting about the movement. And she let herself be taken into another place. Somewhere this man still existed. Living a vibrant fulfilled life. Having cheated death.

'Tell me what you want me to do?' she whispered softly, closing her eyes. Longing to hear his voice. To give her direction. And make sure that any decisions she might make would be approved of by her father.

'Find out who wanted to take down my company.'

She opened her eyes sharply and jerked her head upwards. Did he say that? She wondered, asking herself the question and wanting to believe it. But then she chided herself for being foolish, imagining the spirit of her father was still with her. And that she could hear him speak. And sense his personality. And know him once again. Even though she had only lost him a matter of days ago, she was desperately lonely for him.

David and Cian were both late for the meeting with their solicitor, John, although Bill was on time as she was herself. They sat in the foyer of the office after making some brief comments about the funeral.

'Did you see the London contingent?' Bill asked, in a sarcastic tone.

'I did.'

'Wonder what they want?' he smirked.

'They're relatives. They felt they should come to show respect.'

'All that way?'

She didn't reply. At that moment, the door opened and two of the first cousins of the London family appeared. 'How are you Bill, and Alva.' They shook hands.

'Fine thanks,' she smiled.

'David told us that the reading of the will would happen this morning so we thought we would come along,' they grinned at each other.

'We're waiting for my partner and brothers,' added Alva, taking her phone from her bag and calling Darren.

'Where are you.'

'On our way.'

'How long will you be?'

'About five minutes.'

'Hurry.'

She went into reception, and explained to John's secretary about the delay.

'I'll just tell him,' she said.

The solicitor took them to the board room and they sat around the large table, an air of nervous energy between them as they watched him leaf through various documents and when he had chosen one, he wasted no more time.

'This is the Last Will and Testament of Francis Gabriel Purtell, and hereby revokes all former wills and testamentary dispositions made by him.'

He went on to name the one executor - Alva - and continued.

'I give devise and bequeath the whole of my estate to my Trustees to dispose of on the following trusts.

To pay my debts, funeral and testamentary expenses.

To pay the executors an amount to cover the costs of administration over and above any Executors' expenses incurred.

I direct that my assets be liquidated and that my Trustees dispose of the assets in three equal parts to my three children – Alva Sophie Purtell, David Patrick Purtell, and Cian Trevor Purtell. Dated this 21st day of September, 2010.'

'But I just need to mention,' he said slowly. 'Your father was to come in to me to draw up a new will. He told me that the company is in trouble and as he is the main shareholder it could affect the final assets. But he never came in to sign it.'

'How soon will we get our share,' demanded David impatiently.

'It will take some time for probate to go through.'

'Are there are any other bequests?' Bill asked.

'No.'

'But he promised me money. Are you sure?'

'I'm certain.'

'Maybe he went to another solicitor.'

'Frank has dealt with our company for many years. We have handled the family business since the very beginning, and his father before him.'

'We know that, John,' Alva smiled.

'Where's my money? I told you he promised to leave me something in his will.'

'And where's our money?' the cousins who had come from London asked.

'There are no other beneficiaries in the will.'

'We must have our share. I'm going to contest it,' Bill shouted and banged the table.

'Bill, please. This isn't the place to discuss this,' Alva said gently.

'I want to see that will,' he insisted.

'You can't, without the permission of the beneficiaries but you can apply when probate has been granted,' John explained. 'There is a particular form to use, and you'll find out the gross and net value of the estate.'

'Let me see it, you're not going to protest, are you Alva. Or you David or Cian?' He leaned across the desk towards them in an aggressive manner.

Alva looked at her brothers, a questioning in her eyes. She didn't want to show her uncle her father's will. He should believe the solicitor.

'It's private, Bill, there are no other beneficiaries in Dad's will, it's just the three of us. To be honest I don't remember him ever saying that he had left money to anyone else, and he did discuss it with us. So the three of us are in agreement with our solicitor,' she said.

'We are,' David and Cian said.

The meeting finished. And a copy of the will given to each of them. They didn't hear any further from Bill. He had obviously decided not to contest the will. Or the London cousins either.

She went back to the office, and immediately talked with Hugh, David and Cian. Things had changed now.

'What's going to happen to the company, Hugh?'

'You may have to offer a portion of each of your inheritance as collateral so that the company will not be forced into liquidation.'

'I'm willing to invest my inheritance,' Alva said.

'I've no intention of giving up any of my money,' David said bluntly.

'If you don't, then neither will I,' added Cian.

'But that means the company will collapse,' Alva protested. 'My inheritance may not be enough.'

'Maybe it's time for that to happen, Dad's gone now and it was his baby,' David said.

'I want to carry on his work. It was everything to him,' Alva insisted.

'Look at it now, it's not profitable.'

'I'm going to set up my own company,' David said. 'I want to put my own stamp on it.'

'But Purtell Vintners has been established for so long we can't let it just diminish into nothing.' She was angry now.

'Let's close up the company and set up another,' Cian said enthusiastically.

'Yes, you and I, Cian.' David thumped his younger brother on the arm and he laughed.

'I don't know how you can do that, after all Dad did for us over the years.' Alva was very upset. 'And I'm going to find out exactly why we're in this position.' she vowed.

Chapter Six

Alva didn't know how she had arrived at this point. It was as if her father was directing her. Refusing to let her forget about those suspicions which were always in her head. Pounding on her brain like a bad migraine. Don't let it go, her Dad said. At the oddest of moments. As if he thought she might temporarily put it away. Under a pile of filing. Or at the end of a *to do list* Always intending to get to the end of that list. But Alva always got to the end of her lists, and didn't let things get lost in their complexity. So she promised her Dad that she wouldn't let that happen. She felt he was always with her wherever she happened to be.

Her first move was to investigate that company Tichanko Inc. She checked it out once again, but as before couldn't find out anything about it. It was a blank. A non-existent entity. She was puzzled. But immediately decided she would have to go to the address listed on their records. She didn't want to tell Hugh or David where she was intending to go but decided to fly out to Bordeaux early one morning and return that evening. As she didn't want to be quizzed by Darren, she invented various meetings, aware that there wasn't a lot of time to waste, this had to be done quickly.

The offices of Tichanko Inc. were in the city of Bordeaux in France. It was a city on the River Garonne and she was enthralled by the graceful narrow cobbled streets and beautiful architecture and wished that she was here for another reason.

She had arrived in the mid-morning and after catching a taxi from the airport, she ate a quick breakfast of *café au lait* and a croissant in the centre of the city and then went in search of the address.

She was not really sure what type of building she was looking for. Many of them were old and there were offices on every floor. Eventually, she found number thirty-five on Rue Ecole. She looked at the list of bells of what seemed to be apartments. But there was no sign of the name Tichanko Inc. She was disappointed and frustrated too. Had they moved address, she wondered. She went to the next building and searched the names on the bells, but couldn't see the name she was looking for. She did the same on every other building on that street, but found nothing. Then she went back to number thirty-five and went into a shop on the ground floor. It was a delicatessen and she hoped that she would be able to explain her predicament.

The bell rang as she opened the door, and a man dressed in a large black apron smiled jovially at her from behind the counter. The shop was literally stuffed with goods of every sort. At a glance she could see a very wide range of cheeses, pies, meats, olives, and so many other deli foods she would have loved to browse around.

'*Bonjour ...pouvez-vous m'aider s'il vous plait?*' she asked hesitantly, praying the man would understand her limited French.

'*Oui.*'

'Do you speak English?'

'*Oui, petit peu.*'

She was relieved.

'I am looking for a company called Tichanko Inc. at thirty-five, Rue Ecole, she asked, handing him a piece of paper on which she had written the name and address.

He looked at it, and raised his eyebrows.

'No, no,' he said slowly. 'I not know,' he shook his head.

'Thank you.' She was disappointed. 'Maybe I'll go to another shop.'

'*Oui, bonne idée.*'

'*Merci*,' she smiled at him, and left.

After that she tried every other shop on the street, and on some of the other streets as well. But no one had any idea of where that company might be located. Then she took out her phone and checked listings of companies. Eventually finding The Bordeaux Wine Council. Maybe they could help.

She had to take a taxi there, and found a man in the office who spoke English and was more than willing to help when she explained her problem. But unfortunately, while he searched through the listings of local vinyards, he could not find any mention of a company named Tichanko Inc. He waved his hands in the air and said that the name wasn't even French and that anyway he had never heard of it, and he knew all the companies in the area. After that, he dismissed her abruptly.

She felt very down as she made her way to the airport, and caught her flight for home. What did it mean if this company didn't exist in Bordeaux? Was it possibly a fictitious company? Had someone created it deliberately in order to carry out a financial fraud?

What had her father died for? A man who put everything he had into the business only to be swindled by some fraudster of his money. As she sat there in the plane, her mind began to consider various angles. It had to be an inside job. It would be impossible for an outsider to do such a thing. Now that she was sure that it was probably fraud within the company, all sorts of options were presenting themselves.

Who had access to money? She jotted down a list of names. At the top was Hugh, their accountant. She couldn't imagine that he would do something like that for his own benefit. And if he had taken money, was he gambling, or drinking or making bad investments using company money? And whether they could have been carried out by more than one person. That was a shock. Was it perhaps a group? And how did it actually work? She didn't know how she was going to find out.

It was about ten o'clock when Alva arrived home and drove into the apartment block. Darren's car was parked in the carpark. She went into the foyer, and took the lift up. As she reached the front door of their apartment, she hesitated before she put her key in the lock. Did she still love him? Did she want to continue living with him? These questions demanded answers and she didn't have them.

She went in, but there was no sound of Darren coming to welcome her home. In the living room she found him lying on the couch fast asleep. She was glad of that, reluctant to face him and be forced to talk about how she felt. Now she went to the spare room, lay on the bed and closed her eyes, a slight sense of guilt that she hadn't woken Darren to let him know she was home. But after a few minutes she put on her robe and went into the living room again. He was awake now, and turned with surprise when he heard her behind him.

'Alva, love, you're home.' He stood up and swung his arms around her.

'Yeah, it's me,' she laughed.

'It's so good to see you, I thought you'd never get here,' he grinned widely. 'What can I get you, glass of wine, coffee, or something to eat?'

'Coffee thanks.'

'I've opened a bottle of wine.' He picked it up.

'No thanks, I'm tired, it's been a tough day.'

He went into the kitchen, brought out a cup of coffee and handed it to her.

'Thanks.'

'What were you doing today.'

'Meeting with the auditors again.'

'What do they suggest we should do?'

'It's complicated, the boys don't want to use their inheritance to prop up the company, so it just leaves me and I mightn't have enough.'

'But what will we do?'

'We may have to set up another company.'

'How will we raise the funds?' Darren asked.

'The three of us will all inherit from Dad, so maybe I can set myself up in a smaller way.'

'I don't agree with that.'

'You don't have any say in the matter, I inherit, not you,' she pointed out.

'Surely we'll share the money, I am your partner.' Darren was surprised.

'We can set up business together, but I'm not giving you half to throw away.'

'Why not?'

'It's needed for a business.'

'I'll do something with my half. Maybe invest it. And make a lot of money.'

'No, I won't do that.'

'Mean shite,' he grumbled.

'I'm sorry.' She wasn't but she just said it to keep him quiet. 'I'm off to bed now, I'm exhausted.'

'I'm with you love.' He stood up.

'Goodnight, see you in the morning.' She went into the spare bedroom again.

'Alva, what are you doing in there?' he asked belligerently, trying to prevent her closing the door.

'Going to sleep.'

'Come into our own room,' he coaxed and tried to keep the

door open.

'I want to sleep, and I know I won't if I sleep with you.'

'What does that mean? I want to make love with you, it's been so long, I've really missed you.' He reached to kiss her.

Alva moved back.

'When are we going to be together again, I can't wait for ever.'

'You'll have to wait. Until I make up my mind what I'm going to do.'

'You just want to keep me dangling on a string. Is that it?'

She didn't answer for a moment.

'Well?' he demanded.

'Go to bed, Darren.' She wanted him to leave her alone now.

'Come on, love. Don't be like that,' he groaned.

'You've done something which has hurt me deeply, Darren, and I don't know if I'll ever get over it.' She found it hard to even say the words.

'I know I have, but I've said I'm sorry, tell me what else I can do to sort it out?'

'I don't know.'

'There has to be something.'

'You'll just have to give it time.'

'For God's sakes, how much time?'

'I can't tell you that. Look let's just leave it for now. I need sleep.'

'Go on then, sleep. Do whatever you want.'

He marched into their bedroom and banged the door.

Alva lay in bed. Her thoughts a confused medley. She still couldn't decide what she was going to do about Darren. Up to this, he had been everything to her. But now her heart was breaking at the thought that he had found another woman more attractive. The mix of emotions made the loss of her Dad even worse, and the problems with the company didn't help either.

But those problems had to be sorted immediately. The company must be saved. This was the first night that she actually managed to get some sleep, and she felt somewhat refreshed when she awoke in the early morning. The most important thing in her mind was the company and now she concentrated on working out how she might discover more facts about the purchasing side of the business. While she knew everything about the company in general, she needed to examine the warehousing department to check on orders coming in. She needed to know where the product coming from Tichanko Inc. was stored.

She went to the warehouse and spoke with the manager in charge.

'Are you familiar with the name of this company and these wines?' She handed him a sheet of paper.

He examined it. 'No.'

'You are sure?'

'Certain.'

'But of all the wines and sherries we stock how could you be so certain.'

'I know them all.'

'You've never seen these?' she insisted on asking the question again.

'No.'

'I'll look for some photographs and show them to you,' she said, wondering where she would find them.

'That would be a help. I'm sure I'd know them then.'

'Leave that to me, I'll get back to you as soon as I find some photos.'

But unfortunately, David couldn't produce any photographs of the wines at all.

In the meantime, she went back to the office to see Hugh. He was free, and she was glad of the opportunity to talk to him and sat down at his desk. 'Hugh I'm going to find out who took the money from the company. Someone did, that's certain. And I'm sure it's an inside job.'

'What?' he was surprised.

'It had to be an inside job,' she emphasised. 'There's no other way that our company funds could be depleted to such an extent.'

'It was just one of those things.' Hugh pointed out. 'I'm to blame to some extent I admit.'

'What do you mean?'

'I must have missed something. And as you mentioned, David and I didn't take the letters from the bank as seriously as we should.'

'Yes, why was that? It seemed crazy not to inform Dad and myself about it.'

'I suppose it was the pressure we were under at the time and we didn't realise what would happen.'

'But the letters from the bank should have highlighted that there was something major going wrong, you must have realised that.'

'I know,' he admitted.

'There is something else.' She had to mention the subject of Tichanko Inc. yet David had seemed to be quite aware of the existence of this company. It was then she decided to call him into the meeting. It needed both of them.

'I haven't got much time,' David said immediately he came in. He was drawing a line, and she knew it.

She took out a file and opened it, aware that there was a change of mood in the office.

'It's about Tichanko Inc.' she said.

David looked at Hugh.

'I've investigated the company, but we have no telephone number or email address on our files. So I flew over to Bordeaux yesterday. But there is no-one at that address. No one has ever heard of them. I went from street to street in case they had moved. Called to shops. Made a lot of enquiries. I even called to the Bordeaux Wine Council but they knew nothing about the company. I've talked with Mick in the Warehouse but he isn't familiar with the name of the company or the products.'

'I can't understand that,' Hugh said. 'We will have to investigate.'

'Then do it immediately, Hugh. I want answers now.'

'This is a waste of time,' David said. 'We should be getting on with running the company, trying to get back into profit and keep the banks off our back.'

'Give me the name of your contact in Tichanko Inc. You said you deal with them regularly.'

'I don't know the name off the top of my head.'

'Look it up then and I'll call him or her.'

'I haven't time now, I've a meeting.'

'Do you have the name, Hugh?'

'No, it's one of David's clients.'

'What time will you be finished your meeting?'

'It will be later this afternoon.'

'Then text me the name and number.'

'Sure.'

'Don't forget.'

'Must go.' Her brother left the room.

'Hugh, how many people would have access to David's clients.'

'Various sales people, and the Accounts Department of course.'

But while she waited anxiously she didn't receive the name or the number from David as he promised so she called him that evening.

'Sorry, I forgot.'

'You'll have to give it to me. Is there anyone else who would have it?'

He was silent.

'What is wrong with you David?'

'Nothing.'

'Then why can't you give it to me?'

'I've lost the files.'

'What?' She couldn't believe it.

'My computer crashed and while I found most of what I need, I can't locate those particular files. I have one of the IT guys working on it.'

'Why didn't you say that in the first place?' She was annoyed with him.

'I felt foolish.'

'Anybody's computer can crash. But do you have their details somewhere else?'

'No. I'll just have to wait until they place another order.'

'But I need the information now. I don't want to wait that long. There are payments there, over €20,000 last month, but no details.'

'The IT guys will have it fairly quick I'm sure.'

Alva sighed with frustration.

She examined the information she had on her computer again. She could see the various orders and made lists of the dates and particular wines their company had ordered over the past couple of years. Then she looked at the bank payments made to the company. Among the bank details, she was able to see the amounts transferred and the number of the account. But she was puzzled to see that there were three different bank accounts credited. And there seemed to be no logic as to which invoices applied to which account. She was still frustrated. Would she ever find what she was looking for?

Chapter Seven

On her way home, Alva stopped off at a bar to meet her friend Naomi. They often got together for a chat, although Naomi was a Garda Inspector and like herself extremely busy all the time. But she was someone Alva knew since they started school together, and they had a longstanding arrangement which she didn't want to break.

All day, she had thought about what she should do. Her relationship with Darren had disintegrated suddenly. It was like she had fallen into a black hole and was unable to get out. The biggest question was whether she could ever trust Darren again. She had always believed in him implicitly, loving him so much, but now what lay ahead?

She ordered a coffee, and sat in shadow in an alcove watching out for Naomi.

'I'm so sorry to be late, but as usual someone caught me as I left the station. It's always the same,' she smiled apologetically.

'Coffee?' Alva asked.

'Yeah, I need it. What a day.'

'Latte?'

'Thanks.'

Alva waved to a waitress and when she came over ordered a latte.

'How about you?' Naomi asked. 'You must be very upset since your Dad died.'

'There's a lot happening,' Alva admitted.

'You seem exhausted.' Naomi looked at her.

'I am, haven't been sleeping well.'

'It will take a while to get over the grieving.' She was very sympathetic. 'I'm sorry I hardly saw you at the funeral there were so many people there. Although I talked to Darren.'

'Darren and I ...have problems,' Alva admitted.

'That's awful. How long has that been going on?'

'Just recently.'

'Can I do anything for you? Maybe talk to him perhaps?'

The waitress brought over the coffee for Naomi.

'Thank you but I don't think there's much can be done. I just have to deal with it.'

'Difficult.'

Alva sipped her coffee. It felt good. 'But it's nice to see you, and have a chat. How are you getting on these days? Any unusual cases?' she laughed. 'Not that you'd be telling me anyway.'

'I'm involved in a tough case all right, but we're not making much progress yet.'

'Is there pressure from the top?'

'Course. They're always on our backs. And then I'm putting pressure on the rest of the team who aren't too happy with me.'

'You've got it coming from all sides. I don't know how you put up with the stress of it, day to day, morning and night, twenty-four seven.'

'Your situation is personal, that makes a difference, mine is just a job and I could walk out if I felt like it. That's if I could afford to do such a thing. There is the mortgage to pay and other stuff as well, so I'm probably stuck. Still I like the job most of the time, as you know,' she laughed.

'But for me, it's nice to chat to someone neutral,' Alva said. 'I can't really tell people in work what's going on with us as Darren works in the company, and it's not something I want to talk about generally. And then there are problems in the company as well. The bank is on our backs.'

'Financial stuff?'

'Yeah.'

'You really are having a bad time.'

'I won't talk any more about it. Bore you to tears. Any bit of romance in your life?'

'Not a sign. Where would I get the time?' she laughed.

'You'd make it if someone appeared on the horizon.'

'Sure I would, but I don't think that's going to happen in the near future.'

'There are quite a few men in your workplace, fancy any of them?'

Naomi shook her head. 'Since that last relationship I had, you know I vowed never to mix business and pleasure ever again.'

'You're right, look at me now with Darren. It could prove very awkward at work.'

But as she took a sip of coffee, she saw the door of the pub open and a man walk in. Her heart leapt. It was Darren. For one crazy moment she thought that he was coming in because he guessed where she may be, but that possibility was dismissed immediately when she noticed a woman following him. Her heart dropped. It was that bitch he had taken into their bed. She leaned forward in the chair. Her eyes following the two figures as they made their way through the tables, found a vacant one and sat down. Bastard, she whispered, as a surge of anger swept through her. She was numb with shock and watched as a waiter came to take their order.

'Excuse me, Naomi, won't be a minute.' She stood up and walked through the tables to where they were sitting. She was going to have it out with him.

'Darren?' She stood in front of them.

'Alva?' He looked bewildered.

'What are you doing here with her?' she demanded.

'I …' he stuttered.

'Well?' She felt like screaming but kept her voice down. Staring all the time at him, ignoring the woman.

'I thought you said that she meant nothing to you.'

Her attention was then drawn to the woman when she placed her hand possessively on his.

He didn't say anything.

'Tell her to F off, Darren,' the woman said, moving closer to him.

'Alva, just go please?' he said.

'How dare you,' Alva said.

The barman came over with their drinks and put them on the table.

'Stay with her then,' Alva said. 'Don't bother coming home.'

She turned and walked back to where Naomi was sitting, but by the time she sat down again and looked in their direction, Darren and the woman were already leaving.

'You handled that very well,' Naomi said.

'Could you hear me?' she asked, feeling embarrassed.

'No, but I could guess what you were saying.'

'Bastard.' Alva was furious.

'That's a difficult situation,' Naomi said.

'Maybe it's good that I caught them together again. He was in bed with her the first time and denied there was anything in it. It was just sex. Meant nothing.'

'Bet you feel like having a drink after that,' Naomi grinned at Alva.

'I do, but I'm driving, and as you're a Garda, you're going to catch me before I get into the car.'

'The job has its disadvantages sometimes. So now what will you do?' she asked.

'I told him not to come home.'

63

'Do you think he'll stay with her tonight?'

'Don't know. But it proves he's still involved with her, so all his protestations mean nothing. Now I think I might change the locks.'

Darren didn't come home. A feeling of sadness crept over her. Such loss. First her father. Now Darren. The company. She couldn't imagine how this had all happened in such a short space of time. Was it her own fault?

But she had to continue searching through the accounts again. At the references. A long string of numbers and letters which listed the account detail into which the payment was lodged. She printed off some of them and tried to see if there were any connections between them. Particularly searching for groups of letters which might indicate the name of the person who held that account. It had to be here somewhere, she thought. A little clue which would give her an idea that would help her find out who was the fraudster behind the problems with the company.

Darren burst into her office.

'Alva ...'

She stared at him.

'Darling, I'm so sorry, but last night I was just letting her know that it was finished. That is, her and me.' He sat on a chair and leaned towards her. 'But it was difficult, she wouldn't accept it and it took me ages to persuade her. You were so angry I went to a hotel, I couldn't face you last night.'

'If she wouldn't accept it then that's your problem,' Alva said.

'I don't know how to deal with her.' He held his hand over his forehead in a defeated way like a child.

'For God's sake, Darren, you're pathetic.'

There was a knock on the door and Hugh came in. 'Alva, can we have a meeting? Oh, sorry to interrupt ...' he said when he saw Darren.

'Won't be long, Hugh,' Alva said.

He closed the door.

'What else do you have to say?' Alva asked Darren.

'I was trying to explain what happened last night.'

'I don't need your explanation. We're finished, Darren. You and I.'

'No, she and I are finished.'

'You can do what you like. I own the apartment so you're not entitled to any part of it.'

'But I want to live with you, Alva, I love you.' He reached out with his hand and covered hers. 'You can't put me out.'

She immediately took her hand away.

'Alva, don't do this.'

'I'm doing it. You crossed the line by sleeping with that other woman, and it's something I'll never tolerate. I want to be able to trust you completely. If I can't then I'm not interested in continuing to have any relationship with you.'

'But we work together. That could be difficult.'

'It will be just as normal. You do your thing, I'll do mine.'

'But I can't come in every day and have to keep my distance like you were my boss or someone, and not to be able to touch you, or kiss you, that would be hell.'

'Get another job.' She threw that out with flippancy. He deserved it.

He stood up and walked around the desk.

'All I need is forgiveness, Alva, can't you see that?'

She wondered now did she ever love him?

'I've a meeting, Darren.'

But he was there again at home when she arrived.

'How are you?' he gathered her gently in his arms. 'I've been waiting, thought you'd never get here.'

She extricated herself from his embrace, but said nothing.

65

'Can I get you anything?'

'No thanks, I'm going to bed.'

'Come on Alva, I've just poured a glass of wine.'

'Drink it yourself.'

'Just one, you'll enjoy it.'

'No, Darren, I told you, I'm going to bed.'

She pushed him away from her, and walked to the spare bedroom.

He followed her. 'I want to talk to you, love. We need to work through everything.'

'Tomorrow.'

'I can't wait that long.'

'I'm tired, Darren.'

'There won't be time tomorrow,' he grumbled.

'I'll be home early.' She sighed.

'Alva?' he shouted.

She didn't respond. Just opened the door of the bedroom and disappeared inside. It was all she did these days. She hardly made a cup of tea in the place.

'Alva?'

She heard his voice but to get it out of her head, she went into the bathroom. Took off her clothes and stepped into the shower. His voice faded and she was glad of that. She couldn't bear the whining. He must think she would come around and be persuaded to forgive him. Just like that. What a nerve. Anger churned. He hadn't a clue how she felt. She stood there. Letting the water flow over her. The warmth somehow soothing.

She wrapped herself in a towel. Went over to the door, put her ear close to it, and was relieved that she couldn't hear his voice any longer. She sat on the bed and took out her laptop. She opened the folders in which she had saved the bank statements related to Tichanko Inc. She searched through the bank transfers, examining the reference numbers again and again. In a notebook, she jotted down sections of the numbers. She felt like a code breaker in Bletchley Park during the war. She wondered if that place still existed and laughed. She could ask her computer to find similarities among the reference numbers. It was possible, she was certain about that. But she couldn't ask anyone in IT to do it for her.

Then suddenly, her idea went somewhere. One of these numbers or letters were going to help her to find out who had taken their company to where it was now. She left at six-thirty in the morning before Darren had got up. She didn't want to talk to him. It would only mean a row and she couldn't face the day if that happened. She would be better prepared to discuss their relationship later this evening.

He was in the office that day. Mostly tied up with meetings in his own department. So they had almost no contact other than a brief meeting as he came into her office.

'What time will you finish?'

'I'll be home about seven.'

'Ok. Seven.' He nodded.

She didn't meet his eyes during the brief conversation. She couldn't.

She went back to her lists again as she took a break at lunchtime. Now looking at their register of employees and comparing their names with the references on the bank statement. It was slow and painstaking. Her eyes were tired from concentration.

As she folded away her papers, something made her glance at one of the pages and she noticed that a group of letters in a particular reference was the same as that of Hugh, the Chief Accountant. Hugh O'Carroll. The letters HOC suddenly stood out and screamed connection. But shock horror too. Surely not. It couldn't be Hugh.

She refused to believe it. She stared at the letters for a long time, making the links, only eventually forced to dismiss the possibilities which she saw there.

But that suspicion grew and grew in her mind as the afternoon went on, and when she got home in the evening, she had even forgotten to order food. She wasn't cooking anything for Darren ever again.

'What would you like, Chinese or Indian?' she called out to him from the hall.

'Indian.'

'The usual?'

'Yeah.'

She called in the order.

'I've opened a bottle of red,' he said. When she went into the living room, she noticed he had set the table, and was pouring the wine.

She changed her clothes, and when she heard the doorbell almost collided with Darren as he came into the hall at the same time.

'I'll get it love,' he said.

'Put on the oven to keep it warm,' she said.

'It's already on.'

He came back into the living room. 'Come over and have a drink,' he cajoled. The tone in his voice irritated her.

He handed her a glass. They clinked.

'Sláinte,' he said. 'I'll plate up the dishes,' he went into the kitchen.

She could hear him clattering inside, and then he came in and put the plates on the table.

'Thanks.'

'Looks good,' he tasted it.

She took a forkful of the lamb korma. But suddenly wasn't sure if she would be able to eat much more.

'Mango chutney?' he offered. 'Or spicy?'

'No thanks.'

He continued eating, and she sipped her wine. A voice on the television droned in the background.

She took another couple of mouthfuls of korma and rice. She had to eat. Hadn't eaten all day and knew she wouldn't sleep properly if she didn't.

'Bread?' Darren asked.

She took a piece of naan and bit into its crustiness.

'More wine?'

She shook her head.

'Come on.'

'I've enough.'

'You haven't finished your dinner.'

'Not hungry.'

'Are you feeling all right?'

'We have to talk, Darren.' She pushed the plate away from her. He sipped his wine.

There was a moment of tension between them. And a lot of questions.

'Can you forgive me?' he asked.

'No, I can't,' she said finally. 'That night in the bedroom…and in the bar last night …I couldn't bear to go through that again.'

'How many times do I have to apologise and promise that I will never see her again?' His eyes begged.

'But you said that once before and then I see you in the bar. So that promise didn't last long.'

'I was telling her that we were over.'

'I don't believe that, and I don't trust you. That's the basic problem, Darren, don't you realise that?'

'You have my promise.'

'I don't want another one. I think we need to separate. I need space to be on my own.'

'But we work together, I see you every day. I couldn't bear it

69

if we weren't getting up in the mornings, or going home in the evenings. I want you in my life.'

'I'm sorry.' She had to say it.

'Look, let's see what we can do. Why don't we take a few days off and you can get your head straight. Maybe we'll go somewhere exotic. Please give us another chance?'

'There's too much happening at the moment.'

'Every time I suggest something you knock it on the head,' he burst out angrily.

'It's the way I feel, Darren. I just don't want to live with you anymore.'

Chapter Eight

She didn't say another word to Darren that night. She was very frustrated. Somehow, no matter what she said, she didn't seem to be able to get through to him. He couldn't understand how she felt.

As she lay there, she longed to turn the clock back in time. Before all those days, those grim dark days, which had dragged her screaming silently to where she was now. She felt there was no way out.

The call came through just after nine thirty. The solicitor. She took it.

'Hallo John? How are you?'

'Fine thanks. Alva, could you call in to see me, there's something I need to discuss with you,' he asked.

'Sure. Just let me have a look at my diary.' She pulled the desk diary towards her. 'When would suit you?' she asked, anxious now.

'How about later on today?'

She ran her finger down the list of appointments, glad to see a gap in the mid-afternoon.

'Between three and four, how would that be for you?' Her fingernail, silver painted, hovered over the only free time in this day. She had been holding on to it. A break. A few minutes which offered respite. And now it was gone. It had drifted away like a cloud on the breeze and disappeared

'That would be fine.'

'Do you want to tell me what you want to talk about? Should I bring any files?'

'Eh …no …I'll explain when I see you.' He seemed hesitant. And she wondered what exactly he was on about.

At three-thirty precisely, she walked into the reception. Glad she had managed to get through the rest of the day without undue delay. John's secretary took her into his office straight away.

'Thanks for coming.' He stood up with a smile from behind his desk, hand outstretched. 'Sit down.'

She liked John. Had known him since she was a young girl, often brought in to see him by her Dad if he had business to discuss.

'Your father is going to be a big loss,' he murmured.

She nodded, but had no words to follow his remark. All of a sudden feeling so emotional she had to try hard to hide the tears which threatened to well up in her eyes. Suddenly, she didn't feel confident that she could talk about her Dad with John.

'I'm sorry, it all got to me there for a minute.'

'Don't worry.'

'What did you want to discuss with me?' she asked, hoping it wasn't going to take her to another emotional impasse.

'This is something which could prove to be very awkward for you.'

The lump in her stomach dropped even further.

'Someone has made contact with me,' he said slowly. 'Through another legal firm.'

She listened, puzzled.

He stared down at the file in front of him.

'How long has it been since you had contact with your mother?' he asked softly.

She stared at him. Shocked.

'I'm not sure, I was very young,' she hesitated.

John pushed a box of tissues across the desk towards her and she took one and dried her eyes, glad that it blocked his view of her face.

'Yesterday, I received a phone call from Julie,' he said.

She couldn't believe it. Her mother had disappeared from the family home when Alva was five or six, and her brothers, David and Cian, were both younger. And according to her father her mother had not wanted to take her children with her. Alva had never heard the full details of why this had happened, and when she had asked her father as she grew older he never answered her and she was left frustrated. The only memento she had of her mother was a photo of her taken when she was a young woman. She didn't know who had given it to her, but she kept it secretly all these years and told no-one of its existence. In Alva's family home, there were no photos of her mother.

'What did she say?' Alva asked, tremulous.

'That she wanted to discuss the estate.'

'What?'

'They never divorced and that means she is entitled to one third of your father's estate. The balance, two thirds, is divided between you and your brothers.'

'How do we know they never divorced?' Alva couldn't believe this.

'I've checked. No formal separation or divorce between them.'

'How much did Dad tell you about Julie? Did you know her? I know you were good friends with Dad.'

'I knew her and Frank told me he was devastated when she left and couldn't understand why. But assumed that there was another man in her life.'

'Did she go to live with this other man?'

'He never found out anything about him and couldn't get over the tragedy of it. He threw himself into looking after you and your brothers. That was all he wanted to do in his life after what happened.'

'What exactly did she say to you?'

'She's been living in Spain and she's coming in to see me tomorrow morning.'

'Did she ask to see us?' Alva was shaking.

He shook his head.

'So she just wants money?'

'I don't know that.'

'I never knew where my mother was, you know, I used to ask Dad, but he would never answer my questions.'

'That must have been very hard on you. Have you talked to your brothers about her?'

'No. We never go there.'

'I see.' He nodded.

'What time is she coming in to see you tomorrow?' Alva asked. A kernel of an idea forming in her mind.

'I'm afraid I can't tell you that, client confidentiality.'

'She wasn't mentioned in the will, does that mean that she will have to contest it?'

'No. The executor will have to write to her to tell her the amount to which she is entitled.'

'I'm the executor,' Alva murmured.

'Yes.'

After that, there wasn't much more to say. As she walked out of the solicitor's office she was in a daze, and really couldn't concentrate on anything. She didn't want to go home and start arguing with Darren and decided to go over to her old home. Somehow, she wanted to spend time in that place where her father and mother had lived when they were first married, and had their three children.

She did some basic shopping on the way home and let herself

in and went into the kitchen. Making tea and a sandwich which she ate sitting down in her father's armchair in front of the television and watched the evening news programmes. Later, she went around the house, looking for something which would remind her of her mother. Although having lived here most of her life she had never found anything other than that photograph she had in her wallet. She took it out and looked at it. Her mother was beautiful. A vibrant dark-haired smiling woman. And Alva wondered now would she recognise her if she should happen to meet her. It was only then that the idea which occurred to her earlier today when she was sitting in front of John, her solicitor, came back to her.

The following morning, by nine on the dot, she was sitting at a window table in a café beside the solicitor's office. Her eyes watching the comings and goings of people along the street. She was very nervous. Every now and then she looked at the photo in her hand. But didn't imagine that a mature person would look anything like the young woman depicted there. She wondered if she was wasting her time. Her mother might have no interest in meeting her, particularly as she had left her children when they were so young and hadn't shown any interest in them in the intervening years.

As she sat there, a number of people had gone into the building where the solicitor's office was located and she could easily have gone in. Then a taxi drew up, and a woman and a man climbed out. Alva peered. Standing up to get a better vantage point. There was something familiar about her. A look of herself almost. Alva's shoulder length hair was dark, and this woman's hair was much the same colour but was cut in a shorter style, and was slightly grey. Her heart raced. For a moment, she didn't know what to do. They went into the building through the automatic doors and Alva grabbed her handbag and followed at a distance. They stood at the lift doors which slid open and they went inside. The doors closed again. Alva stared at the number which indicated the floor at which the lift had stopped. It was the fourth floor, and that was where John's office was located. Immediately, Alva was about to take the lift as well but stopped. There was no point going into John's office. He wouldn't allow her into the meeting if that woman happened to be her mother. She knew that. So she walked across the foyer and sat down in a seat to take a breath. She relaxed, and leaned into the soft leather back, prepared to wait. In the meantime, she watched the people going up to the fourth floor. Examined every person who passed. Their faces. Features. Walk. Style. Reminders of the woman who's photograph she held in her hand.

She picked up the Irish Times and flicked through an article or two just to pass the time. But she wasn't really concentrating, her eyes constantly moving around the foyer as people came in and out.

When the same couple actually came out of the lift, she was prepared, and stood up immediately, turning to face the woman first.

'Julie?' It was the only name she could call her, feeling that to call her by anything else would be inappropriate.

The woman stared at Alva who could immediately see recognition in her eyes.

'Are you Julie?' She had to capitalise on that one moment. Although she could see a likeness in her eyes of her Auntie Cass, Julie's sister, who had died some years before. Also, there was a look of Alva's brother, David, in her face as well.

The woman nodded. 'I am Julie.'

'I'm Alva.'

'Alva?' The woman breathed her name and smiled widely. Put her arms around Alva's shoulders and embraced her.

Held in a wave of delicate perfume, Alva burst into tears, quite unable to move. She was stunned and wasn't able to say anything to Julie.

'It's wonderful to meet you.' Julie touched her tearstained cheeks with her manicured fingers. 'Can I introduce you to my partner's son, Carlos.'

Alva turned her eyes to meet those of the tall dark eyed man who stood beside Julie.

'It is my pleasure, Alva.' He held out his hand and took hers.

'My darling daughter. You are so beautiful,' Julie whispered, in tears also. 'I cannot believe I am meeting you at last.' She dabbed her eyes with a wisp of a fine cotton handkerchief. 'Can we go somewhere to talk?'

Alva nodded. She still couldn't say anything she was so emotional.

'You have time?'

She nodded again.

'Is there somewhere we could have a cup of coffee nearby?' Julie asked, putting her arm through Alva's as they walked out through the doors together.

'Yes.'

They went into the café Alva had been in earlier and sat down at a table, and it was only now she was able to finally speak.

'My solicitor told me that you have been living in Spain, is this the first time you have been back in Dublin?' Alva asked gently. Still feeling utterly emotional and finding it hard to keep control. To have her mother close to her after all this time was amazing.

'No. I have been back occasionally with Carlos and Nuria, his sister.'

'Both of us studied here and now I work here, so we know Dublin well,' Carlos said.

All Alva could think was how astonishing it was that her mother could have passed her by any day in town, although it had often occurred to her as she grew up.

She ordered coffee and scones.

'This is so lovely.' Julie gazed around her, a broad smile on her lips.

'I was in Spain a little while ago,' she said, thinking how much of a coincidence that was.

'Where?' Carlos asked.

'Jerez de la Frontera, when the Flamenco Festival was on.'

'We live near Seville.'

'I was there too,' explained Alva, laughing.

Julie smiled. 'I cannot believe it.'

'Did you go to any of the concerts in Jerez,' Carlos asked with a smile.

'I went to one and really enjoyed it.'

'Which artist was performing?' asked Julie.

'María Moreno.'

'She's a wonderful dancer. Every year I go to some of the concerts, and we often see performances in small bars as well. There are a lot of different places which present Flamenco in Jerez,' Julie said.

Alva was glad to chat about that, and her threatening emotions were held in check. There was a slight pause and she asked another question. She had to talk. To keep the thread of conversation going, however inconsequential it was.

'Do you dance Flamenco?' she asked Julie.

'I do, although I'm not very good, but I enjoy it, and often take a class with one of the dancers who present their shows during the festival,' Julie said.

'I'd love to learn, but I'm sure they wouldn't want a complete novice in their classes,' she laughed.

'You could take classes in Dublin.'

'I've never heard of anyone holding Flamenco classes in Dublin.'

'Look up online, there's bound to be one or two, I'm sure.'

'I've never thought of taking dance classes, there just isn't time.'

It was a very strange feeling to meet her mother like this, and to talk in this light hearted fashion.

The waitress arrived with coffee and scones, butter, blackberry jam, and whipped cream.

It was pleasant, although there were no revelations. While Alva wanted to ask questions about the past, she held back, aware that the amazing mood at that table would splinter like shards of glass and allow the darkness which she knew must exist at the depths of their lives free rein.

'How long …will you stay in Dublin, Julie?' Alva asked hesitantly.

'I leave the day after tomorrow.'

Alva wanted to know why she was here. Was it because of her father's will? But she was afraid to ask that more pointed question. While Julie hadn't told her anything, she knew that the solicitor would let her know the exact reason why her mother was here in Dublin. But she was glad to have met her at last. To fill all those years of loneliness with something tangible.

She tried to pay the bill, but Carlos insisted that he would get it. They walked outside.

'I'd love to see you both again if you have time before you return?' Alva asked. Although she wasn't sure whether Julie had any interest in seeing her again.

'Why yes, that would be lovely.' Julie responded with enthusiasm. 'When would suit you?'

'Tomorrow perhaps?' suggested Alva. 'Would you like to meet for dinner? And I'll see if Cian and David can come as well.'

'That would be perfect, I would give anything to meet them.'

They made the arrangements and as soon as she arrived back in the office, Alva phoned her solicitor, John, and told him she had met Julie and Carlos.

He seemed surprised.

'It was very strange. I wasn't sure whether Julie wanted to meet me again at all. Our conversation was very light, as if we were just acquaintances. I couldn't believe it. You hear so many stories about people meeting parents, and many times they don't get on at all.'

'I have to say she was very pleasant,' John said. 'And the man who was with her.'

'What did she say to you? Can you tell me what she wanted John, exactly?' Alva asked.

'She just wanted to know what happened to Frank, and you, David and Cian. But apparently, she has kept in touch with her own legal people over the years, and they have informed her about what was happening with your family, and how you were all getting on.'

'My God, that's astonishing. She knew what we were doing?'

'So she said.'

Alva was very surprised.

'As Julie will receive one third of your father's estate, it will make a considerable difference to your own inheritance and that of David and Cian.'

'And I was going to invest my money back into the company so that we won't be forced into liquidation, so that will make it less effective. The lads don't want to do that. They don't care about the company as much as I do, particularly David, and that causes me a lot of sadness, particularly when we have just lost Dad.'

'I can understand.' John nodded.

'Still it's wonderful to have met Julie after all this time. I'll be meeting her and Carlos tomorrow evening for dinner, but I'll talk to the lads in the meantime and see if they would like to meet their mother.'

'I'd recommend that.'

'It's going to be a shock to them.'

She walked down the corridor to David's office and was glad to find that he was there.

'Can you spare a few minutes?' she asked with a smile.

'Anything up?'

'No, not exactly.'

'You have me full of curiosity now. I know by your face that there's something. You can't fool me,' he grinned.

'There is, I'll admit.'

'It's not that bee in your bonnet about the company in France, is it?' he laughed.

'That bee is still buzzing,' she said. 'I haven't forgotten about it, but it's ...' She hesitated for a moment. 'I've asked Cian to come up,' she added, unsure how exactly she was going to introduce the subject of their mother.

Cian pushed open the door and came in. 'You were looking for me?'

'Yeah, there's something I want to tell you both.'

'What is it?' he asked.

'It's a bit difficult.'

They stared at her, their faces puzzled.

Alva took a deep breath and slowly spoke. 'It's about ...our mother, Julie.'

Cian sat down on one of the chairs, but he said nothing.

David's mouth fell open with shock.

'John, our solicitor, told me that she had been in touch and that he had a meeting arranged. I decided to wait until their meeting was over and as she came out of the lift I just walked up to her.'

'How did you know her?' Cian asked.

'She looks a bit like our Auntie Cass, and David actually.'

'That must have been a very strange experience for you.'

'It was amazing. And she behaved like we had only met last week. She put her arms around me, and was so affectionate, I couldn't believe it. And there was a man with her.'

'Who was he?' asked Cian.

'Carlos is his name. He is her partner's son.'

'So she did end up with another man, bitch.' David was angry.

'Apparently. But I often wondered whether we had the full story,' Alva said. 'Did Dad ever talk to you about it?'

'No,' Cian said.

David shook his head.

'Anyway, we're meeting for dinner tomorrow night. Would you like to come along and meet Julie? She's very anxious to meet you both.'

'She has some cheek,' David seemed bitter. 'Walking away when we were so young.'

'I didn't actually mention that.'

'Why not? I'd have torn strips off her.'

'Cian, do you remember our mother?'

'I've a vague recollection of her. I seem to remember her hugging very tight, I think she always did that.'

'Would you like to meet her?'

'Oh, I would,' he smiled, instantly delighted with the idea.

Chapter Nine

Alva and Cian arrived at the restaurant early. She wanted to talk with Cian before meeting with Julie, but there was no opportunity as she also happened to be early.

Alva stood up when she saw Julie walk through the doors, as did Cian. She waved to her and their mother walked towards them, smiling.

Julie enveloped Alva in a close embrace. 'How lovely to see you again.'

'This is Cian,' she introduced him.

Julie turned and stared at him. 'Cian,' she said softly, and stretched out her arms towards him. They held each other tightly without words for a long moment.

Alva sat down and waited. Again, she could hardly believe her eyes.

'It's wonderful to meet you both.' Julie stood with her arm around Cian.

'Sit down.' Alva moved along the bench seat in the alcove. Julie sat between the two of them.

'Is David coming?' Julie asked, looking around the restaurant.

'No, unfortunately he has a meeting this evening.' Alva murmured. But when she enquired about Carlos it appeared that he was working this evening as well.

The waiter came with the menus and handed one to each of them.

'Julie, would you like something to drink? Glass of wine?'

'I don't drink alcohol, so I'll just have a juice, that would be fine thank you.'

'Me neither,' laughed Cian. 'We have something in common.'

'We have a lot in common.' Julie put her hand on his. 'We are of the same blood.'

Cian smiled.

The waiter arrived and when they had given him their orders, they chatted about their family.

'Do you have a partner, Cian?' Julie asked.

'Yes, Natalie is her name.'

'I'd love to meet her too.'

'We'll arrange that.' Cian seemed really happy.

'And Alva, what about you?' Julie asked.

'To be honest, I've just separated from my partner.'

'I'm sorry to hear that.'

'It's for the best,' Alva said, reluctant to talk about it.

'And David?'

'He has a lovely wife, Sarah and two gorgeous kids, Jon and Sisi, they're eight and six,' Alva explained.

'My grandchildren, I'd give anything to see them. Maybe you might persuade David to meet me before I fly out tomorrow afternoon?'

'I'll call him,' Alva said, but didn't feel there was much hope of that.

'And your company? Is it going well?'

'Not really, there are few problems there, but we won't talk about that today,' Alva hedged. This was a very happy day and she didn't even want to think about the company.

Alva had some questions to ask her mother but decided to wait until they had eaten. The meal was delicious and they all enjoyed their choices.

It was at the coffee stage that Alva decided to ask those questions which were burning through her.

'Julie, all of us would really like to know what happened between yourself and Dad, and why you left us? We've had to live with that.' She looked into Julie's face, praying she would give them some explanation.

'I can understand why you want to know this. What did your father tell you?'

'He said nothing at all,' Alva said.

'Nothing?'

She shook her head.

'I was at fault mostly,' Julie said slowly. 'And I was sure that Frank would have blamed me, and rightly so.'

Neither Alva or Cian spoke.

'Unfortunately, I had a problem with alcohol.' Julie continued. 'I was very difficult to live with no doubt in that I tried to hide my addiction, secretly drinking at home.'

'Is this difficult for you?' Alva asked. Thinking that it had to be.

'No, there is some therapy in assuaging my guilt at last. I must admit my responsibility. My first thoughts were that I had to get out of that house to deal with whatever was wrong with me. I didn't think I could do that on my own with Frank overlooking everything. He was very critical of me, and really whatever I did was never quite up to scratch. While on the surface we were happy, but underneath ...' her voice tailed off.

'I'm so sorry that you felt that way, but it was such a pity you couldn't sit down and discuss it then.'

'Of course, the final outcome wasn't expected when we did talk and tried to come to a decision. But I offered to go somewhere and get treatment and Frank was delighted with that. But I was very upset leaving you Alva, and David too. But at that time you weren't born Cian.' There were tears in her eyes, and she put out her two hands and held both of theirs.

'How did you get on?' Cian asked.

'I did well after treatment, and came home, but it didn't last.

'That's sad.' Alva felt for her.

'Then I had you, Cian,' she smiled at him. 'But sadly I went back drinking again a few months later. It seemed to be a waste of time. Then, to my utter shock, Frank told me he wasn't going to put up with me and my problems any longer.'

'But, from the point of view of marriage, he had a responsibility too. Fifty-fifty today, sixty-forty tomorrow and so on.' Alva pointed out.

'But then sometime later he met someone else.'

'What? He certainly never mentioned that to us and never brought a woman into the house as far as I can remember, but then we were only young kids,' Alva was shocked.

'Remember the first housekeeper, Sally?' Reminded Julie.

Cian and Alva looked at one another, puzzled.

'He never wanted me back after she came to look after you, they were definitely together,' Julie said.

'Are you sure?' Cian asked. 'I knew nothing about that.'

'Your father told me.'

'And Sally was there until we were teenagers,' he said.

'Then Nora came to look after the house after Sally died, I was about fifteen,' said Alva.

'But how could you leave without any of us?' asked Cian, puzzled.

'He gave me no choice.'

'Why didn't you go to court and look for custody?' he asked.

'I can't understand why you didn't,' Alva murmured emotionally.

'Neither can I,' Cian said.

'It was blackmail. I had no money, no job, and nowhere to live, so a court was never going to give me custody of three children.'

Alva began to understand.

'So you can see how there was no choice for me. But still I have always felt very guilty that I allowed it to happen.'

Tears flooded Julie's eyes.

'It has been with me ever since.'

'Did things improve for you?'

'I did manage to get a part-time job, but it didn't pay very well and I couldn't save enough to offer you children a home, or look for custody. And your father had a successful company and was able to give you everything you needed. Eventually, I went to Spain and worked in bars until I met Pedro, my partner, and he needed someone to look after his own young children as his wife had died, and he offered me the job, so I stayed there with him.'

'Did you keep in touch with Dad?' asked Alva.

'I did, but he didn't want me back and wouldn't allow me to talk to you children. He felt it would be upsetting for you. So he kept me at a distance.' She bent her head, obviously very upset.

Cian put his arm around her shoulders.

'Would you like another cup of coffee?' Alva asked gently.

'No thank you.'

'I'm sorry you're so upset.'

'It's not your fault. This is my life.'

'But you had Pedro, didn't you?'

'Yes.'

'And you were happy?'

'I was very lucky to meet him. He is a very nice man and he loves me.'

'It's been so good to meet you. I never expected it to happen. Our father died so suddenly we didn't have an opportunity to talk about you. We should have done that before now,' Alva said.

'I'm so glad I decided to meet your solicitor. I made contact with a solicitor myself and asked him to let me know what was happening to the family over the years. I always read the Irish Times online anyway and I saw the notice of Frank's death there.'

'Would you give us your phone number and we can call you?'

'Here is my card.' She took a small silver box from her leather handbag and handed Alva a card, and Cian as well. They gave her their cards as well.

'My daughter, and sons, I have you again at last. My little children,' Julie whispered.

'We should have known you before now. I can't believe my father wouldn't have made that possible, even when we were older.'

'I think he was afraid of losing you.'

'That was crazy. Did he think we'd all leave home to live with you?'

'Perhaps he did. He wasn't a very confident man.'

'I never would have thought that. He always seemed to be so completely on top of everything.'

'He was afraid of me and what I might do,' she smiled. 'That's why he didn't want me to have any contact with you.'

'If only we knew where you were.' Alva hugged her again.

They parted emotionally outside the restaurant, particularly Cian, and Alva took Julie home to Carlos's apartment.

'It's been wonderful to meet you, Julie,' Alva said, still calling her mother by her name, feeling awkward about calling her Mother or Mum. They hugged again in the car.

'Why don't you come in for a coffee? Carlos may be home.'

Alva wanted to extend the time she had with her mother as much as she could so immediately accepted. To pack all those years of loss into such a short time. All that emptiness. She thought of the time spent with Darren and now faced a future without him as well. Also, in the background was the concern about the company and what exactly would happen with the bank. It was almost too much, but she concentrated on getting to know Julie. That had to be the most important.

Carlos was home and he made coffee for them. Carrying in a tray he put it on the low table, and sat down with them.

'I'll be mother.' Julie grasped the coffee pot and began to pour.

Those few words left a question in the air between them, but neither Carlos or Alva said anything. There was something so poignant about those words, her heart began to thump erratically. Obviously, it was very important for Julie to say it.

They chatted generally, and Alva found out about Julie and Carlos and the rest of their family, and told them more about their lives in Dublin.

'Where do you work, Alva?' Carlos asked with a wide smile.

'At the family firm. We all work together.'

'What do you do?'

'We are in the wine and sherry business mostly in Spain and France.'

'How interesting. I didn't know.'

Obviously, Julie hadn't told any of her Spanish family about her own background, Alva thought. But then, why would she? Her ties with Dublin had been completely cut so long ago, although Alva had been very surprised to hear that Carlos actually studied and worked in Dublin now as a neurosurgeon at Beaumont Hospital and that his sister Nuria had studied in Trinity College.

'What is your own role?' Carlos asked.

'I am CEO of the company.'

'A very responsible position,' he commented.

'Thanks. I enjoy my work.'

'I'm sorry about your father,' Carlos said.

'It was very sad to lose him.' She didn't want to say too much and neither Julie or Carlos made any more remarks. Suddenly, there was an uneasy silence between them.

'I think it's time I went home, I've a very early start.' Alva rose from her chair, and picked up her handbag.

'It's been lovely to see you.' Julie walked with her to the door.

'And for me too. I can't believe I've actually met you at last, it's wonderful,' Alva said, trying to hide her emotions in front of

Carlos.

'Let us keep in touch, I never want to lose any of my children again.' Julie put her arm around Alva.

'I'd love that.'

'It's been good to see you, Alva.' Carlos followed them.

'And lovely to see you too, Carlos,' she smiled.

'Would you like to meet some time?' he asked.

'Why yes.' She was surprised.

He pushed open the door of the apartment.

'I'll see you to the lift,' Julie said.

'Thanks.'

They walked along the corridor for a few yards.

And then Julie spoke hesitantly. 'Maybe you'd give my number to David just in case he …' Her voice tailed off as she took a card from the silver box and handed it to Alva.

'I'll ask him to call you, Julie. And take care of yourself. I'm looking forward to seeing you again soon.' Alva pressed the button on the lift.

Julie embraced Alva and held her tightly.

The lift arrived. The door slid open. The brightly lit space waited for her. To take her away from this woman who now meant everything to her.

She cupped Julie's face in her hand, and could feel tears on her cheeks.

'I am so happy to have met you, I love you,' Julie whispered.

'For me too.'

Julie reached to kiss her. 'I never want to lose you again.'

Alva had made no mention of the will or money and neither had Julie. She would leave all that to the solicitor.

'Go home now. It's late. Sleep well my baby.'

Alva stepped into the lift reluctantly. 'Goodnight Mum.' It was the first time she had used *Mum*.

She had to glance down for a couple of seconds to press the

button for the ground floor, but raised her eyes immediately to lock on to Julie's blue eyes again as the doors closed slowly. Her mother was gone. She had a very strong urge to press the button and return to the floor but didn't.

Alva had to drag her mind back to what was happening in the company. There was so much going on, not one thing could gain precedence over another particularly this recent development of meeting Julie. And she had to deal with the situation with Darren, but didn't know how she was going to handle that. A mix of emotions threatened to destabilise her life.

'We met Julie last night, she's a lovely person.' Alva saw David the following afternoon.
    'Oh?'
    'Why are you so much against her?'
    'Do you need to ask?'
    'I understand how you might feel a certain resentment, but I don't think she's looking for anything, although she is entitled to a share of Dad's estate.'
    'Yeah?'
    'She didn't say anything to our solicitor at the meeting. Although John will have to inform her solicitor.'
    'She's knows it. That's why she turned up.'
    'It's hard to know.'
    'You can say that again. It's too bloody obvious.' David voice rose.
    'Why do you feel like that?'
    'She'll split up our share of the estate.'
    'It's the law. And you should have come to see her last night. She is our mother, she deserves that.'
    'I don't want to know her, Alva. And I think you're mad to even think about taking things any further. And Cian should take a

step back as well. We're only letting her into this family to cause disruption.'

'We know nothing of what happened between Julie and Dad. He should have told us …anyway there's a back story.'

'What difference does that make?'

'It makes all the difference. There were problems between them.'

'If a woman leaves her family behind, there's a back story all right. What sort of woman does that, tell me?'

'I told you there were reasons …' she insisted, but was slowly realising that she was wasting her time trying to persuade David to see Julie.

'And Julie asked me to give you her card.' She handed it to him. 'She's leaving tomorrow afternoon but hoped you could meet her in the morning.'

'Yeah, yeah …' He threw it down on the desk carelessly, his voice already holding a degree of boredom which couldn't be hidden.

She sighed. 'I'm sorry.'

'No, I'm sorry that I can't go with you on this.'

'Maybe you'll change your mind?' she asked, forcing a hopeful tone into her voice.

'Don't think so.' It was a blank refusal.

Chapter Ten

As Alva let herself in the door, she saw the light curl under the door in the living room. These days Darren was always home before her. Waiting to see her. Beg her. Implore her. To give him forgiveness. To continue on living together.

The door opened and he appeared. Looking dishevelled. His blue shirt flopped below the belt of his trousers and he wore no shoes. 'Alva?' he asked. It was a vague question as if he didn't know her at all.

She didn't reply.

'It's great to see you. Want anything?'

'No thanks.' She didn't want to drink or eat. Anxious to stay in full control. So much had happened over the last couple of days she almost didn't know where she was. Who she was. That most of all. And now she had no one to ask. The one person who could have told her what had happened in the past was gone. And he had taken his secrets with him.

'Sit down love. Let's talk.' Darren stood behind her. Too close. She thought.

He reached to kiss her, but she pushed him away. She couldn't bear him to touch her.

He laughed and walked across to the couch, flopped into the soft cushions, and picked up the glass he had been drinking. 'Cheers.'

She sat down at the other end. 'I've wanted to talk, but we've just been too busy and it's frustrating,' she said. Thinking she hadn't had a chance to tell him about Julie. But she wasn't going to go into that now. He would probably have the same attitude as David and she just couldn't deal with it.

'Alva, I hate this situation between us.'

'It's your own fault. You deceived me by telling lies. Sleeping with that woman and then meeting her again.'

'I told you that she doesn't matter. Over and over.'

'And I told you that I don't want to live with you any longer,' she said bluntly. 'So we have to make a decision about what we're going to do.'

'But I don't want to lose you,' he insisted.

'You've already lost me.'

He was silent. His head down.

'You'll have to leave.'

'But where will I go?' He looked at her, questioning.

'Find somewhere else to live.'

'This is my apartment as well. I'm entitled to half.'

'I own this apartment.' She pointed out. 'And you have no entitlement to any part of it as we're not married. And we are only together for four years.'

'We'll have to sell and split the proceeds. Don't think you can hang me out to dry.'

'We won't be doing that. And you've only yourself to blame.'

'I won't be able to buy an apartment with half the proceeds anyway, there's no property out there at the lower end. Although you'll inherit from your Dad's estate so you'll be all right,' he spoke as if he hadn't heard what she said.

'You know I want to invest any money I receive into the company so I won't benefit at all.'

'I'm sure you'll easily be able to raise a mortgage.'

Suddenly his earlier panic about losing her had disappeared and was replaced by a colder attitude.

She had been so involved with Julie that she hadn't really

thought through the practical side of breaking up with Darren. Although he had obviously given it plenty of consideration. But if she couldn't forgive his deceit then there seemed to be no other way out of the situation. He had to go.

It was Alva's final decision. And she hoped that he would leave. Whether she would ever forget the memories of that night was another thing, but she would have to try. It would always be a marker in her life. Something awful. Something traumatic. But in contrast, the happiness she felt on meeting her mother at last, helped her to face her life which had taken such a downward turn this last while.

Now that Julie had gone home, she planned to pick up where she had left off on her investigations into the fraud which she suspected had gone on in the company. Seeing Hugh's initials in one of the reference numbers of the payments made to the French company Tichanko Inc. had given her a start.

But she had to meet with the bank today as well. This was the last chance she would have to discuss their financial position. Would they be prepared to extend their credit until probate was granted on her father's estate.

She went down the corridor to Hugh's office, and knocked.

'Come in,' he said and she put her head around the door. 'We'll have to head to the bank. Are you ready?'

'Sure, just give me a minute.' He didn't look at her, but bent his head and continued reading the documents in front of him.

'I'll remind David.' She continued on to his office, but found him on the phone and just waved at him.

In her office, she gathered her papers and had a quick chat with her secretary. Over the last while she had been considering what exactly could be done about the company's finances. It was frustrating and it seemed that reducing the wage bill would be the most effective thing to do. Hugh also agreed with her as well on this move.

'But how will we run the company without the usual complement of staff?' she had asked.

'There has to be room to trim.' He had taken out a list of staff and they had looked at it together.

'But how could we make any redundancy payments? We have very little money,' she pointed out. 'It would be impossible.'

'The Department would do that if we can't.'

'I hate the thought of being forced to choose who should leave.'

'It's very difficult.'

'If only we hadn't got into trouble financially.' She stared at the list.

Hugh didn't say anything.

Alva wanted to ask him about his initials being in the reference number on the bank statement, but hadn't got the courage. It sounded like an accusation somehow and she wanted to be certain of why she was asking him this question in the first place.

David burst through the door. 'There you are, we'd better head. I'll drive.'

They sat into David's Mercedes.

'What are we going to say to the bank?' she asked.

'I'd like to tell them to fuck off. We've been with them for years. Not to support us now when we need it most is shit.'

'There will be money when Dad's estate is finalised. That should keep them happy.'

'I'm not giving my share of the estate to shore up the company,' David said.

'But it's the only way.' Alva was adamant.

'You can invest your share if you want.'

'I will,' Alva said defiantly.

They arrived at the bank, and were ushered into the office. The official they were dealing with brought up the details of their accounts on her screen.

'Have you been able to work out a plan which will bring your accounts into credit,' she asked immediately.

'Firstly, I will be in a position to provide collateral for a loan when probate is granted on my father's estate,' Alva said.

'When do you expect that to happen?'

'It could be some months,' she had to admit.

'And how much?'

'I'm not sure yet, but it could be somewhere around a quarter of a million euro.'

'That's far short of what your company owes to the bank.'

'But we have looked at cutting costs as well. We're looking at the possibility of redundancies,' Alva said.

'How many?'

'We're not sure yet.'

'You'll have to decide on the numbers and see if you can reduce your wage payments realistically so that your outgoings can be reduced.'

'How long will you give us to do this?' Hugh asked the bank official.

'Let us have the plan and then we will make a decision. As it is, your overdraft is way above your facility and it has to be reduced.'

'We will work on it.'

'I'll need to see it by Friday.'

'You'll have it.' Alva stood up. She hated the woman. So cold and unfeeling. If they were lodging funds she would be very different. Now the shoe is on the other foot, she thought, determined to leave that bank as soon as she could.

Alva printed off the list of names and titles, thinking about everyone individually. There was no one she wanted to lose. All of these people meant a great deal to her as they worked alongside both her Dad and herself over the years. She was so fond of many of them.

'Have you made any decisions yet?' Hugh came into her office.

'No, it's very difficult.'

'You can't be emotional about it.'

'I know, but when I see the names on a list, and they're not numbers, they're people, and with the stroke of a pen we're going to wreck their lives. They have families. Homes. Mortgages. They don't deserve this.'

'No, but if we don't make some of them redundant then we're all out of a job. There have to be sacrifices.'

'It's so cold and calculated.' Alva shuddered.

'Let's get on with it. Who's first on the list?'

'Allen, Maureen.'

'What do you think?'

'She's been working here for a long time.'

'Maybe she might be glad to retire early?'

'Can she live on the amount she would receive?'

'I hope so. She would have to wait until she is entitled to a pension.'

'The rest of the staff must accept a reduction in their salaries. And that includes ourselves.' Alva sighed. Her finger moved further down the list. 'I hate the way they're listed, the surname first and Christian name second. It's so impersonal somehow.'

'It's the computer.'

'The computer is a machine without feelings.'

'Come on, we'll never get this done,' Hugh said.

They continued on, and drew up a list. Everyone else on the staff had to take a twenty-percent reduction. When they totalled up the figures, it seemed that the amount saved would bring the bank accounts almost into credit. But it would take some time to reach that point. They hoped that the bank would accept the plan.

Darren was away from the office today but she needed to have the same conversation with him soon. She scrolled down the list of payments in the bank statements, searching for another set of initials which might give her some clue as to who else might be involved in the fraud. She found no one else, noting that credit transfers occurred regularly at the end of each month. There had to be a connection between them.

Now she was faced with a dilemma. Had someone inserted the initials, and made it seem as if Hugh was responsible. She thought of calling an EGM, but as her evidence was so flimsy, she didn't think they would take the slightest notice.

Chapter Eleven

Alva was only back to the unpleasant task of deciding who was to have their salary reduced, or to lose their job altogether, when her phone rang. She put her hand out and picked it up, but then noticed that a name didn't come up on the readout. She hesitated then, suddenly reluctant to answer. It could well have been a con, one of those hoax calls when a person was asked trick questions in the hope of fooling someone into giving them their bank details. She let it ring out deciding to avoid any confrontation and went back to her work.

The phone rang again a few minutes later. She thought it was the same number, but then took a chance and answered, thinking it was new business perhaps.

'Yes?'

'Alva?'

The voice was deep, and it had a foreign tone.

'Yes?' She was almost ready to press the off button.

'This is Carlos.'

'Hallo …' she was very surprised.

'How are you?' he asked.

'I am well.'

'Would you like to meet me for dinner some evening?' he asked.

She hesitated. Unsure.

There was a silence between them.

'Yes, why not,' she smiled to herself and accepted.

'I'm free on Wednesday night and I wondered if that would suit you. I'm looking forward to seeing you again, we didn't have a chance to get to know each other when we met with my mother.'

'No …' She was stalling for time. 'Yes Carlos, thank you, I think Wednesday will be fine.'

'Will I pick you up?'

'Sure …I'll text you my address,' she said that so she could give herself a chance to cancel if she changed her mind. Although that might upset Julie if she heard about it. Still, she wasn't going to be forced into meeting with Carlos. Maybe he just wanted to get to know her because of the connection with Julie. Maybe Julie has even suggested it? Her rational mind intervened. Just meet him for dinner and get to know him. She thought. That's all. And he's really family.

She went back to the files. Faced the dilemmas. She looked down the list again and this time actually ticked names. Coldly. Trying to make herself feel that she didn't know them. They were strangers. Mary, Tom, Liz, Brid, Paddy, but they weren't strangers. Tears flooded her eyes. How could she tell them that they weren't needed in the company any longer. The thought of that cut through her.

Hugh came in.

'We'll have to announce the salary cuts soon. But I think we'll have to talk to the people whose jobs will be made redundant before that. They will need to know,' Alva said.

'If we present the plan to the bank then it should keep them off our backs until the staff serve their notice. Only then will we see a result. But in the meantime, I've been wondering what other cuts we can make? How about the expenses?'

'They're mostly only paid on invoice, so if you travel there's not much more to be made. Not like it used to be in companies years ago.'

'Credit?'

'Most accounts pay on time.'

'We could tighten up, refuse to give people ninety days, when they should be paying in thirty days.'

'That would make a huge difference. will you let me have details of the companies we're talking about please?' Alva asked.

He made a note of that.

'It's a pity we don't have any assets other than this building here.'

'At least we don't have to pay rent,' he said.

'I'm glad Dad bought this building but we still have a mortgage.' She felt grateful to her father, although thinking about him brought back the emotion of his loss.

Alva felt like bringing up the subject of the fraud, but resisted that. She had no proof. It was a quandary. Who could she talk to about it? Who could she trust? That was the problem. She needed advice. Good advice. As she pondered, she thought about their solicitor, John. Could she trust him. Solicitors were meant to protect their clients. But if he suspected fraud as well would he be inclined to report it to the Gardai.

They chose the jobs which could be done without. Including her own secretary, Hugh's secretary and David's. The top directors' secretaries, and other jobs at the lower level. Alva felt particularly sad that she would have to tell her secretary, Cara, that she had to let her go. She had worked for her for over six years and now to tell her that she had no job cut Alva to the quick. But it had to be done soon, and she wanted to talk to everyone personally. She went to her office, and found Cara in her adjoining office. Immediately, she drew her attention to the various messages which had come in.

'Thanks.' Alva sat down. 'I'll sort them out. But before that, I need to talk to you.'

Cara looked at her expectantly, a smile on her face.

'This is very difficult.' Alva clasped her hands together tightly. 'The company is in trouble,' she said, trying to find the right words.

'My God.' Cara was shocked.

'And I'm sorry to say some jobs must go.'

Disappointment swept across her face.

'I'm not going to have a secretary any longer.'

'That's going to be tough.' Cara was sympathetic.

'I don't mind that, I just regret having to tell you this. You don't deserve it. And on top of that, we can't pay you redundancy. You'll have to accept statutory. Although if anything changes, I'll certainly make it up to you. Please believe me.'

'When will this happen?' Cara asked.

'I'll be giving you notice as of tomorrow. I'll put it in writing to you. And give you an excellent reference. Although if you are applying for another job just ask them to give me a call.'

'That's just a month?' Cara was shocked. 'I can't believe it,' she said.

'I'm so sorry.' Alva felt guilty. 'But as well as that, the rest of the staff will have to accept a drastic cut in their wages. Or perhaps work a shorter week. Because the company is in such a state, we have to cut costs drastically or else we're in liquidation.'

'That's awful.' Cara was genuinely concerned.

'Anyway, I'm full sure you'll be snapped up, and if I can do anything for you, I promise that I will. I do regret the situation with all my heart.'

'Thank you.'

'We'll be having a general meeting tomorrow and making the announcements.'

'Am I the only person?'

'No, there are a number of staff at the same level.'

'I don't feel so bad then.'

The idea is that I can work alone, I'll have to, and the same

103

goes for others in my position.'

'I feel useless ...suddenly.'

'I hope you won't feel that way for long.'

Cara looked lost. 'I hate change.'

'None of us like change. Even I ...' Alva hesitated. And thought how her life had been totally transformed in recent times.

'I hope the company survives,' Cara murmured.

'So do I. It was my father's life.'

'I could see that Purtell Vintners meant everything to him and to you.'

She met the other employees on her list, and it grew even more upsetting. There was horror, shock, anger and tears too and although she tried to explain that there was a chance that the company could collapse, they didn't all understand and quite a few of them refused to accept the course of action which the directors had taken.

But when they had a staff meeting the following morning, it was only then she could really sense the level of uncertainty among them. The board were all present, and both Alva's brothers, and Darren too, but she still felt this was the most difficult situation she had ever been in and was very glad it finally came to a close.

'That will get us over the hump with a bit of luck,' David commented.

Alva didn't reply. She couldn't.

Darren walked beside her, and reached for her hand. But she shook him off and hurried back to her office.

Later she sat down with Hugh and David and they prepared the plans for the bank. As they calculated the figures it looked as if there would be some advantage when cuts in salaries and redundancies became effective but would it be enough for the bank? That was the big question. And it would take some time before it would show results.

Then she had to write the letters to those staff members whose jobs were to be made redundant. By the end of the day she had to make a supreme effort to try to diminish the anxiety which dogged her recently. She was meeting Carlos this evening but would have preferred to cancel the arrangement she was in such a state. But decided it was too short notice.

Darren had left the office earlier, and she was home before he arrived which was unusual. It was strange to find the apartment empty and silent, but she was glad of it. Able to have a shower and change without any interference from him. In the dressing room she pulled a dress out of the wardrobe. A red mini off the shoulder. Held it up in front of her for a moment. Then flung it on the armchair. Next a black and white stripe full length was flung on the floor. A beige top. A clingy cream elasticated number caught on the door handle. They came out of the wardrobe fast and furious, given less and less time for consideration and ended up in the growing pile around her feet. Finally, she held the utterly plain midnight blue with long sleeves up to her. Gave it more time than any other and finally decided it would have to do. So when she put on the diamond earrings which had been the last present from her Dad she felt a little better. Would you like this, Dad, she whispered as she circled, staring at her reflection in the mirror. She moved closer to the glass, wondering had the sleepless nights imprinted those dark shadows around her eyes. She touched up with her Yves Saint Laurent concealer and hoped she looked a little better.

This was the first time she had a date or whatever you might call it with any man since before Darren had moved in with her. And that was over four years ago.

She grabbed a black jacket and pulled it on as the doorbell rang. There was no time to make any more changes. She refreshed her lips with bright red lipstick. Grabbed her handbag and hurried along the corridor on her six-inch heels, taking the lift down to the foyer aware that her heart was racing at such a pace she didn't think she could stop it.

She had told Carlos she would see him at the entrance and now he stood there waiting for her, dressed in dark trousers, and a grey jacket. She smiled.

'It's good to see you,' he said.

She was surprisingly pleased to see him. He had those dark Spanish good looks and she prayed she looked all right now after all her effort.

They walked out to see Darren coming towards them. Alva didn't know what to do for a moment, but continued walking with Carlos towards the carpark.

'Alva?' Darren ran after them. 'Where are you going? Who is this guy?'

'I'm going out,' she said.

'What does that mean?' he stuttered.

'I'm going out, Darren,' she repeated.

'Who's he?'

'None of your business.'

'Where are you taking my partner?' He turned to Carlos and shouted into his face.

'As Alva said, it's none of your business.' He held out his hand towards her. 'Let's go.'

She took his hand and they walked towards the car.

'Alva, Alva,' Darren shouted, running after them, his voice echoing loud.

She ignored him. Carlos held the passenger door of the Audi open for her. She climbed in.

'I'm sorry about this,' she said, pressing the remote for the gates.

'Don't worry.' He glanced at her with a smile. 'Forget about it.'

'I'll try.'

'I've booked a table at a restaurant in town, I hope you'll enjoy it.'

'I've had so much going on over the last few days, it will be lovely to put it out of my head.'

'We will do exactly that.'

'Thank you.'

He ordered drinks for them as soon as they arrived in the restaurant. She had a gin and tonic although he just had a non-alcoholic beer. They sat on cushioned couches, and she sank into their softness, now determined to enjoy herself this evening despite meeting Darren.

'I'm sure you are wondering about the situation with my partner, my ex-partner.'

'You don't have to tell me. But I'm sure it was upsetting for you.'

'I've told him to leave but he won't go.' That was all she could say.

'That must be very awkward for you.' His dark brown eyes were sympathetic.

'It is.'

The waiter arrived and took them to their table. It was quite a small restaurant, and there was a warm vibrant atmosphere.

They looked at the menus and ordered. Alva chose a prawn starter and salmon for her main course, and Carlos had prawns as well and monkfish.

'Wine?' he asked.

'Maybe a glass of white.'

'I'll just have the beer. I don't drink alcohol when I'm working.'

'It was wonderful to meet Julie when she came to see the solicitor with you,' she said. 'I couldn't really believe that I was meeting my mother after so long.'

'It must have been very sad for you when Julie left home,' he said.

'We were all very young and my father never told us the reason why she left.'

'We were also very young,' he murmured.

'Julie told me the reason why but we never understood that at the time.'

Their food was served, and they both enjoyed the delicious dishes.

'We were very lucky to know Julie, and she really looked after us. I suppose we must have been a substitute family for her,' Carlos explained.

'Did you know that Julie had another family?'

'No, until she came to see the solicitor about her husband's death. She told me then.'

'When she told us how she lived, I was glad that she was with your family, and that she loves your father and he loves her.'

'They always seemed very close to each other, not that we noticed things like that as children, once we were happy enough, we didn't question. But she is a lovely person, warm, loving, and my father was very lucky to meet her. Our mother died when she was only in her early thirties.'

'That was tough on all of you children.'

'We were young, like yourselves.'

'Dad had housekeepers and they were very fond of us.' Alva was glad to know more about Julie's life through Carlos.

'It must have been a surprise to know that your mother had come to Dublin.'

'I was astonished to hear that from my solicitor, and I was determined to meet her if I could.'

'She was delighted to meet you that day in his office, she told me she really couldn't believe it.'

'But why did you decide to study medicine in Dublin?'

'We always spoke English at home and the Irish university system is so good both my father and Julie were keen for us to study here.'

'Do you enjoy medicine,' she asked.

'Yes, I really enjoy it. It's what I've always wanted to do.'

'Does Julie come over to visit you regularly?'

'Yes, she loves to come back to Dublin.'

'It's a pity Julie didn't decide to make contact with us before my Dad died.'

'I think she was afraid, as she didn't know if Frank had a new partner. That would have been very awkward if she had made contact.'

'I understand.'

Finished his meal, he placed his knife and fork on the plate, and it was immediately taken away by the waiter, as was Alva's. They continued talking, mostly about Alva's life now.

'Unfortunately, we have problems in the company.' She had to admit.

'I'm sorry to hear that.'

The waiter came back with the dessert menus.

'Would you like dessert?' Carlos asked.

'No thanks.'

'I'm going to order cheese, we can share it between us.' He ordered. 'Coffee?'

'Yes please.'

The waiter topped up her wine glass from the bottle which was kept cool in the ice bucket. She sipped it with pleasure. As the evening had progressed, she had become more and more relaxed and she did like Carlos. He seemed to be a really nice guy.

He dropped her home.

'Will you be all right?' he asked, turning towards her after he had switched off the engine.

She stared at him, taken aback, but was immediately aware that he was referring to the earlier incident with Darren. 'I'll be fine,' she replied, and laughed.

'Do you want me to come to the lift with you?' he offered. 'Just in case your partner is waiting for you?'

'Oh no thanks, there's no need.' She opened the car door, and stepped out. 'Thanks so much for dinner, I've really enjoyed myself.'

'We must meet again,' he said.

She hesitated and smiled. 'Call me.'

She was slightly nervous turning the key in the door. Expecting Darren to appear at any moment. But he didn't. She went into the living room and stopped abruptly. A suntanned hand holding a glass of wine dangled into view over the arm of the couch. And she could hear Darren laugh. She walked further into the room. It was her again. The blonde woman. They were lying on the couch and she was giggling. An empty bottle of wine stood on the coffee table, and another was half full. He looked up at her. Said nothing. Then lowered his head and kissed the woman.

Alva turned and left the room. Closing the door softly. Wanting to keep them in there. Imprisoned in their selfish uncaring lives. She went into the spare bedroom. Aware that she would never sleep in her own bedroom again, or be able to sit in their living room, tainted by the touch and smell and sound of that person. Darren obviously wanted to get his own back on her when he saw her leave the building with Carlos, and brought his girlfriend over later in the hope that she would see them together when she returned. Although she had to admit that she had done the same thing by going out with Carlos, but it hadn't been deliberate.

She thought about them now. Just a few metres away from her. Every sound she could hear was accentuated and all she could think of was the two of them together. She wanted to get up and leave. Go and stay somewhere else. But this was her own home and if she left then Darren would be able to keep possession of the apartment and she might never be able to live here again.

Even if Darren moved her in Alva wasn't going to allow her take over altogether.

Her phone rang. It was Carlos. She had put his number into her Contacts list.

'Alva, is everything OK? I was worried about you.'

'Everything's fine, thank you.' She was grateful to him for his concern.

'Your partner was very angry and I thought perhaps he …'

'I'm all right.'

'I'm glad. I waited here for a while.'

'In the carpark?'

'Outside.'

'Thank you for being so considerate.'

'It's no problem, I'll head off now.'

'It's late and I think you said you've an early start.'

'Yeah,' he laughed.

'Thank you so much. I appreciate that you waited.' She was quite amazed that someone she hardly knew would take the trouble. Still, he was connected with her mother so was family in a distant way.

She lay back down on the pillow, still listening for whatever was happening in the living room down the hall. Suddenly, there was a shriek of laughter and footsteps came closer. She tensed up, pushed her legs out on to the floor and stood up. Were they coming in? She moved closer to the door and listened, aware that Darren could do such a thing just to annoy her. But the footsteps passed the door and she heard them run on into the bedroom. Her bedroom. She could hear more laughter and then the door banged closed.

Was this going to be her life from now on, she wondered. Which of them was going to leave? Why should she be the one forced to go? It was her apartment. Although Darren would probably want to have a share of it, he didn't have any legal right. As she lay there, she decided that if Darren was going to behave as he did tonight then she couldn't see how it would be possible to continue to live in this way. He would have to leave. Set up home with his new girlfriend if that was what he wanted. She intended to spell it out to him tomorrow in no uncertain terms.

Having to endure another night of disruption really drove Alva almost mad. She closed her eyes but her mind kept going around in circles. Everything was exaggerated. Taking her into strange places. Darren was in those nightmares of course. But she didn't always recognise him. The scenarios played out were weird, outlandish, and frightening. Eventually, she made tea at five and wrapped in her robe sat at the kitchen table staring out through the window at the dark night sky. Later she went back to the bedroom, reluctant to stay in the kitchen in case Darren and his girlfriend happened to get up early. That was the last thing she wanted. To be face to face with this woman who had taken her place and intended to oust her permanently no doubt.

Chapter Twelve

In the office it was quiet. The work stations empty. She strolled among them. Knowing the names of each occupant. She stopped. Aware of their personalities by the different little mementos stuck on screens, or desks. And felt guilty that she was the cause of this upset in their lives. A blow which was totally unexpected. For those whose jobs were to be made redundant, and those whose salaries were to be cut, all would face a shortage in their finances. And there would be major changes in their lives. They would have difficulty in paying their everyday expenses. Mortgages. Electricity. Gas. Food. Clothes. And after that would there be any disposable income left for a social life? That question slashed through her and only enhanced the guilt.

She sat staring at her computer screen at those lists of bank lodgements, still puzzling over whoever had fraudulently decided to cripple their company. What was she going to do about the fraud? She had no answer to that question. And what was she going to do about Darren? She had no answer to that question either.

At lunchtime she rang her friend Naomi. Just to talk. She couldn't think of anyone else who might listen.

'Let's meet for a chat. It's been a while,' she suggested to her.

'I've left you a few messages.'

'I'm sorry, but I've been very busy.'

'Not to worry.'

'There's been so much happening since Dad died.'

'I can imagine.'

They met at a café close by.

'I'm sure there is a lot of work connected with the estate and all that sort of thing.' Naomi sipped her coffee.

'Probate takes quite a while to go through and the house will have to be sold.'

'That's a pity, you always loved that house and I'm sure you'd have liked to live there.'

'It's to be divided between us.'

'You could buy out the lads.'

'I'll have to invest my inheritance to support the company.'

'Will that be enough?' She seemed surprised.

'I hope so. We're making a lot of cuts so hope the bank will be prepared to back us.'

'That's tough.'

'But there's something else which is amazing.' She went on to tell Naomi about Julie.

'That is wonderful,' she said.

'I can't believe it.'

'Course I still have to deal with Darren. And I didn't tell you what happened that last night we met.'

'No, what about him?'

'He's still with that one. Even last night I arrived home to find her there with him.'

'What?' She stared at Alva, her eyes wide with astonishment.

Alva admitted that he had seen her go out with Carlos on one evening.

'Who is Carlos?' Naomi asked.

'Julie's partner's son.'

'Darren is a bastard,' she exploded. 'You weren't kissing this Carlos I presume, and he could just have been a friend.'

'That's all he is, not even that, he has a family connection although I haven't told Darren about Julie yet, never could get around to it with him.'

'But you've told him to leave?'

Alva nodded.

'When is he going?'

'Don't know. He doesn't want to.'

'Just put his clothes in black bags and leave them outside the door, and then change the locks.'

'It will probably come to that.'

'Get on with it then, girl.'

'I will.'

'Promise,' Naomi insisted.

'Yeah,' she smiled. 'But at least there's one good thing and that's meeting our mother.'

'Do your brothers feel the same?'

'Cian does, David doesn't.'

'That's a pity, maybe he'll come around.'

'Maybe.'

'When will you see her again?'

'She's living in the south of Spain, Seville, so I don't know whether that will be possible.'

'What's the son like?'

'He's very nice.'

'Do you fancy him?' she giggled.

'Not at all, Naomi. He's probably only being polite because of the connection with Julie.'

'Is he free?'

'Don't know. He never mentioned a partner.'

'Alva, you're all over the place. He's probably gone back to Spain too I suppose, so there's not much scope for you,' she laughed.

'No, he's a neurosurgeon in Beaumont and has a very busy life.'

'Wow. So maybe there might be something in it for you after all. I'd love to see Darren's face when he finds out you have another man.'

'He's hurt me and doesn't know how much. Hasn't a clue really.' Alva couldn't hide the bitterness which welled up inside her.

'Bastard,' Naomi said again.

'Bastard,' Alva echoed her word with even greater emphasis.

'But be careful of the rebound, that can pose trouble and that's when mistakes are made,' warned Naomi.

'I have no intention of getting involved again,' she laughed.

'But?' Naomi wagged a finger.

'There's too much happening. And I'm sure my new found mother wouldn't approve of me having a relationship with Carlos.'

'Have you heard from her since she went back?'

Alva shook her head. She had sent an email to Julie the evening she had left. So very grateful to her for spending the time with them. A dream come true. She had been swept backwards in time to when she had had a mother. To know this woman who had given birth to her. Who had loved her in those first years of her life. Held her close. Whispered stories to her when she went to bed at night. Sang songs. Promising always to be there for her. I'll never leave you. Those few words apparently repeated over and over to a small child who didn't really remember those days as an adult. Did she remember, she asked herself. Did that actually happen. Julie had told her she said it. Now she didn't know whether to believe or not. She wanted to, but since she didn't hear anything from her mother a gap was widening day by day and it supported that negative belief.

'I'm sure she will make contact, maybe she needs time to get things into perspective. It must have been a surprise for her to meet you as well. She hadn't planned to see you there that morning in the solicitor's office,' Naomi pointed out. 'And you have to think about her partner. Maybe he doesn't know anything about you at all.'

'You're right. But I had hoped that we would get together again, but since she hasn't responded, maybe she doesn't want that, but she's always in the back of my mind.'

'It's the most natural thing in the world. She is your mother after all.'

'I've thought about going out to see her in Seville, but I can't turn up unless she invites me. Anyway, I don't know where she lives so there would be no point wandering around the city looking for her,' she smiled wryly 'Also, as you know, my financial situation isn't good and I couldn't afford to take a trip out there at the moment.'

'Yeah, you were telling me.' Naomi nodded.

Alva went on to explain what had happened in the company in more detail now.

'You think it's fraud?' Naomi whispered.

'It's the only explanation. I've been looking into the accounts and there is a suspicious thing I've spotted.'

'Do you want me to look into it?'

'I don't know that it warrants that. I'd have to be very careful as it involves a person in the company. But it could be all in my imagination.'

'Tell me. Sometimes another head can help, and needless to say I won't pass it on, and I really don't know anyone in the company that well.'

While Naomi had met the accountant Hugh at dinner parties in Alva's own home, he was just an acquaintance. But just sharing the problem with Naomi meant a lot to Alva. She was a detective in the Gardai and as they had known each other since schooldays she really trusted her. Although she hadn't planned to talk about her suspicions, now that she had opened up, she felt better as

Naomi had promised that she would investigate the company, Tichanko Inc. and see if she could find out anything about it in her position as a trained investigator.

Chapter Thirteen

What to do? The question echoed over and over in Alva's head. She knew she had to speak to Darren. A final decision had to be made about their broken relationship. And she didn't know exactly what that should be. If she found that woman still in her home when she arrived back then she could see herself losing her head altogether. He would have to go and it would have to be soon.

There was a meeting that afternoon and he was there in his position as Sales Manager for Ireland. It was hard to give the impression that all was fine between them. A struggle. And she never met his eyes as she discussed the agenda, hoping that no one would notice. As they left the board room and went back to their offices, he followed her.

'I'll talk to you later, now is not the time,' she said abruptly and turned to go into her own office.

He stared at her but said nothing.

'What was he thinking?' she wondered. Up to now, he had been so apologetic about his behaviour. Promising that he would never be with that woman again. That it meant nothing. She meant nothing. In the beginning she had wanted to believe him. But as time passed, she began to realise the truth. Darren was a liar. A deceitful character. And couldn't be trusted. But she knew her own life was going to be difficult. They worked together, and although he travelled quite a lot all over the country, he was back in the office at least a couple of days a week. She sighed.

Dreading the thought.

She actually did some shopping on the way home, intending to cook for herself. But he was there before her.

'What's for dinner?' he asked.

She didn't answer, just pushed past him into the kitchen. Turned on the cooker and began to make a meal. She shouldn't have been able to eat with the stress she was under, but oddly now she was suddenly ravenous. He followed her and stood behind watching as she peeled potatoes, scraped and chopped vegetables and put them in the steamer to cook. Then placed a piece of salmon for herself in the oven.

He set the table with glasses, cutlery, and opened a bottle of red wine. Just like they would normally do in the past.

She watched him out of the corner of her eye, but chose to ignore him. She knew what he was at. Just the same old routine. She hardened her heart. He wasn't going to get away with this.

'That looks delicious,' he said, as she plated up.

She sat down at the table.

He poured two glasses of wine.

She sipped.

He sat down and clinked his glass against hers.

She began to eat.

He looked around. 'Where's my dinner?'

'Haven't you cooked it?'

'Well …no…I thought.'

'See what thought did,' she laughed, taking another sip of wine.

'That's mean, you know I can't cook,' he sulked.

'You're going to have to learn or get your woman to do it for you.'

'Alva …' he sighed dramatically.

'It's over, Darren. And I want you to move out.' She finished her meal, and poured some more wine. She was suddenly stronger and better able to tell him how she felt.

'But where will I go?'

'Go and stay with *whatever her name* is.'

'I told you before, I can't do that.'

'Bunk down with one of your friends, Darren, I don't care where you go.'

'You'll have to give me a chance to find somewhere.'

'You've had chances. Now you can go in the morning and that's it.'

'I'm not, this is my home as well as yours.'

'Darren, this is my apartment, you don't own it.'

He looked at her, astonished. 'What do you mean, I've often bought stuff. What about that coffee table there, and other things around the place?'

'You can have anything you want I don't care. Just load up the stuff and take yourself off and be gone. The quicker the better as far as I'm concerned.' She was beginning to lose it.

'No Alva, please...' he begged.

'As I said, I want you out of here by tomorrow morning.'

He was silenced.

She stood up, and put away the dishes in the washer. Then left the kitchen. She said no more.

It was the end of their relationship. She had said the same to him before since she had found him with the woman, but somehow now she felt she hadn't made it clear to him that she wouldn't put up with it, as he continued doing whatever he wanted. She had looked at him this evening and wondered what had attracted her to him in the first place. He had probably been playing around with other women all along. He didn't even seem to feel guilty when she caught him with that woman. Now she decided she would definitely be better off without him.

She couldn't stop the fierce rush of feelings which dominated her. He needed to understand, and stop making excuses for his behaviour. He was such a disappointment. She didn't think she would ever be able to forgive him. And now she felt she would never be able to tell anyone about it, particularly her colleagues in the company. People who knew her well would hardly believe it had happened. Just as well if they turned against him. But maybe they might turn against her and refuse to believe that it was all his fault. The men might side with Darren. Even though she was CEO for a number of years, since her father had died she had become more aware of levels of resentment in the company from some of the men particularly.

But maybe it was because of her suspicions of fraud. Had that leaked out from Hugh or David? Perhaps she should have kept it to herself. She regretted now that she had let herself become paranoid about it. But she had to find out who was the culprit. She had to. She wasn't going to let the company go down the tubes without a fight. She wondered had Naomi found out anything about that French company, but she called her later and her friend confirmed that she had no success in discovering anything about it. It seemed it was a mystery.

Now Alva needed time to herself. Time to plan. She stared around the living room. Part of her regretting that her relationship with Darren was over, and that he would be gone tomorrow. Part of her relieved that she would have her apartment to herself once again and there was no chance of Darren bringing that woman into her home without her knowledge. She checked her phone to see if there had been any reply to a text she had sent earlier in the day and was delighted to see that the locksmith had confirmed that he would be here first thing in the morning to change the locks. It helped to know that at last she could keep Darren out of her apartment. And hopefully out of her life.

As arranged, the locksmith arrived, and she explained what needed to be done. She had to stay there, just in case Darren happened to turn up, but she did some work on her laptop while waiting. She went through the suspicious list of lodgements once more, always searching for something which she had missed.

To her surprise, she noticed that there were no more invoices received from that company in Bordeaux since her father had died and therefore no more lodgements to those bank accounts. That was unusual and now she planned to discuss the subject of her suspicions about the company with David, Hugh, and Darren, as soon as she had an opportunity.

Later, she met Darren at work. She stopped abruptly.

'Alva?' He stared at her.

'I'll talk to you in my office.' She opened the door and went inside. He followed her.

'Close the door,' she sat down.

He sat opposite.

'I told you I wanted you to leave the apartment, but your stuff is still there,' she said.

'And I told you I don't have anywhere to go.'

'Whatever, I want you out by this evening. Come around and take all your stuff. If you don't remove your clothes, I'll take them to the recycle centre or to one of the charity shops, they'll be delighted with them.'

'Alva, please don't do that.'

'Where did you sleep last night.'

'I slept on a couch,' he grimaced. 'Had too much to drink.'

'You can stay there tonight as well.'

'But I can't …I wasn't really invited.'

She shrugged. 'What's your schedule today?' she asked, wondering what time he intended to be back.

'Last appointment is at four, should be home about six o'clock.'

She winced inside at his mention of *home*. 'I'll make sure I'm there. See you then.' She wondered what he was thinking. Up to this he had refused to see things the way they were.

She made sure she was home in the early afternoon and brought down his clothes and other things into the hallway. She packed them in suitcases, and bags. Lastly, she went through the bedside locker on his side of the bed. There were various papers there, and she leafed through them. Then she took a large bag and put them in. She was almost through when she noticed a sheaf of bank statements stapled together at the bottom of a drawer. Suddenly her eyes widened as she noticed that one of them happened to be a bank in the British Virgin Islands in Darren's name. A second in Hugh's name and a third in David's. And the balances in each were exactly the same. One hundred and sixty-six thousand US dollars.

'My God,' she whispered. The total of the three balances was roughly the amount by which their company bank balance had been reduced – five hundred thousand euros. Her heart raced, and she could feel perspiration dampen her hair line.

The bell rang once. And then twice. And she knew instantly who that was.

She quickly took a photo of each of the bank statements on her phone. She wanted to take a proper copy, but hoped that he wouldn't look for them before she had a chance to do that. Then Alva put them into her own bedside locker in the spare room.

She went to the front door.

'I can't get in, my key won't work,' Darren shouted from outside.

'Don't know what's wrong with it.' She could hear him grumble.

She opened the door.

He burst in and almost fell over the cases she had in the hall. 'What's this?'

'Your things. If there's anything else, you can come back later and collect them.'

'For God's sake, Alva, what are you doing?'

'Isn't it obvious?'

'But you can't just throw me out?'

'That's exactly what I'm doing. How many times have I told you?'

'You can't do that to me.'

'I'm doing it now. Take your things. I'll help you into the lift.'

'Thank you,' he replied with heavy sarcasm.

She picked up a couple of bags and brought them into the lift. Then came back and took some more.

Eventually, they finished, and stood looking at each other.

'Goodbye Darren.'

'I don't want to leave, Alva, you know I still love you,' he said.

'Go on.' She stepped back out of the doors of the lift and they closed slowly. Suddenly she felt glad to see the back of him and couldn't believe that he suddenly seemed to have accepted the situation.

She hurried into the apartment and locked the front door. Rushed into the bedroom and grabbed the bank statements from her own drawer. Immediately, she scanned them and printed off copies of each. Now she knew what had happened and that Darren was involved as well. It was like the final piece of the jigsaw had been fitted into place. Everything was clear as day.

She called a meeting with Hugh, David and Darren for the following morning. She hadn't said anything to Cian yet as there had been no mention of his name anywhere. She emailed Darren but he didn't respond. Then she called him on the phone but the call went on to his voicemail. She left a message.

Alva was glad to see that the accounts in the British Virgin Islands were all in credit and was so relieved that it seemed the money could be returned. Why Darren had left such incriminating bank statements in his bedside locker amazed her. What an idiot.

But then, perhaps he assumed that rather than putting such information in the office or in a locked filing cabinet where it might have been found, at home there was only the two of them and really she would never have rooted through his stuff, always respecting his privacy. It was only now in these exceptional circumstances that she even looked in his locker.

Now she called her solicitor, John, and while she didn't go into very much detail, she requested him to arrange to freeze the account in the British Virgin Islands because there was a possibility of fraud. He agreed to apply for the appropriate court order which would ensure that the money could not be withdrawn from the account by the people named on the accounts or anyone else.

The following morning, she met with Hugh, David and Darren as arranged.

'What's this meeting about?' Darren barked as soon as he came into her office.

'Sit down,' she said quietly, determined that she wasn't going to take any nonsense from him.

'I've had to cancel my appointments for this morning,' he complained.

The others said nothing.

Alva picked up her hard copies of the statements, and invoices from Tichanko Inc. and handed each of them a set.

There was silence in the room for a few minutes, broken only by the crackle of paper as the pages of the statements were turned.

'As you can see, I now have proof that the money which was paid to Tichanko Inc. was for false orders, and the payments were then transferred to three separate accounts in the British Virgin Islands. And it is quite clear now that there were three staff members involved in this fraudulent activity,' Alva stated, opening her own copy of those bank statements.

'Where did you find these statements?' Darren exploded.

'If you leave things around where they can easily be found, then what do you expect?'

'How dare you go through my stuff,' he raged in an incoherent manner.

'It was purely by accident,' she said smoothly.

She didn't want to be drawn on the subject, and was reluctant to discuss her personal life openly at this stage with the others.

'This could be a made-up thing.' He waved the statement in the air. 'Not an ounce of truth in it.'

'Currently, our legal people are applying for a court order to freeze the accounts in the British Virgin Islands,' she said.

'But they have no right to do that.' Darren was the most voluble. The other two said nothing.

'If they are representing our company, Purtell Vintners, they have every right.'

'I don't agree with that.'

'I'm hoping that this matter can be dealt with amicably,' said Alva. 'I'm only interested in having this money returned. At this stage, I have no intention of taking a legal case against the staff members who were involved. But I expect you all to resign, and if that doesn't happen then I will take a legal case against each one of you.'

David and Hugh looked at each other.

'Just one question. Why did you do this? It seems that the amount in the British Virgin Islands accounts equals the amount we lost in the company but I'm not too sure that it's all the money which was stolen or how long this has been going on. But our solicitors are investigating that. Have any of you got an answer for me?' She looked at them straight. Each one directly. Their eyes lowered and they seemed ashamed and tongue-tied.

'And there is another thing. Who else is involved? While there are only three people mentioned as account holders on the bank statements, I want to know how many other people have been implicated in some way or other. Did they take some part in it? Are they paid? Is this whole thing a business of sorts? Who is going to tell me?' she waited for a reply.

They didn't speak.

'I don't see why I should have to resign,' Darren burst out.

'Your name is on one of the accounts,' reminded Alva. 'You are involved.'

'I don't accept it. You're just making a scapegoat of me for your own personal reasons,' he grimaced. He stood up and stomped out of the office.

As the meeting came to a finish, Alva addressed Hugh and David.

'This will have to be done without any delay. I want all the information about this fraud and I will give you until ten o'clock tomorrow morning to supply me with your explanations.' She gave them that ultimatum, hoping that the matter could be resolved quickly. Obviously, if they admitted culpability then they would have to resign from their positions and be let go from the company. And Purtell Vintners wouldn't be involved in a long drawn out court case as the staff members tried to prove their innocence, and the money held in those British Virgin Islands accounts would drain away on legal fees. If they didn't resign, then they would be suspended in the interim, and the company would have to go down the legal route.

The next thing to be done was to call an EGM. The decision to suspend would have to be agreed by the board. And they would have to be informed of what had happened. She couldn't believe she had found those bank statements, as the other evidence she had on bank account numbers was flimsy to say the least, and it would have been very hard to make it stick. Perhaps Hugh had been the person who set it up and therefore his initials were in the account number. She would have had to be very sure before she had taken on legal cases against the three of them and possibly hadn't a hope of winning. Now she dreaded the outcome of the meeting which would take place the following morning.

The following morning, Hugh, David and Darren were at the meeting, and this time, the three had their own solicitors with them, and her solicitor, John, had come along to represent the company.

She opened the meeting, and waited for them to let her know what decisions had been made overnight. She wasn't going to say any more.

Hugh's solicitor was first to speak.

'My client has come to a decision,' he said.

Alva waited.

'He will admit his culpability in the fraud, and will resign immediately. And he will also confirm there is no-one else involved other than the two people present here.'

Alva gave a huge sigh of relief.

David's solicitor spoke next.

'My client has also come to a decision and will admit his culpability in the fraud and resign immediately, and he will also confirm there is no-one else involved other than the two people present here.'

Darren's solicitor said almost the exact same words and announced that Darren would resign as well.

'I accept your resignations,' Alva said. 'But my solicitor has drawn up a document which I need signed by all parties. It is to allow the sum of money in the British Virgin Islands accounts to be transferred back into the Purtell Vintners bank account.' She opened a file, and handed a document to Hugh who signed it, David signed next and Darren after him.

'I also need any ID numbers and passwords which were used

on this account in order for us to transfer the funds.' She picked up a pen and waited for them to give her the information. It took a while but eventually all three gave her what she needed.

'I'm sorry to have received your resignation, Hugh, but under the circumstances perhaps it is the best way of dealing with the matter. I have to say that I'm very disappointed with your actions after all the years you have worked here for my father. As for you David, I'm speechless. Our Dad was a more than generous man and yet you still felt you had to steal from him. And I have no words for you, Darren. None at all. I'm sorry to ask you all to clear your offices immediately and leave the building. But I will allow you to keep your company cars.'

She let it go after that, she would probably never know the reason why they did it, beyond greed.

She had already had a chat with Cian and let him know what had happened. That evening he came around to see her.

'Had you any idea of what was going on?' she asked.

'No, I'm astonished. Do you know what they were going to use the money for?' he asked.

'I couldn't get an answer even though I asked more than once.'

'Gambling or investments or something like that?'

'Perhaps.'

'You must feel very upset about Darren. What will you do?'

'I won't be doing anything as we're not living together any longer so it won't make any difference.'

'I'm sorry to hear that.'

'I only found out he was involved in the fraud quite recently.'

'What about David?'

'Again I'm shocked. I relied on him so much. I hate the thought that he has resigned. I'll really miss him. To lose all those people in our lives is heart breaking. And to know that they were prepared to behave in such an underhand manner makes me feel sick. If Dad actually knew the names of the three culprits then I know he would never have been able to handle it.'

'I'm surprised I didn't pick up something earlier. I do work in IT but I'm not even aware of that company you mentioned, Tichanko Inc.'

'Neither was I until I did some investigation. By the way, do you want to come over tomorrow evening. I'm going to ask David as well. We need to talk. In spite of all of this I don't want to fall out with him, and I'm sure you don't either. We've always been very close as a family and we can't let this incident break us up. Although he may feel that I've forced him to resign and mightn't want to have anything to do with me, but I'm going to try anyway.'

'What time?'

'Say seven?'

David agreed to come over and Alva was glad about that. She had been worried that he wouldn't, and that a rift would develop between them and never be repaired. She hoped that she could persuade him that she had no option but to take the action which was needed. She was responsible for Purtell Vintners.

She welcomed David into the apartment as normal, although there was a distinct detachment between them. A coldness. She was very much aware of that, but decided to ignore it for now, hoping that things would change soon.

'How are you?' She led the way into the living room. 'Would you like a drink?'

'No thank you, a cup of coffee would be fine.'

'Cian is coming over as well,' she said.

'Family reunion?' he asked with a slightly sarcastic tone in his voice.

She ignored that and went into the kitchen to make the coffee. As she busied herself there, she wondered how she was going to open up a conversation after what had happened yesterday.

The doorbell rang and she went down the hall to press the intercom and waited until Cian came up in the lift.

'How are you, love, David is already here.'

He hugged her.

'I'm making coffee, or would you like a drink?'

'Coffee is fine thanks.'

Within a minute or two she took in a tray. They sat down.

'I'm very sorry about what happened yesterday, David.' She decided to be the one to apologise but actually felt it should be him who apologised.

'Yeah, I'm sure you are.' Again, that underlying tone of sarcasm from David.

'Of course, I am. I'd much prefer that such a thing had never happened.'

'It could have been handled differently. You were so certain that you were right when you came to us with your suspicions.'

'I knew there was something wrong. Tell me, what was the point of it all. Did any of you owe a great deal of money that you needed so much?'

'No, we just had plans for it. Our future you could say. And the company could afford it.'

'Don't think so, if the bank had pulled the plug we'd have been bankrupt by now.'

'Purtells could always have borrowed more.'

'As you know, the bank were not prepared to continue to facilitate us.'

'No, but I'm sure we could have shopped around.'

'You're naïve David.'

'Well, you've got your money back. You're happy. And I'm out of a job.'

'There had to be some censure. I couldn't treat you, Hugh and Darren any differently. It would have been unfair.'

'And your own partner was sacked as well, I almost laughed at that.'

'He resigned.'

'And you offered your resignation,' Cian said.

'What do you know about it?'

'Alva told me.'

'Keep your mouth shut, you weren't there.'

'What are you going to do now?' asked Alva.

'Don't know yet.' he shrugged.

'You can always move to another company, I was glad that you didn't go the legal route. You'd never have got over the publicity, even if you'd have won your case. I just wanted it dealt with quickly without any fuss and damage to Purtell Vintners.'

'You wanted us out of the company,' David accused.

'I did not. I had to get to the bottom of it. I had to do it for Dad.'

'Anyway, we'll all get our share of his estate.'

'You can use that to set yourself up again,' she suggested.

'I'm glad to be out of the company. I'd like a new challenge.'

'I hope you get on well, truly I do.'

'Me too,' Cian added.

'There's plenty of business in our field.'

'So you'll have no trouble getting established,' Cian said, looked awkward.

'Cian didn't get involved in your little scheme,' Alva said.

'He wasn't asked.'

'It's a wonder you didn't ask me to get involved,' quipped Alva with a grin.

'It should have been a much bigger project only for you.' David was still angry.

'If it had been bigger, you don't know where you'd have ended up. Doing time possibly.'

'Fuck you, Alva.'

'Thanks.' She felt that the conversation was getting out of hand now.

'How are Sarah and the kids?' Cian asked.

'They don't know what's happened yet.'

'I hope Sarah doesn't take it badly.' Alva was worried about her sister-in-law.

'I won't tell her everything.'

'Maybe you shouldn't …' Alva agreed. 'Will you take some time off?'

'Yeah, since you don't want me in the office.'

'I won't mention it to Sarah if I meet her. I don't want to upset her. But if you're stuck for money, let me know, I wouldn't like to think the family are suffering,' Alva offered.

'You should have thought of that before you decided to start this whole thing.' David's lip curled.

'I feel the same,' Cian said. 'Just let me know if I can help in any way.'

'I don't need anything from you two. Keep your money. Goodbye.'

He stood up abruptly and left.

Alva and Cian stared at each other.

'I didn't expect him to accept our offers,' said Alva.

'I knew he wouldn't take any money,' Cian agreed.

'I hope he makes good with his portion of Dad's estate when he gets it.'

'He's lucky to have it.'

'At least I don't have to invest my inheritance in the company as I had intended. With the money from the account in the British Virgin Islands we can get the bank off our backs. Maybe we can re-employ some of the people who were made redundant, although that mightn't be possible. But the changes in salary levels could be reduced perhaps.'

'We'll have to fill the three positions which are now vacant.'

'I'll talk to HR in the morning. We need an accountant quickly. And someone to replace David and Darren too. But I hope David's mood will improve, I hate this situation between us now. We were always so close,' Alva said. 'Although I can understand why he is so resentful.'

'I don't know if that's going to happen any time soon. He's very stubborn,' Cian added morosely.

'He hates us now. And I'm sorry you've been dragged in. You didn't have anything to do with it at all.'

'We can't have a rift in the family. How will Sarah explain that to the kids. It will be so difficult for them. They won't understand.'

'How long will it take to heal do you think?' she asked worriedly.

'God knows.'

Chapter Fourteen

Back in Seville, Spain, Julie waited for the right time to mention that she had met one of her sons and her daughter while she had been in Dublin. She decided to talk to Pedro one morning after breakfast when they would usually chat about the day ahead. But she hadn't been careful enough and when he heard what she said he threw his napkin down on the table and stalked out of the sun-filled room in a fury. Tears flooded her eyes, and she was glad that her daughter Pacqui hadn't come down yet. She had wanted to talk to Pedro on his own but seeing his reaction, she realised that wasn't going to be possible. She was very disappointed.

A maid came in carrying a tray of churros and croissants and put them down on the table. The door was pushed open loudly and Pacqui burst in. She always did that in the morning. Usually receiving a loud rebuke from her father Pedro at which she always laughed and was forgiven. She leaned across the table and picked up a round of churros, and chomped. Then poured a cup of café con leche for herself and sat down.

'What's wrong, Mama?' She looked at her. Her dark eyes quizzical.

'There's nothing wrong.' Julie turned away.

'But you have tears in your eyes.'

'It is just dust, or something.'

Pacqui reached and put her hand on Julie's. 'I'm worried about you.'

'Don't worry about me.' Julie pushed back her chair and left the room. Pedro had probably gone out to the stables and she wouldn't see him again until luncheon. She talked to the cook about the menu for dinner, and then went upstairs. Looking through the shuttered windows she could see the horses being exercised out on the paddocks. Suddenly, she looked forward to getting out there herself. She changed quickly and drove to the stables, asking one of the stable hands to bring out her horse. He was a beautiful chestnut stallion and Julie put her foot in the stirrup and pushed herself up on to the saddle, gripped the reins, and trotted out. She took a route along an avenue bordered by trees which led around the outer reaches of the large sprawling estate. It was a quiet place and she loved it. Generally, she didn't see anyone else at all and was glad of that. Now she needed peace and quiet, that above all. She had been building up to this morning since she had returned from Ireland and hoped that she would be able to persuade Pedro around to talking about her family. There had never been any mention of Frank, Alva, David and Cian, although she had felt obliged to tell him that Frank had died and he knew she had gone to see the solicitors in Dublin about his will. Now to receive such an aggressive response as she had this morning really upset her.

She was immediately reminded that she should email Alva, but she had been waiting until there was something positive to say about her Spanish family before she made contact. Now she had nothing to say.

She dug the heels of her black leather boots into the horse's side and he responded with a leap forward, ears flat, tail flying out behind, taking Julie along at such a pace she just let it happen and her negative feelings whirled away with the pounding of the stallion's hooves and the movement of the animal beneath her. She felt like she was in a race and that she was winning and hung on so tight she almost didn't know where she was. For an hour she let the horse run, and she was full of enjoyment until she reached the top of the hill and stopped in the shadow of a copse of trees. It was restful, with an unexpected breeze cooling her at this height. She slid off the back of the horse and holding on to the reins they followed a narrow pathway which meandered through the trees. Again, those fleeting thoughts returned. She wanted to talk with Pedro about Alva and her other children in Ireland. Wanted to introduce him to them. She wanted to. So badly. And decided to try again later.

As they sipped their coffee after dinner, there was a short lull in their conversation and she looked out through the window into the garden, brightly lit by flickering lamps set among the shrubbery. She took a deep breath.

'Pedro?'

'Si?'

'I mentioned my family in Ireland to you this morning, I'd like to talk about them.'

He didn't reply. The only sound the clink of the china coffee cup as he put it down. It was sharp somehow, and heralded defeat.

'Why now?' he asked curtly.

'I met my daughter when I was in Dublin.'

'Was this arranged?' he asked.

'No, it was an accident.'

'How so?'

'At the office of her solicitor. We went there …Carlos and I, to talk about Frank's will.'

'Did he include you?'

'We weren't divorced, so I automatically inherit part of his estate.'

'Oh?' He raised his eyebrows, dark with flecks of silver now. 'How much?'

'It is one third and could be substantial.'

Pedro seemed surprised.

'When I arranged to meet with Frank's solicitor, it really wasn't to find out how much money I would receive, if anything at all, it was just to make contact and through him to try and meet my children. Now that Frank is dead I was very hopeful that my children would want to know me too. But the solicitor didn't tell me very much and the meeting was short. The executor will inform me of the exact amount when the estate has been calculated.'

'You don't need Frank's money, you and I have enough, querida,' Pedro reassured.

'Thank you, my love.' She pressed his hand, grateful.

'When I met my children, I didn't say anything about money or the will, and neither did they. It was such a surprise for me to meet my two children that it was all I cared about. I am not interested in how much money I will receive. That doesn't matter to me.'

'I don't want you to receive such money from your husband. I am the one who will provide for you. You can have anything at all that you wish. Has it not been that way in all our years together?'

'Yes, Pedro, you have always been more than generous to me.'

He knew that she had another family before she came out to Spain, she hadn't kept that a secret. Although she did write to Frank every so often, she never received a reply from him or any of her children, and their existence had faded from her memory somewhat. She never wanted that but knew it was necessary. She had a new life here with Pedro in Seville and had no life at home, so there wasn't any choice really. But all the time she waited to hear something. Over the years, even the smallest few words would have kept her happy. But that never happened. It was as if she had been written out of history. Someone had put her name down once and that of her children, but they had used invisible ink and it had slowly faded and left no imprint as if they had never existed.

'It is strange, but suddenly I feel that I am being pushed to one side with this mention of your husband. Of course, he is dead now, but your children are aware of you for the first time and perhaps this will make changes in our lives.'

'Nothing will change, Pedro, I will always love you and our children,' she insisted. 'Knowing my other children will have no effect on our lives.'

'I want to be sure about that.' Pedro gripped her hand. 'They are of your blood.'

'You can be very sure, I will always be here for you.' She kissed him, her lingering touch on his lips tried to persuade him that she meant every word of it.

He turned towards her, and pressed himself close. Undoing the buttons on her shirt, he kissed the soft skin below her neck. Searching for that sensitive little spot he knew kindled her desire. She never could refuse him. There was something so dynamic about Pedro she always found him impossible to resist.

'Let's go to bed.' He took her in his arms and drew her with him into the lift which brought them up to their bedroom on the second floor. Inside, he continued kissing her, his lips gripping hers with such intensity she let herself go as they took their clothes off.

'*Mi querida*,' he murmured.

'*Te amo,*' she replied, wanting him to know how much she loved him and how strongly she felt.

'*Te amo*,' he whispered. And held her even closer.

After they had made love, Pedro went downstairs and came back up with two glasses of Fino. 'Enjoy that, *querida*.' He handed one to her and raised his glass. 'To us!'

The crystal pinged. It made her feel better. Making love always did that. It seemed to reassure her that her life was good and that the uncertainty which hovered around the edges of her heart when Pedro had been so scathing this morning had disappeared.

'I'm sorry I seemed so difficult this morning, but ...I just got out on the wrong side of the bed.'

'It's my fault.' She took the blame.

'Sometimes I am in a bad mood in the mornings as you know. I apologise.' He kissed her. 'It was just the thought of your children looking for you.'

'If they had wanted me, they might have made contact before now, but I do not think they wanted me.'

'It is very strange. I found it hard to believe when you told me that.'

'I did not know the situation in Ireland. My children were very young and had been told that I had left them. They knew no better.'

'My children were very lucky to have you here to look after them. They love you,' he said.

'I love them.'

'I am glad that you feel that way.'

'I've always loved them.'

'Will you have more contact with your own children now?' Pedro seemed concerned.

'I told my daughter that I would contact her but I wanted to talk to you first.'

'Thank you for that. But I don't know how ...my ...our children will react to hear that you have another family.'

'Carlos knows of it already. But I feel it may be difficult to tell the girls.'

'Is there a chance that your daughter Alva might arrive here?'

'She doesn't have our address, although Carlos may give it to her. She's a very strong-willed young woman. I'm proud of her,' Julie insisted.

'There could be problems with the family if she comes,' Pedro pointed out.

'Surely they will understand. Carlos had no problem meeting her.'

'But what if all three of your children arrive together?' Pedro asked.

'It's highly unlikely, particularly as David, one of my sons, doesn't seem to want to know me.'

'That may change when you inherit.'

'I can't imagine it.'

'Money changes everything, Julie.'

She thought about that, but didn't know if she had the strength to stand up and claim her inheritance, or maybe it would come to her automatically, the administration handled by the solicitor, and she would have nothing at all to do.

'I'm glad that you don't object if I keep in touch with my children. That was why I needed to talk to you before I make contact with them.'

'I can't say I'm very enthusiastic about it, but I feel it's not up to me to object or otherwise.'

'You have a right to object.'

'You're a grown woman and you have to make up your own mind about such things.'

'I don't want it to change things between us, you know I love you and our children. You are my life.' Julie tried to impress this on Pedro as tears flooded her eyes. 'I never expected to see my first family again, this is as much a shock to me as it has been to you.'

'I'm glad that you told me about meeting your daughter, it's never a good thing to discover secrets at a later stage in our lives.'

'I would never try to hide anything from you,' she said. 'I promise.'

'Thank you. But now what are you going to do?'

'If it's all right by you, then I'll email Alva, though I will have to word it very carefully until our girls know about my previous life.'

'And the wider family too.'

'Oh yes …' Her heart thumped. She hadn't thought about that. Pedro's family were very close. He had three brothers and two sisters. His grandmother was still living here on the estate, now in her nineties. Julie would also have to take her feelings into account. Abuela had never queried whether herself and Pedro had actually got married and to announce that they were living together all this time would probably shock this very conservative family. Suddenly, it seemed that there was a lot more to this situation than she had expected.

Chapter Fifteen

Alva continued to live in the spare bedroom and the living room only. That was it. She hadn't told many people about her separation from Darren but it would leak out eventually, she was sure of that, but for the moment she was content to let it be. But that afternoon he called her. A long angry tirade accusing her of locking him out of the apartment, and forcing him to resign from his job. He went on and on about the fact that she had no right to do that.

'How dare you, Alva,' he had threatened. 'I'll get my own back, you stupid bitch. Just you wait. You won't know what hit you.'

She turned off the phone. It was too much to be forced to listen to him. Lately, Darren's aggression had annoyed her. He thought he could control her. And she wasn't going to be controlled. Never wanted that. Even when they knew each other in those early days she hadn't wanted him to assume that he could be the stronger of the two of them. She hadn't wanted any man in her life to feel he had more strength than she had herself. Now she felt free. She could make all her own decisions about everything in her life.

In the middle of her musings, her phone rang, and assuming it was Darren again, she was about to put it back in the pocket of her jacket, when she noticed the name *Carlos* on the read-out. Now a pleasant sense of surprise swept over her as he invited her to meet him for a drink on the following Thursday. She wasn't quite ready when he rang the bell, but she pressed the intercom and he came up in the lift.

'Sorry, I've been working, I'm just back,' she apologised.

'No problem,' he grinned, and put out his hand to her.

His soft warm grip sent sudden darts of excitement through her. She had liked him that first time they had dinner, liked, but not much more than that. She wasn't the type of person to fall in love with men without warning. Darren was the first man she had loved. And now she wondered what she had seen in him. Carlos was very different and she had to prevent him ever knowing that her reaction to his touch meant any more than friendship.

'I just need a few minutes,' she said, aware that she needed to comb her hair and spray some perfume. 'Would you like a cup of something or a drink?'

'No thank you. It's no problem to wait for you.'

In his car, they drove towards Dalkey. It was a pleasant evening, and they stopped at a pub which overlooked the sea and sat chatting.

'It's beautiful here,' she murmured, sipping a gin and tonic although he chose a non-alcoholic beer as usual.

'*Si,* I come here sometimes, just to get away from the city. There is something very relaxing about it. And it's never too busy.'

'How is Julie and all your family in Spain?' she asked, although she didn't want to appear to be too curious, she really wanted to know.

'They are well.'

'Julie sent me an email a few days ago, it was lovely to hear from her. She spoke about your father, and sisters, and how things are going with them.'

'She told me,' he smiled at her.

'It's amazing to know her now. Can you imagine how it feels?' she asked him. Anxious for him to understand.

'It must be wonderful for you,' he nodded. 'And Cian too.'

'Extraordinary,' she murmured. 'All of a sudden we have another family. I hope that they will accept us.'

'I have,' he laughed. 'Why shouldn't they?'

'Thank you. I really appreciate that.'

'Don't worry, when they meet you, it will be a very natural thing.'

A text came in on her phone.

'I'm sorry,' she ignored it.

'No problem. Would you like to have something to eat, the restaurant here is quite good.'

'Yes, why not, just something light.'

'I'll ask if they have a table. Pardon me.' He stood up and went into the restaurant.

While he was gone, she checked her phone. It was Darren asking if she would call him. She didn't respond and ignored his message.

Carlos returned with a broad smile on his face. 'Ten minutes, they will call us. Would you like another drink before we go in?'

'No thanks, I'll just finish this.' She sipped the last of the gin and tonic.

Another text came in.

'Do you want to check your phone, perhaps it is urgent?' he asked.

'Thanks, I will. Sorry about this.' She opened up her phone to find that it was Darren again. She pursed her lips with annoyance. 'No, it's not urgent.'

The manager of the restaurant came out and called them in to their table.

'This is lovely,' Alva smiled.

'It is a nice place, and I'm so glad to see you again,' he said.

She didn't know what to say.

'I wasn't sure whether you would want to see me also so I didn't want to rush you,' he said.

She wasn't sure what to say, interrupted again by another text. She glanced at the phone again and suddenly wondered if perhaps it was urgent. Had something happened to Darren? She was suddenly worried.

'I'll have to make a call, I'm worried now. But let's order first.'

'Sure.'

Alva didn't take long to decide on a vegetarian pasta dish which sounded tasty. Carlos ordered a fish dish.

'Excuse me, I'll just call.' She went out into the foyer and pressed Darren's number.

Almost immediately he replied. 'Took you long enough,' he snapped.

'Is something wrong, Darren?' she asked, suddenly concerned.

'Of course, there's something wrong, how could you ask such a stupid question. I've just called around and I can't get in, and you're not answering the doorbell.'

'I'm not home.'

'Where are you?'

'Out.'

'Out where?'

'None of your business.'

'Your car is in the park.'

'I didn't take it.'

'Who are you with?'

'Again, it's none of your business.'

'It fucking is, I'm your partner.'

'You are no longer, Darren. It's over.'

'It is not. I won't accept it.'

'You will have to. We're finished.'

'I refuse.'

'Goodbye Darren, and don't text me again. I want no further contact with you.' She turned off the phone, and put it on silent.

Carlos smiled when she reappeared in the restaurant. 'I am

hoping it was not a problem,' he said.

'No, it wasn't.'

'I'm glad of that. Ah here is our food.'

The waiter placed the dishes in front of them.

'Would you like some wine?'

'No thanks, water's fine. It would be nice to share a drink but as you're driving, there's no point.'

'One cannot take chances when drinking particularly in my career. I do not even drink at home as there can often be an emergency call with one of my patients and I cannot afford not to be one hundred percent sober and ready to operate should it be necessary when there are lives are risk. The only exception is when I am at home on holiday and there is no chance of such emergencies occurring.'

They chatted on, enjoying their food. She encouraged him to talk about Spain and what he loved about the country. It gave her an image in her head of their lives and also that of Julie's. It was a very pleasant evening.

They sat into his car, and for a few minutes enjoyed the view over the sea. 'Imagine living here and having this view every time you looked out,' she said, smiling.

'There is something magical about it. Although I am quite close to the sea where I live, and sometimes walk out to Howth.'

'Your work must be very stressful,' she remarked.

'It can be but to save a life gives me a sense of purpose.'

'We're lucky to have you.'

'I am lucky to be in Ireland. And with you tonight.' He leaned towards her and touched her lips with his. Softly warm. So very intimate. She didn't hesitate and clung to his mouth with her lips, heart pounding. Senses screaming. Longing to know him even more. His arms encircled and folded her closer to him. She swam in the delicate aroma of his after shave. Feeling the softness of his skin on hers, a slight roughness on his chin. His dark brown eyes looked down into hers and he smiled.

'You are very special Alva.' He cupped her cheek in his hand and kissed her again. She lay against his chest and could feel his body warmth through her light blouse. Just sitting there with him meant so much after all that had gone on recently. The comfort of having someone who cared about her was an amazing feeling and she wanted to thank him just for being him. Whether he felt deeply about her, or not, didn't matter, she was just thankful to him.

Driving home, she began to worry if Darren was going to be waiting for her at the apartment, although she was reluctant to tell Carlos that it had been him on the phone earlier. So her mood changed to some extent and she became apprehensive. She was very quiet but couldn't think of anything light to chat about dreading the thought of possibly meeting Darren at the apartment.

Carlos drove into the apartment block, and pulled into the place allocated for visitors. 'Thank you for coming this evening,' he said smiling. 'I really enjoyed it.'

'I must thank you for such a lovely dinner.'

Suddenly, there was the sound of someone rapping on the window on the passenger side.

She looked around and her heart dropped when she saw Darren peering in at her. He mouthed something but she couldn't hear him.

'I'm sorry Carlos, that's Darren, I'd better go.' She opened the car door.

'Is this your ex-partner?' he asked.

She nodded.

'Perhaps you should not get out until he leaves,' he suggested.

Darren pulled open the door fully, reached in, grabbed her arm and tried to drag her out.

'Darren, please go away.' Alva begged, as she tried to close the door.

'I was looking for you, where have you been?' he yelled.

Carlos reached across Alva and managed to pull her door shut, locking all the doors. 'Don't get out. He is very dangerous.'

Darren banged on the door again and continued doing that.

'We should call the Gardai.'

'No, I don't want to involve the Gardai.'

'He is very angry. I think we should go. Would you like to come to my apartment and you can stay there tonight?'

'Thank you, Carlos, maybe that would be best. But I'm sorry to be a problem.'

'I could not leave you here with him.' He started the car, and reversed it. It left Darren nonplussed and he rushed after it, but Carlos shot forward and managed to drive towards the main exit but the high wrought iron gates had closed. Alva took the remote control from her handbag, but by then Darren had caught up with them and he continued banging on the back of the car, and yelling her name. Then he came around to her side but the gates began to open slowly and there was just enough space for the car to slip through. With a quick glance left and right to check that the road was clear, Carlos swung out and drove away.

Alva gripped her hands tight together. She was so nervous. But very grateful to Carlos. Darren's behaviour was very worrying. Was he going to continue harassing her until he managed to force his way back into her life? She said little as they drove to the north side. Although on one occasion, as they were stopped at the traffic lights, Carlos put his hand across and gently he covered her hand with his just for a moment. It was comforting for Alva and she was grateful to him.

The apartment block Carlos lived in was very similar to Alva's, and she remembered it from the occasion she had gone there with Julie.

'Come in, Alva, and sit down. Would you like a cup of coffee?'

he asked.

'Thank you, that would be nice.' She sat there, feeling rather worn out. She couldn't believe that Darren was behaving in that way. What was the point refusing to accept the situation, she asked herself. She took out her phone and could see that he had sent quite a number of texts over the evening. The wording in all of them happened to be the same, demanding to know where she was. And why she had gone out with someone else and left her car? And who was he?

They had a cup of coffee, and then Carlos took her into the spare bedroom.

'There are some clothes here belonging to my mother, so you can certainly use what you want.' He opened a drawer. 'She won't mind. The en-suite bathroom is in here with fresh towels, soap, etc.'

'Thank you, Carlos.'

'I hope you'll be comfortable.'

'I'll be fine.'

'Can I get you anything else?'

'Thank you, no, but I wonder could you see if your phone charger might fit mine?'

'Let us have a look.' He went to look for one and they tried it, but unfortunately it didn't suit.

'Turn off the phone completely and you'll save the battery, then it will still be working for you in the morning, and when you go home you can charge it.'

'I'll do that, I have one in the office anyway.'

'What time do you want to get up?'

'I have to go home first and change.'

'I leave at six, is that too early for you?'

'That's fine, the traffic will be too heavy if we leave later.'

'I'll say goodnight then, I'll call you in the morning.' He reached to kiss her. It was a soft gentle touch of his lips which held a lot of promise.

All Alva needed was underwear for tomorrow, and she had to look at Julie's clothes, and chose a pair of lace panties, which were definitely designer and brand new with the label still attached. But she hoped Julie wouldn't mind. She would buy her a new pair.

To her surprise, Alva slept well most of the night. She felt relaxed here with Carlos. And there was no threat of any sort. She had already awoken before six, and taken a shower, so when he knocked, she was ready.

'What would you like for breakfast?' he asked.

'Coffee, and some toast maybe.'

'I'll do that.'

They sat together and she found it very pleasant to be with him.

'Drop me off at the Dart station and I'll go straight into work.'

'Are you sure, I could drive you home, it's no problem,' he offered.

'At this time of the day it would take ages to get across the city and then back to the hospital.' She pointed out, reluctant to delay him.

'If that's OK for you?'

'It is, I usually go into work early, so I'll be ahead of the posse,' she laughed.

'I hope everything works out for you when you get home this evening. Do you expect your ex-partner to be there?' Carlos asked as they drove to the Dart Station.

'I hope not,' she smiled. Trying to make it seem she wasn't too concerned.

When they had arrived at his apartment, she had given him some idea of what was happening in her life, and why Darren was behaving in such a violent manner towards her so she was glad of that. If she was going to see him again, then he should know where she was at. Now there seemed to be a greater chance, although she wondered how much their shared kisses actually meant.

Alva's first meeting today was with HR and they had already been given the task of finding new staff to replace those who had resigned. But in the meantime, there were assistants who could carry on with the various jobs. Still, a lot of the work would fall on Alva. She had a responsibility for every department in the company and was always anxious to ensure that the operation of the different areas ran smoothly.

The next thing she planned to do was to arrange a meeting at the bank with the assistant accountant, who was now taking over Hugh's position. She opened up her laptop and the account in the British Virgin Islands. The money was still there, frozen, but all she had to do was to get the bank to unfreeze it and transfer it into their own company account, and then their credit balance would look the way it should at last.

Chapter Sixteen

In Seville, Julie waited anxiously to tell her step-daughters, Pacqui and Nuria, about her Irish family. But she would have preferred to mention it to them both at the same time, and was delighted when Nuria called and told her she had decided to come down from Madrid for the weekend. Now she would have both girls together. But she didn't know what reaction she would receive from them. That was an unknown. When they spoke as a family about the past and she was asked by them about her own mother and father and where they were from, she was always evasive and never gave away very much information. She had decided when she had been employed by Pedro at first that she would keep her past a secret. To have spoken of her children and not be able to put her arms around them and hold them close, would have broken her heart. So she hid them in the shadows. In that place where their voices whispered low, and she could barely hear their sweet tones cry out to her, as they must surely do at her loss. Had they missed her, she wondered. Or was her husband Frank enough for them. Or had that other woman, Sally, been a mother figure so their memories of her would be forgotten altogether in their young minds. She had been so sure that her face, her eyes, her smile, would have faded so much as the years passed that if they ever met her they would not know her. Yet her thoughts were twisted, and she was recently proven wrong when her daughter Alva knew her immediately when they met. How strange that was, she thought. She had recognised her son,

Cian, instantly too, but knew by the uncertainty in his eyes that he didn't know her on that night. But now she prayed that when they would meet again, he would know her. And David too, should he ever agree to meet her at some point in the future. She prayed that he would not refuse to recognise her as his mother.

She talked again to Pedro.

'You must be prepared for a bad reaction from the girls, especially from Pacqui, she is very close to you,' he pointed out cautiously.

'How will I deal with that if she is very upset?' she asked him, worried.

'I do not know. It is a difficult situation and must be carefully handled.'

Julie thought of what Pedro said. It put her off so much she began to think she should talk with Carlos on the phone, but then she decided against that. His reaction to meeting Alva had been quite normal, but then he was older than the girls and more mature and that might have made a difference. Still, she didn't want any delay. Since she had met Alva, she was anxious to have the rest of the family meet before long.

When Nuria had arrived from Madrid the following evening, Julie took a chance to broach the subject.

'Pacqui, Nuria,' she said hesitantly.

They looked at her curiously.

'There's something I want to say to you both now that you have arrived, Nuria.' She decided to plunge in straight away. If she hesitated, she might never be able to tell them.

Pedro cleared his throat noisily.

'Before I came to look after you here in Spain, I had another family in Ireland.'

Nuria seemed the most surprised of the two.

'Many years ago I separated from my husband, and was forced to leave my children. I came to work here in Seville, and as your Papa needed a person to look after you he asked me to work here.'

'Qué?' Pacqui was astonished.

'My husband didn't want me, and wouldn't allow me to see my children.'

'How horrible he must have been,' Nuria whispered.

'Why did you not tell us?' Pacqui asked.

'I was afraid. It was like I had left behind my other self.'

'I'm so upset about this,' Pacqui murmured. 'It seems impossible to have happened. Did you know about this, Papa?'

'I did, Pacqui.'

'Why did you not tell us?'

'I …we…your father decided it was better,' Julie said.

'So you wanted to hide it from us.'

'Only so that we could all live a new life without a hindrance, because I was going to act as your mother and I was to look after you. I loved you.'

'What did your own children think of you?' Nuria burst out.

'They were very young and didn't knew why I had left.'

'It seems so sad.'

'And it was only a short time ago that I met my children after all these years.'

'How did that happen?' Pacqui asked.

'My Irish husband died. And I met my eldest daughter and my youngest son when I went to Dublin that last time. It was very surprising for them to meet me after all those years.'

'Can we meet them too?' Pacqui asked.

'Carlos has already met Alva.'

'That's unfair, he's one up on us.'

'He didn't tell us that he'd met them.'

'I asked him not to.'

'How many children do you have?'

'Three.'

'There's three of us in each family?' Nuria was excited.

'Yes.'

'Then we should get to know each other.'

'I want that, more than anything.' Julie was eager.

'I don't think it will prove to be so easy,' Pedro said.

'Why not, Papa?' Pacqui asked.

'I don't know what your grandmother is going to say.'

'Abuela will say nothing.'

'You are Spanish, they are Irish.'

'I love Irish people,' Nuria enthused. 'They are so warm and friendly. You should have told us about your family, we would have made contact a long time ago.'

'I'm sorry. I didn't have the courage.'

'Please let us meet,' begged Pacqui.

'Soon. I want to.' Nuria was equally enthusiastic.

'Will they come over to see us?'

'I'll try and organise that when we are in Cadiz.'

'That will be wonderful.' The girls were delighted.

'Thank you for telling us about your family.' Pacqui stood up and threw her arms around Julie.

'It means so much to us.' Nuria was next and hugged her too.

'Thank you.' There were tears in Julie's eyes.

'I hope they will come to Cadiz, we will have a lovely time together,' Pacqui smiled widely.

'I will invite them,' Julie said.

'I'm looking forward to seeing them all.'

'What are their names, Mama?' Nuria asked.

'My eldest girl is Alva, my eldest son is David and the youngest is Cian.'

'We will be a real family now.'

'I don't know what your grandmother is going to say or the rest of the family either,' Pedro said.

'We won't tell her,' Nuria responded immediately.

'She is very conservative, and may not understand,' Julie warned.

'You tell her, Papa,' Pacqui smiled at her father in a winning way.

'No, I will tell her. It must be me.' Julie put her hand on Pedro's, and was very happy when he squeezed it affectionately. At least he agreed and that made her feel more confident. The girls' reaction was amazing really, and utterly surprising.

That night as Julie and Pedro lay in bed, they talked about the family.

'Will it be very difficult to tell everyone?' she asked. 'I feel that I have created this problem for you.'

'No, it is out now and better for that. It's difficult for the older generations.' She lay her head on his shoulder and he put his arm around her and held her close.

'Don't worry too much. It will not be a problem.'

'I don't know, you know how your grandmother is.'

'Abuela has very strong opinions.'

'She's amazing for ninety-three. I'll tell her tomorrow.'

'Nuria and Pacqui won't keep the secret for long.'

'They're bound to let it out. You know how much time they spend with Abuela particularly now Nuria is home.'

Julie felt good about the decision. If she could tell some people about her Irish family then it would mean a great deal to her, and at last she could soon begin to speak about them openly.

Pedro's grandmother, Abuela, lived in a small house on the grounds of the estate, and as she was elderly she had a nurse taking care of her. But while she was slightly infirm, she still had a very sharp mind, and Julie was always a little intimidated.

Nothing passed dear Abuela, the Spanish name they used for grandmother and she was very pleased to see her. Julie had brought some delicious petit fours as a gift and Abuela was delighted.

'I have not seen you for a few days,' Julie said. 'I have missed you.'

'You must all come for dinner soon, both you and Pedro, and the girls,' Abuela suggested.

'We would love that,' Julie said.

'How is Carlos, will he be coming home for vacation this year?' Abuela enquired.

'I have already asked him,' Julie said. 'And he is hoping to come home.'

'That will be wonderful, we have not seen him because of Covid.'

As Seville was very hot in summer, the family spent the months of August and September at their home near the beach in Cadiz, and in the back of Julie's mind she was hoping that Alva, David and Cian, might come to spend part of the vacation with them, and she could then introduce all of them to her Spanish family.

The maid brought in a trolley with coffee and pastel and served.

'This pastel looks delicious.' Julie chose one, picked up her coffee cup and sipped it.

'You are very lucky to have your pastry cook still, we have lost ours,' Abuela said. 'She was very good, but someone realised that and offered her more money and now she has gone.'

'There are always better positions for good people,' Julie agreed.

'Now, what other news do you have for me?' Abuela fanned herself although the air conditioning was on and the house was kept cool.

'I have something to tell you, but I don't know what you will think.'

'Tell me quickly, is it a secret?' Abuela clapped her thin little hands excitedly.

'It was a secret,' admitted Julie.

Abuela looked at her in puzzlement.

'As you know, when I came to Seville at first, Pedro offered me a job to take care of the children after their mother died.'

'We were very lucky to find you, and for Pedro too. Look how happy you all are now,' Abuela exclaimed.

'I was very lucky to find you, as my life was quite difficult at that time.'

'I did not realise that,' Abuela murmured.

'In Ireland I was married.'

Her mouth fell open in shock.

Julie went on to tell her about the children.

'How sad for you.' Abuela was very sympathetic.

'When I came here, and met Pedro and his children I was very happy, and somehow over time the children became like my own, and of course Pedro and I are very close now.'

'Did you ever hear from your husband and children?' asked Abuela.

'Julie shook her head. 'He died recently, but I met my daughter and one of my sons when I went to Dublin that last time to see Carlos.'

'That's wonderful. Were they happy to see you? I'm sure they must have been.'

'Oh yes.'

Abuela smiled. 'You will have to introduce me to them,' she said.

'I will.'

'Does everyone in the family know about this?' Abuela queried.

'No. Just Pedro and the children. And you now.'

'Thank you.'

'But I don't know how the rest of the family will accept it.'

'Don't you worry. They will,' Abuela laughed out loud.

'I was amazed that the girls have shown no resentment. I only told them last night.'

'Why should anyone object? You weren't someone without a family. Everyone has a life. A past. I'm not surprised to hear that you had a family, but sad that you lost them.'

'Thank you so much, Abuela, I really appreciate everything you've said.' There were tears in Julie's eyes.

'I'm looking forward to meeting your children,' Abuela said.

'I hope it can be arranged.'

'And soon.'

Chapter Seventeen

Alva was kept particularly busy today. Most of her work connected with banking, and the transfer of the funds which had been frozen, and she knew that once a credit balance was shown in the bank accounts, their business could continue to operate in a proper manner and they would be solvent once again.

But as the day continued on, she noticed that she had received a number of texts from Darren although she hadn't opened any of them. She wasn't going to read the rubbish he had written. She was becoming more and more angry as the texts increased in number. How dare he write so many. It really was too much to bear. If he kept it up, she would have to do something about it. And if he was at the apartment when she arrived home she would explode. She had to do some shopping on the way and as she drove in she couldn't see his car and was relieved about that. So she slipped in quickly, taking the lift up, and banging the door closed. But after a few minutes, her heart almost stopped as she heard the doorbell ring. But she didn't answer it.

Then the texts started again. Alva stared at the phone as text after text came through. It was then she decided that she would have to keep a record of them. Obviously, Darren was outside. Waiting for her. Watching. In case she went out. The thought of that was sickening. She had to go out. To work. To meetings. To visit friends. To do whatever she had to do. And she couldn't allow Darren to make her afraid to put a step outside her door. It just wasn't on, and no way to exist.

Her phone rang again. Her heart thudded He was making her frightened. Why should she be frightened by him. She looked at the phone. But to her great relief it was Carlos.

'Are you safe? Is Darren there?'

'No, he just keeps sending texts and I'm sure he's outside the door.'

'What does he say?'

'Threatening stuff.'

'Perhaps you should call the Gardai?'

'No, I won't do that yet. I want him to stop doing it.'

'But if he doesn't?'

'Then I'll call them.'

'Record them. They will want evidence.'

'I have the texts on my phone.'

'I am worried about you. He seems dangerous.'

'I'll be fine.'

'Do you want to come over here?'

'No, not tonight.'

'Do you want me to call when I am off duty. But it will be late.'

'Thanks, but he might over-react if he's outside and sees you. I don't want anything to happen to you, Carlos.'

'Nothing will happen to me. Do not worry, Alva.'

'Please don't come over. I appreciate that you are concerned about me, but I'll be scared if you do. But thank you so much for offering.' She felt very grateful to him.

'Call me if you have a problem, but I won't be able to talk as I will be on duty, but I'll come back to you as soon as I can. But I think that you should call the Gardai if you feel threatened again by him.'

'I will,' she agreed.

'Promise me?'

'Promise.'

'And leave me a text message if anything should happen.'

'Thank you.'

'If it's not too late, I will talk to you later, *querida,* I look forward to that.'

'But I will have to put my phone on silent, Carlos, I can't keep listening to all the texts as they come in and I won't pick up a call from you.'

'Send me a text when you are going to bed,' he asked. '*Buenos noches.*'

They finished their conversation and she had been surprised to hear him add that word *querida* at the end of the sentence. That meant *darling* in Spanish. A warm feeling swept through her. Now she wondered if perhaps he did like her more than she had expected. He certainly seemed to care about her anyway, and was worried about her safety.

With the phone turned off, she eventually went to sleep, although part of her was still listening for the doorbell to ring. But there was no sound, and it was only when she turned on her phone in the morning that she saw the number of texts. She didn't count them, but couldn't believe there were so many, realising that Darren must have been sending them all night. Maybe they were automatic repetitive texts, she decided, that would certainly explain the high numbers.

She left home early as usual, even more conscious of avoiding Darren. But there was no sign of him and she made it into the office without any hassle. When she arrived in and checked her inbox she was delighted to see an email from Julie in Spain. It was the first she had sent and Alva was delighted to be invited over to join with the family on their holiday in Cadiz in August or September. September would suit very well thought Alva, now that Purtell Vintners had managed to shake the bank off their backs which was one problem solved. Alva was looking forward to it already. Julie had said she would email Cian personally, but wanted Alva to invite David too.

There was one good thing about the invitation and that was the fact that she would be able to afford to go now as she didn't have to invest any part of her inheritance in the company. While her salary had been reduced, the board had decided to leave these reductions in place until the company was totally solvent again. But on the other hand, as David had shown no interest in meeting Julie when she was over, he probably wouldn't be keen to join with her family in Spain which was such a pity. But Alva determined that she would talk to him and try to persuade him to make contact with Julie, she was his mother after all, and he may well regret not meeting her in the future. Of course, he wasn't speaking to her or maybe Cian either, so probably wouldn't want to spend any time with them in Spain. She decided then that she would let him know how she felt, as she didn't want the situation to remain the way it was. While he didn't want to have anything to do with their mother, Alva would have done anything to help Julie reconcile with him. It would be very sad if that didn't happen.

Alva replied to Julie, thrilled to have received her email. Saying she was delighted to be invited to Spain and was really looking forward to meeting her again and the family. She also asked who would be there, anxious to know the names of people. She made no mention of Carlos. Unsure whether he had spoken to his mother about her. She didn't think he would have gone into detail about their dates in Dublin and perhaps may not have wanted anyone in the family to know.

This morning, she had texted Carlos, letting him know that all was well, but immediately she turned on *silent* on her phone again. Alva realised she would have to let people know that she had it turned on, but then she decided to buy a new phone instead. Let Darren keep texting on the old number as long as he liked.

She slipped out at lunch time and managed to buy a new phone with a new number. The people in the store were able to transfer most of her contact numbers so she hadn't lost those, and she was glad of that. Later, she texted everyone on her Contacts list, and WhatsApp and let them know. And had the satisfaction of deleting Darren's number. She was on Facebook and Linkedin too, but now decided to close both accounts. She had been threatening to do that for a long time so now it suited her to do it. The first persons she texted were the family, and other business people who would need to contact her. And of course, Carlos too.

She sent out a general email to the staff, and informed them that she had lost her phone, and gave them her new number. Adding that no one in the company was to give her new telephone number to anyone who would enquire according to GDPR. She wasn't sure whether that would work or not, but hoped it would.

Darren was a popular staff member on the sales team and he could easily request her new number if he suspected she had changed hers. Now she decided to occasionally reply to his texts to keep up the impression that she still using the old phone. Maybe that might work. She had every intention of keeping the phone anyway, just to have a record of how many texts he was sending on a daily basis, it seemed to be almost in the hundreds.

As she worked, she kept an eye on her phone. And could see the numbers of texts building. She opened one. It had a stream of words describing her. Vulgar. Disgusting words. She couldn't believe that Darren would write such vile stuff. What had got into him? She wanted to write back in a similar vein, but wasn't going to lower herself to his level. She didn't know this person now. He had changed radically, and she thought if he kept himself at a text level and didn't bother calling to the apartment, then she could probably keep him at a distance and hope that he would tire of this eventually.

But he didn't and was at the apartment when she arrived home.

The minute she parked he was out of his car and waiting for her. She climbed out of her own car and locked it. She stood looking at him. Maybe she could talk to him. Persuade him that sending all these texts was crazy.

'Darren, how are you?' She began by speaking in a friendly fashion, and smiling.

'I'm not good. What do you think? I'm out of work and I've nowhere to live.'

'I'm sorry about that.'

'It's all your fault.'

'What was the reason for stealing the money? Did you plan to invest it in some project with Hugh and David?'

'Yes, we were planning to build a small hotel, and that money was enough to make a start on the build.'

'Why didn't you talk to me about it. We could have looked at other avenues of raising funds. As it is you could be in court now for fraud.'

'We didn't really think you'd take us to court,' he grinned.

'You were pretty sure about that?'

'Yeah.'

Alva looked around. Someone else had arrived into the car park and was pulling into a space, and she didn't want to be overheard.

'Anyway, this has nothing to do with us. You're free now to go to your new woman, and do whatever you want.' She lowered her voice as a man walked past.

'You don't care about me. Whether I have a cent or not,' he moaned.

'Look, you'll have to make your own way in life. I'm sure you'll pick up another sales job. There's plenty of them out there now. And, for heaven's sake, give up sending me those ridiculous texts. You're like a schoolboy sending them every minute. And the language is vile. You should know better.'

'Fuck you,' he spat.

She turned and marched into the main entrance closing the door behind her. She pushed her key in the lock, and opened the door, hurrying in to press the button for the lift. It came down quickly. She stepped in and stared at herself in the mirrored walls, shocked to see that her face looked pure white. God, what was he doing to her? She wondered. But was so relieved that he hadn't followed her and that she had made the lift alone. It arrived at her floor, and just before she was about to step out, she hesitated. What if he had run up the stairs after her. He was fit enough. The doors swung apart and she looked out. He wasn't there. She ran then, nervously pushing her key into the lock of her own door and throwing herself into the hallway almost falling against the hall table and knocking over the lamp, only hanging on to the edge of the table to steady herself. She took a deep breath, went inside and sat down. Staring around the living room. Wondering now was this a safe place for her to be any more. If Darren was going to constantly harass her, how could she live a normal life?

Chapter Eighteen

Alva drove down Westminster Road towards David's house. It was in Foxrock, and now she wondered how he was going to pay the mortgage on his home, a detached four-bedroomed on a large site. She didn't know how friendly he would be, as there had been no contact between them since that night in her apartment.

She rang the bell.

The noise of children laughing could be heard from the hall.

She was very fond of the family.

The door opened and David's wife Sarah smiled at her.

'Alva?' the two children both screamed with excitement, and rushed towards her.

'Sisi, Jon, hallo, how are you?' she smiled and hugged them.

'Come in, Alva, it's lovely to see you.' Sarah welcomed her in, and kissed her. 'It's been a while.'

'Yes, I'm sorry about that but you know …' she hesitated.

'Don't worry, would you like some tea or coffee?'

'I feel like tea today, that would be lovely.'

Alva handed a bag to Jon and one to Sisi as well as Sarah. 'A few chocs for you.'

'Thank you, Alva.'

The two children pulled the presents out of the bags, and were already playing excitedly with the toy car and the doll.

'Is David here?' she asked, her voice deliberately low.

'He's inside, watching television.'

'How is he?'

Sarah shook her head.

'Will he see me?'

'I don't know.'

'I'll go in.' She walked into the living room.

'Hi David,' she asked with a smile. 'How are you?'

He didn't look at her and continued watching television.

'I just thought I'd call over to see you all. I've missed you.'

He shrugged.

'And probate will come through eventually,' she said softly.

He nodded.

'And we have a meeting with John next Monday, at two.'

'OK.'

'Perhaps it will be better to make a new start,' she said.

Sarah came in with the children and they had their tea and cake. Now Alva was glad that she had called around and that David's anger towards her seemed to have eased a little.

When they met at the solicitors the following week, David's mood had improved even more and he spoke amicably with Cian. The meeting went well, until the solicitor informed them of the way the estate was to be divided up. Then when Julie's name was mentioned Alva could see the expression on David's face change, and he certainly wasn't pleased when the solicitor mentioned that she was entitled to a share of their father's estate.

Afterwards they went to lunch together, and David asked about Darren and was there any chance that he and Alva would get together again.

'Was it because of the money?' Cian asked.

'No, we've had problems for a while and Darren has moved out. Although he's been texting me a lot, and driving me mad.'

'Sorry to hear that, I thought you were the perfect couple.'

'So did I,' she said bluntly. 'But he was playing around.'

'Is there anything we can do?' David asked.

'Not really, although …'

They waited.

'There is something,' she ventured hesitantly.

'What?' Cian asked. 'Say it.'

'Darren has been trying to get back into the apartment.'

'You're saying he won't leave?' David was astonished.

'He doesn't want to, and keeps sending texts. Hundreds.'

'Do you want me to have a word with him?' David asked.

'No, he's very angry.'

'Probably because he had to resign.'

'It happened before that and it's hard to feel sorry for him.'

'Bastard,' Cian exploded.

'Anyway, I wondered if you might agree that I move into our home for a while until it's actually sold. He won't realise I'm there and it will give me some peace.'

'Of course, you should Alva,' both of her brothers agreed.

'Thank you. I appreciate that.'

'I feel like beating his brains out,' David said furiously.

'How long do you think he's been playing around?' Cian asked.

'God only knows.'

'It's tough on you, there's enough going on without that on top of it.'

'On a happier note, I received an email from Julie and she's told her family about us, because up to this they were unaware. So we've all been invited over to Spain to meet the family when they go to Cadiz in August and September, they've a house there. All of us. Partners. Children. Everyone. It's a big place apparently. Enough space for all the Purtells.'

'I had an email from Julie as well inviting us.' Cian seemed pleased. 'Natalie is delighted.'

'I'm not sure of the exact dates yet, I've to get back to Julie.

But I thought September would be the best time for me. Ask Natalie anyway, and David, what about you? Sarah and the kids are invited too,' Alva asked, although she knew she had to tread carefully even mentioning Julie.

'I'm not sure what I'll be doing then,' he muttered.

'Yeah, I understand, but maybe you could come over for a weekend, just to meet the family?' she suggested.

'You know how I feel about her.' David's expression was grim.

'I'm sure if you meet her and she explains exactly what happened to her, it might make it easier to understand. You know Dad never told us what happened, and he did have a relationship with our housekeeper. Of course, Julie had her own problems and she has admitted that, although she may not have told the Spanish family all those details, so if we're there we'll have to be careful of what we say.'

'We won't be going,' David said bluntly.

'Please think about it. It's never good to blame someone for what happened in the past. We don't know the exact details.'

'It's a pity Dad didn't talk to us,' Cian said.

'Julie was his wife,' Alva added.

'She's getting more of Dad's estate than any of us and she hasn't been around for most of our lives.'

'It's the law.'

'I could contest this,' David muttered.

'On what basis?' asked Alva.

'That we should get more and that she shouldn't get anything.'

'I don't think she can do anything about her inheritance. She has to accept it,' Cian said.

'And at the moment we don't even know what price the house will make, and there's other monies as well in his estate.'

'I'm going to talk to the solicitor,' David said.

'Maybe you might wait until we meet Julie again?'

'An inheritance will mean a lot to our mortgage,' Cian said.

'And maybe set you up in a new project, David,' said Alva.

They parted amicably, in spite of the disagreement about Julie, and Alva was glad about that. She hated any conflict in the family.

Darren continued sending texts during the day, but she was able to ignore them, and usually stayed in work late, catching up. Tonight, it was just after ten when she left and drove home to the apartment, praying that he wouldn't be there. As soon as she went inside, she gathered the clothes and other things she would need for the next few weeks, and before long, was driving over to her old home.

It was a while since Alva had been here, and as she made her way to her old bedroom and put away her clothes she found it deeply emotional. Memories of her Dad whirled around her. She almost thought she saw him more than once. Heard his footsteps on the stairs. His voice call her. And that made her long to put her arms around him and hold him close. Lying in bed, she was back in her childhood. Remembering those early days.

She slept well that night and her worries about Darren receded. If she could only stay here, then maybe she could manage to get her life back on track. Although how long that would last was another thing. All Alva wanted was for David to be reconciled with Julie. To know his mother. Aware that she needed to be close to all her children. Julie had lost them for so many years it was hard for her to deal with their loss. And now she had a chance to meet her children again and Alva wanted to help her.

She had three nights of sleep without disturbance, and when she awoke on the fourth day, she felt so much better she knew she could face into anything. The sign had gone up on the house. *FOR SALE*. And she knew that it wouldn't last long before it was replaced by *SALE AGREED*. And finally replaced by *SOLD*.

They received good offers within a few weeks for their

home and even achieved more than the reserve. But David, in particular, was anxious to try and obtain a better price, so they didn't accept any of them. To her relief she had avoided Darren, but didn't know how long that would last. Now she had the run of the house. All of the rooms. So that she could have freedom to wander everywhere she wanted without any restriction. But then they had to clear out the house. That was the worst aspect of it. Years of their lives had to be waded through and decisions made as to what should be done about the contents. Echoing back in time. To childhood. Growing up. Teenage years. College. To those days of awareness that there were only four of them in this family.

She called David and Cian and asked them to call around to the house and they could go through everything together before the house would be sold.

'You may like something and want to keep it, and I'm not going to know that,' Alva suggested. 'And the same goes for you Cian. I've already spent some time going through the cabinets, just to make a start on it. I've put stuff in boxes so you and David can examine them.'

'I'm not that interested in what's in them,' David said.

'But what about photos, things like that. Surely you'd like a few of them.'

'We've enough photos of our own family.'

'But I might take some, just for posterity. I'll have a look later.'

'There's quite a few around, and I suppose I'm sentimental about a lot of things,' admitted Alva.

'You can keep the rest of them,' David said.

'Well OK,' she agreed reluctantly.

That evening, they went through a lot of stuff.

'It's very emotional,' she admitted.

'Yeah, it is. But you've done a lot already,' David said.

'Would you like any furniture?'

'It wouldn't suit our house.'

'I'll see if one of the charities would like to have it.'

'It's hard to get rid of old furniture.'

'I'll make a few calls.' She leaned back in a velvet armchair and sighed.

'When are you going back to your own apartment?' Cian asked.

'When the new people move in, I'll have to leave then.'

There was a ring on the doorbell.

'I hope this isn't someone wanting to see the house. Sometimes people think that if they make a private deal with the sellers, they'll get the house cheaper.' She stood up and went to answer the door. Opening it, she stared in shock.

'So you're here, are you?' Darren said with heavy sarcasm.

'Yes, what's it got to do with you?'

'Here with your boyfriend?'

'No, Darren. Cian and David are here.'

'Well, when are you coming back to the apartment?' he asked.

'I'm not sure.'

'I've been waiting for you.'

'Don't be ridiculous, Darren, I'm not going back to you.'

'I've sent you texts telling you that.'

'I don't read your texts, so you're wasting your time.'

'Please come back to me. I want you.' He pushed his way in.

'Darren?' Cian appeared behind her.

'How's the little brother?'

'I think you should leave, Darren.'

'Are you going to make me?'

'If you don't leave, I'll call the Gardai.'

'Go, Darren,' Alva said.

He straddled the doorway.

'For God's sake, you're behaving like a child,' Alva said.

'Darren, piss off,' David said, coming downstairs.

'Mind your own business. It's got nothing to do with either of you,' Darren yelled.

'Get out of here,' Cian said.

'I know where you are now, so don't think you can hide away from me.' He shook his fist in her face.

'Darren, will you stop shouting and just go,' Cian said.

'Fuck off, Cian.' He turned and swaggered down the drive.

David was already at the front door.

'Leave him be,' Cian warned.

'And don't come around here again,' David shouted.

All he received was a raised finger in the air.

Chapter Nineteen

Later that evening, Alva received a call from Carlos wondering how she was.

She told him Darren had called around.

'I'm worried about you.'

'I'm hoping he'll just give up eventually.'

'It must be very stressful for you.'

'Yes, but I'll get through it.' She wasn't quite sure whether to mention Julie's invitation or not. Was Carlos aware of it? She decided to wait until he mentioned it first.

'Would you like to have dinner?' he asked. 'I haven't seen you for a while. I've missed you.'

'At the moment, I feel it's difficult. I'd love to have dinner, but Darren's attitude could be a problem. He could hang around wherever I am. Waiting. And I can't put you into that position.'

'I am well able to take care of myself,' he laughed. 'I go to the gym regularly.'

'I'm sure you are, but I can't have controversy at the house here.'

'I can understand that. Perhaps we might meet somewhere?'

'But I could be followed by him, and have a problem when I get there.'

'Perhaps you could ask someone to talk to him on your behalf?'

'He's aggressive so that would be very hard. I may go to my solicitor and ask his opinion.'

'That's a good idea.'

'Thank you for being so understanding.'

'I think you need someone to help you.'

'I'll tell you how my meeting goes with the solicitor.'

'I would like to know.'

'Sorry I can't meet you.'

Alva felt depressed that she couldn't meet Carlos because of Darren. She questioned herself. Why should she allow him to control her life? It was crazy. And if she couldn't talk to him in a rational manner, how was she ever going to sort out their differences. And thinking she might get some help from her friend, Naomi, she called her later. Maybe her expertise might send her down the right road.

She didn't go home after work, and took a taxi to a different bar, hoping Darren hadn't been loitering around outside the office and followed her. They chose a table at the back of the place, partially hidden by a large palm, and ordered their drinks.

'Cheers,' Alva raised her glass of gin and tonic. 'Sorry, I'm like someone in a thriller film hiding here.'

'Why?' Naomi laughed.

'I didn't tell you the latest about Darren.'

'What about him?'

She told her about his recent behaviour.

'He's become very aggressive since he resigned.'

'It must be very difficult for you.'

'I'd like to talk to him, he may have rights, I don't know.'

'Not much,' Naomi said. 'Did he ever contribute?'

'To the apartment?'

'Yeah.'

'No, I own the apartment, I bought it before I met him.'

'But he shared the expenses?'

'Oh yeah, all the usual stuff.'

'He may have rights then. Did he buy any furniture?'

'Maybe an odd thing. But he did buy some paintings.'

'He's probably looking for them. That's part of it.'

'He can have anything he wants. I don't care.'

'Maybe you should tell him that.'

'It's very difficult to talk to him now. I feel very threatened with all the texts coming, I wish he'd stop. It's just his behaviour is so awful it wears me down.'

'That's coercive control you know,' she said. 'And it's against the law. You could take a case against him.'

'I don't think I'm ready to do that yet.'

'It's good to know it's available to you now.'

'Yeah.'

'Another drink?'

'Why not, I took a taxi tonight. Hope he doesn't walk in.'

'He won't, relax.'

'It's only tonight I thought of taking a taxi, but if he's parked outside the house when I get back, how will I get in quickly. That's the trouble, pushing the key in the lock and fumbling with it takes time and he could be on my heels and into the hall behind me like a flash.'

'Do you want me to talk to him?' Naomi offered.

'Thank you, but no. I'd be afraid he would be aggressive and perhaps hurt you, I couldn't put you in such a position.'

'I'm well able for men like that.'

'Carlos said the same thing.'

'He seems to be very supportive.'

'He is, amazing really for someone I hardly know.'

'But remember the Gardai are always there for you.'

'I know.'

'It's not like the old days.'

'What used to happen then?'

'They used to go and fill up with petrol before calling to a house for a domestic disturbance. Then they had no authority to do anything, and nine times out of ten, the person who called the Gardai would deny she had called them even though she was obviously battered and bruised. There's nothing going on here, she would say, as generally it was a woman who needed help.'

'I found them very understanding, although I only mentioned about the texts and the arguments at the door. Anyway, I'm thinking of going to my solicitor. He may also have some ideas as to how I could approach Darren.'

'Good idea.'

Alva made an appointment with her solicitor, John, and the following day went in to see him. He understood about the fraud but when she went on to explain about the harassment and the constant texting, he straightened up in his chair. 'That's very serious. We'll have to do something.'

'I wondered would you write to him, pointing out that it is now against the law and ask that we might have a meeting to discuss the terms of our relationship. I'm prepared to give him money depending on what I receive from Dad's estate because he did contribute to the expenses of the house. He can take back all the stuff he bought if he wants.'

'I certainly will,' he agreed.

'Except I don't know where he is living, but maybe email.'

'Why don't I send you the letter addressed to Darren?'

'Yes, I'll try that and give it to him if he turns up.'

'I'll arrange it today. And give me his email.'

'I've managed to avoid Darren by taking taxis,' Alva told Carlos when he called her on the phone. 'And at least he hasn't popped up anywhere I've been. But he's still sending texts.'

'So we could meet some evening?' Carlos asked.

'We could take a chance,' she agreed, although she still wasn't very confident and dreaded the thought that Darren would follow her.

'Let's have dinner somewhere.'

They met in the city, and Alva was glad that Carlos still seemed to have some interest in her. She had expected that he wouldn't bother with her because of Darren's attitude, but she was surprised to find that there was no difference. If anything, he seemed even more affectionate towards her.

'I believe you've been invited to Cadiz by Julie,' he said smiling.

'Why yes, I was so surprised. She's invited all of us in her Irish family. It's amazing to know she's going to introduce us to all of your relatives.'

'I'm going to try and take some time off when you are there.' He reached across the table and covered her hand with his.

'I was going to tell you that Julie had emailed me, but I felt a bit shy about that, in case you didn't know.'

'I'm in touch with my Mum quite often, and we talked about it when she first asked you. She had to talk to other family members about the trip. I think she was afraid they would disapprove but in actual fact they admitted they often thought that she must have had a family here and wondered why she never told them about it. In a way it was a pleasant surprise for them.'

'What does your father think?'

'He's good too, and my sisters as well. Nuria is really pleased. She loves Ireland, and some of her friends are Irish, so she can't wait to meet you.'

'I'm looking forward to meeting her too. At least when I meet everyone it will be in Spain and I won't have the fear of Darren following me around all the time. That will be such a relief.'

'I'll be there anyway,' Carlos reassured.

'I just hope that he will calm down soon.'

'He hasn't turned up tonight.' He looked around.

'Thank God.'

'More coffee?'

'Please?'

The aroma drifted upwards. Alva added cream, and swirled it with a small silver spoon pensively. She really enjoyed Carlos's company and wished her life could be less complicated. As it was, thoughts of Darren drifted in and out, and took the best out of being here.

Before they finished, she asked him something. She had wanted to do that but didn't like to ask Julie directly.

'Sorry about this, but should we arrange our own accommodation in Cadiz? I feel it's a bit much to expect the family to put us up. Julie has invited Cian and David and myself, I don't know how many bedrooms you have in the house, but there could be a lot of us if David comes.'

'There is a separate villa for guests,' Carlos smiled. 'And you'll be quite comfortable.'

'Thank you, but I might mention it to Julie next time we chat.'

'If you wish, but I know it will be fine. Do not worry. Hospitality is in our blood,' he smiled.

Carlos paid the bill, and they went downstairs and out into the street which was crowded with people. It was warm, an unusually humid evening. He took her hand and they strolled down Grafton Street. His clasp was warm and intimate, and she wished she could respond to him the way she would have liked. Did that mean she was falling in love? She smiled within. He was the typical tall dark stranger with those enigmatic dark Spanish eyes which seemed to swallow her up every time he said something to her. Or, she checked herself, was it a rebound thing? Was she just looking for someone new? A relationship to replace what she had with Darren and which was now finished. Still, it felt strange to be with another person, and maybe she was fooling herself. There was also a possibility that Carlos wasn't serious. Foreign men could be very flirtatious and he could sweep her up into something which wasn't at all what she wanted. And what was that? And why did she say foreign men, she wondered, when there were plenty of Irish men equally flirtatious?

Suddenly, her wonderings were split into atoms when Carlos put his arm around her and drew her into a doorway of a small shop which luckily happened to be closed at the time. He whispered her name, held her close and his lips touched hers, warm, tender.

'*Te Amo*,' he murmured.

Her heart trembled, and she couldn't believe what she was hearing. *Te Amo* meant I love you, she understood. But didn't know what to say in response. With all her musings, she felt totally confused.

He kissed her again. Harder this time. His body pressed against hers. His hand caressed her face. Softly. She was somewhere else. Unable to grasp what was happening. And drifted helplessly like a leaf on water. Tossed. Turned. And wanted him so much, she couldn't prevent her emotions from taking her down a road which would perhaps be a road of no return.

'Am I rushing you?' he asked softly, raising his lips from hers and looking into her eyes. His dark brown eyes questioning her blue eyes which were wide with astonishment at what had happened.

'It is a surprise,' she said hesitantly, smiling.

'I am sorry, I had not intended to bring you into such a place as this.' He looked around the doorway. 'I would have preferred a beautiful Spanish garden with moonlight shining down on us.'

'I don't think it matters where we are,' she said.

'The only thing that matters is that I love you. I don't know if you understood my earlier words, I just said it without thinking.'

'You've taken my breath away,' she said.

'Let us leave this rather ugly place, and look forward to much more beautiful places in the future. Although perhaps I am being too impetuous,' he laughed. 'I have to admit it is in my nature. I sometimes do things without thinking. Forgive me.'

'When you decided to come to Ireland, was that a spur of the moment thing too?' she asked with a grin.

'I always wanted to study medicine in Dublin, but my father was anxious for me to join the family business. It is good that my sister did so instead of me. Otherwise, I would still be in Spain working with the horses.'

'I'm sure you love horses.'

'I do of course, we were raised with them, but it was not for me.'

'Has he accepted it now that you are working as a surgeon?'

'I think so. But he doesn't like that I am so far away. He wants the family around him all the time. He is a typical Spanish father.'

They stopped at a small bar later, and had a drink. Their conversation had swung from love to more general topics and Alva was relieved about that. She had been exhilarated when he told her he loved her, but hardly allowed herself to believe that he really meant it.

'I would like to spend more time with you, but as usual I have an early start,' Carlos admitted. 'But I am looking forward to seeing you soon.' He reached across the small table and kissed her.

'And I.'

'And I'm sorry if I have been too hasty.'

'There's no need to apologise,' she said immediately, laughing.

'I hope that when you go home you will not regret our evening.'

'Of course not.'

'Let us catch a taxi.'

'I'll go on my own. You're going to the other side of the city.'

'We'll just use the same one. I want to make sure you get home all right.' He put his arm around her shoulders.

'Thanks. I hope Darren isn't around.'

'Hopefully he won't be.'

The taxi brought them back to the house, and Carlos asked the driver to wait as he helped her out and they both walked up the driveway. She couldn't see Darren's car on the street outside and was glad that Carlos was with her as she pushed the key into the lock.

'Would you like to come in?' she asked, as soon as the door opened.

'It is late and the taxi is waiting. Goodnight my love.' He kissed her.

'Thanks for a lovely evening.' She stepped inside and closed the door softly. Smiling at him through one of the glass paned windows at the side of the front door.

He touched his lips with his fingers and turned to leave. But as he walked down the driveway, a figure detached itself from the trees which bordered the garden, ran across and flung itself on him. The two of them tumbled on to the flags of the drive.

Alva screamed and rushed out. She knew exactly who it was. 'Darren, stop,' she shouted, and tried to grab hold of his jacket to pull him off Carlos. But Carlos was well able to handle him, and in a few seconds he had Darren underneath him, and took a swing at him, his fist crashing into his jaw. Both of them kept punching each other and it looked as if neither was going to give in.

She stared at them, not sure what to do. She didn't want to call an ambulance, hoping neither would be seriously hurt. But if the Gardai arrived also she didn't want either of them to be arrested for assault. As she watched, Carlos gave one final punch and it seemed that Darren had almost given up. His responding punches weak by comparison.

Carlos pushed himself up into standing position.

Darren rolled along the ground, but seemed unable to get up.

'Darren, get out of here before I call the Gardai. You'll be arrested for assault,' Alva shouted.

'Fucking bastard,' he muttered, trying to get up off the ground.

'How dare you attack this man. You don't know who he is,' she shouted again.

'He deserves everything I gave him.'

'You were lucky he didn't beat your brains out. You didn't come out on top, you idiot.' She took out her phone and held is threateningly in front of him. 'Now I'm going to ring the Gardai.'

'Shag off.' He managed to wobble into a standing position at last.

'Are you going?'

At that moment, a Garda car pulled up in front of the taxi, its headlights shining, floodlighting the driveway and front of the house.

Two Gardai climbed out, and at that point the taximan also climbed out of his car. One Garda went over to him and talked, while the other talked to Alva.

'What happened here?'

'I arrived with a friend and my ex-partner assaulted him,' she said.

The Garda first went to Carlos and talked, and then to Darren who stood shamefaced.

The taximan had apparently phoned the Gardai and now they wanted to know if either Darren or Carlos wanted to press charges. Alva could have mentioned that she had made a complaint to the Gardai about Darren's constant texting, but decided not to mention it.

Neither man decided to press charges and the Garda ordered both of them to leave.

'Are you able to stay on your own?' the Garda asked.

'Yes, thank you.' She would have liked to bring Carlos in to have a cup of coffee, as he looked the worse for wear after the battering the men gave each other, but as the taximan still waited for him outside, Alva assumed that Carlos would have preferred to go home. Darren had already gone up the road presumably to wherever he had parked his car she thought.

'Are you all right?' she asked Carlos. 'You're hurt. I see some blood at the corner of your mouth.' She took a tissue from her pocket and dried the blood.

'It was just a fracas.' He dismissed it.

'I'm so sorry, it was a terrible thing to happen to you.' She kissed him. 'I'm worried about you.'

'I will be all right.' He took her hand briefly and pressed it.

'Let me know how you are feeling when you get home?'

'I will,' he smiled.

'I hope you haven't got concussion.'

'I haven't.'

'Take care.'

'And you, my love. I will talk to you soon.' He kissed her. 'Go into the house, Alva, just in case Darren decides to come back.'

He waited at the front door while she went in.

The Gardai climbed into their car and drove off.

She watched Carlos get into the taxi and waved as they drove away.

He called a short time later.

'How are you feeling?' she asked, very concerned.

'I'm fine.'

'I'm so sorry that Darren assaulted you. He really is a pig. I'm so angry with him. It certainly isn't your fault, and you shouldn't have to put up with it.'

'You will have to be very careful of him. He is very dangerous. It could have been you he attacked.'

'I'll be careful.'

'Promise me?'

'I promise.'

'I will phone you tomorrow,' he said. 'I love you.'

She resisted responding to him. He was telling her he loved her, but that was something that she couldn't take on just yet.

She went to bed, not even undressing, but was in such a state she couldn't sleep and just lay there thinking and wondering where Darren was now. She must have dozed, but suddenly she heard a noise at the back of the house. She sat up and listened. Her heart thumping. She climbed out of bed and ran to the window, pushing back the curtain so that she could see into the back garden which was illuminated by floodlights. She listened again, thinking that it was her imagination but then she heard the sound of broken glass. The alarm went off. Loud. Insistent. She went down the stairs. Grabbed a big umbrella in the hall and crept along by the wall until she went into the kitchen.

She couldn't believe her eyes when she saw Darren half in and half out of the kitchen window, and Carlos trying to prevent him for getting in.

'Darren, what are you doing?' She shouted, although she realised she was wasting her time as her voice couldn't be heard because of the whine of the alarm. She ran to the hall and switched it off and then went back into the kitchen.

The two men were still struggling through the broken window.

Alva ran across the tiled floor and pushed Darren out helping Carlos to get him back on to the patio. 'What are you doing here, the Gardai told you to leave. If I call them again then they'll have you arrested for burglary.'

'I wanted to talk to you.'

'I don't want to talk to you. Get out.'

'You'll have to leave, Darren.' Carlos turned to him.

'You can't tell me what to do,' he said, belligerent.

'I'll be here all night,' Carlos warned. 'So are you leaving?'

'I'll go when I've talked to Alva.'

'She doesn't want to talk to you,' said Carlos.

'Why didn't you knock on the door if you wanted to talk instead of breaking into the house?' demanded Alva. 'And what do you want to say, Darren?'

'I'm not talking in front of him.'

'I'll move away.' Carlos walked around the side of the house.

'Wait a minute,' Alva said, 'There is something I have to give you.' She ran into the hall, took the solicitor's letter from her bag, ran back and handed it to him.

'What's this?' He waved the letter.

'It's from my solicitor.'

'I don't want to read it.' He tore it into two pieces and threw it on the ground.

'It's a warning that if you don't stop harassing me by texting me continuously, and calling, I'll take you to court and get a barring order. It's against the law now and if you continue, you'll end up in prison.'

'Bullshit.'

'My solicitor wouldn't send a letter like that unless there were grounds.'

'Well I haven't read a word it, so it makes no difference to me.'

'He has a record that he wrote it, and I can confirm that I gave it to you. Now, what do you want to say to me?' Alva asked.

He seemed suddenly sheepish. 'I want to get back with you Alva, but you won't talk to me, so that's why I keep sending the texts. I don't know what to do.'

'But those texts are vile. Disgusting. Do you think I would want to live with you again after you've said such horrible things to me?'

'I didn't mean to say them, it's just when you don't answer me I get very angry and I can't control myself.'

'Well, I don't want a partner who can do such things. I never thought you were like that.'

'I'm not really. I'll never do it again. I promise you, Alva. Please forgive me.'

'I don't believe you.'

'Please do, I'd give anything to be together again like we used to, we were so happy.'

'But what about that woman?'

'I don't like her anymore.'

'You've changed your tune.'

'Please give me a chance, Alva, I beg you. That's all I want. One chance.'

'No, Darren, we're finished.'

'I'll kill myself.'

'Don't be ridiculous.'

'How would you feel if I did?'

'It would be your own decision.'

'You don't care about me anymore.'

'No I don't. So please leave.'

'I'll make it very hard for you,' he muttered in a threatening manner.

'I'll make it very hard for you too. But if you agree to leave me alone, then we can arrange a settlement and that will be the end of it.'

'You're a bitch.'

'My solicitor will write to you.'

'Big deal.'

'But it's only on condition that you stop sending me texts and calling to me.'

'Bloody hell.'

'Carlos,' Alva called, and he reappeared.

'Darren is leaving, will you make sure he goes please.'

Carlos indicated to Darren that he must move on.

Alva went through the house, opened the front door, and stood there, watching Carlos walk behind Darren as he reluctantly made his way down the drive.

'Where is your car?' Alva called.

Darren waved up the road.

'Don't come back, or the neighbours will call the Gardai because of all the noise.'

He didn't reply.

A short time later, Carlos returned.

'Thank you so much for all you did.' She was effusive. 'And for coming back. I'm amazed that you did.'

'I never left, the taxi took me around the corner and I paid him there. I had an idea that Darren might come back.'

'Come in, I'll make us some coffee.' She put her arm around him.

They sat chatting in the kitchen. Carlos was very anxious that she shouldn't be in danger because of Darren.

'It's a very difficult situation for you,' he said.

'He tore up the solicitor's letter, so he's going to ignore any warnings in it.'

'Where are you going to live when this house is sold?'

'I don't know. I really need somewhere that Darren doesn't know about. When I inherit my father's money, I could sell the apartment and buy somewhere new. But the problem is that all Darren has to do is follow me from work and he knows exactly where I am living. So there is no point in doing that. Getting taxis to and from the office might work for a while, but he could still follow the taxi. I don't know how to deal with him. He's crazy really.'

'You could stay with me in my apartment,' he offered with a smile.

'Thank you very much.'

'At least I live on the north side of the city and he might not think to search for you there.'

'You mightn't want me living with you. We don't know each other that well,' she laughed.

'The way I feel about you I'd give anything to live with you.' He took her hand. 'Although maybe I'd be pushing you into a situation. I don't know if you feel quite the same as I do.'

'I'm in such a complicated place at the moment, it's very hard for me to make a decision about anything. Can you appreciate that?'

'Of course, I can. But to change your home temporarily might help this situation with Darren. But there is no pressure on you to do that, I just offered. And I don't want you to feel that by doing that I will be asking you to commit yourself in any way to me.'

'I wish I could, Carlos, but I'm very fond of you.' It sounded so lame, she immediately wanted to take it back and say something much more meaningful.

'Pack a bag and come home with me,' Carlos suggested with a smile.

'There's hardly time. I'll be due in work in another couple of hours.'

'I'll stay here with you for tonight, and we'll go to work together by taxi. Come home to me after work this evening then. I should be there about eight.'

'I'll have to do something about the broken glass.' She went over to examine it.

'I'll see what I can do with it. Can I look in the shed?'

She gave him the key, and then she kissed him, and ran upstairs. Quickly she packed all of the clothes and other things she had brought with her recently. Her own car was in the carpark at work so it was safe enough there. The house was rather bare at this stage. Most of the contents had been put away in boxes, which she intended to store when the house was sold. The carpets, curtains, blinds etc. were all to be included in the sale, and even some furniture if the people who bought the house wanted it.

It was strange to see it like that, and she felt a wave of emotion sweep over her, missing her father so much as she came downstairs.

Chapter Twenty

It was strange to move into Carlos's apartment. Like she was on holiday almost. She had her own room with an en-suite bathroom, and he gave her a set of keys that first night so that she could come and go whenever she liked. She was grateful to him and it showed that he had an amazing amount of trust in her to give her the run of his home. He often worked late, and was only coming home early in the morning after spending all night in theatre.

She was equally busy, glad to spend time in her office and avoid seeing Darren. A couple of weeks passed and she didn't see him at all. The relief she felt was palpable, and she wanted to talk to him now and discuss what financial arrangements she might make with him. He was still sending texts, but they were more amorous rather than particularly vile and disgusting. She was glad of that. She had calculated how much money she would give him for the expenses. If he behaved himself, she would be generous. After all, legally, he wasn't entitled to anything which did seem a bit unfair.

The estate agent called later to tell her that there were good offers for her father's house. She knew David and Cian were keen to get as high a price as possible particularly because their share had to include Julie which was an unexpected twist. Alva talked to them and explained what the agent had said, and they agreed to meet to discuss the final figure they would accept.

'We should go ahead with the sale fairly quickly,' she said.

'Yes, the market is high now,' Cian agreed.

'But it could suddenly take a tumble,' warned Alva.

'Of course, we won't get as much as we should because of Julie.' David said bluntly.

'You're talking about your mother?'

'She was on the ball very quickly.'

'The solicitor had to inform her that she was entitled to a share when Dad died.'

'And she jumped at the chance no doubt.' He was sharp.

'I don't think she really needs money, I think the family are well off.'

'Lucky for them.'

'Let's leave it for now. We might get a better price later.' David said.

'It's a pity Dad didn't keep us informed about our mother. He could easily have done that. He must have known where she was.'

'Maybe there was no contact between them at all.'

'Of course, she had problems.'

'What sort of problems?' David asked bluntly.

'Alcoholism.'

'Oh …' He was taken aback.

'While she tried to beat it, she didn't manage that, and eventually Dad forced her to leave. And of course, he had the relationship with the woman who looked after us.'

'I was never aware of that,' Cian said.

'Neither was I,' David admitted.

'Julie was broken hearted when she left.'

'I'm sure she was.' He was harsh.

'She seems a lovely person, and I'm looking forward to going to Spain,' said Alva.

'We'll go too. Have you booked your flight, Alva?' Cian asked.

'Carlos is going to book them.'

'Carlos?' David asked.

'Julie's partner's son.'

'Oh yeah?'

'It's the 5th of September, and I'll be away for two weeks.'

'I'll book my own,' said Cian. 'I'm not quite sure when I can get away. If Alva and I are away together it might be a problem. We're still short-staffed but it's great we've managed to re-employ some of the staff who wanted to come back.'

'It was no harm to trim back the company, our staff levels were probably a bit top heavy,' admitted Alva.

'We'll only go for a long weekend, I'll check with Natalie,' said Cian.

'I feel guilty going for two weeks,' Alva said.

'No, you need a break so make the most of it,' Cian said.

'There's something I have to tell you,' she said.

'What?' asked David.

'I've been seeing Carlos for a while now.'

'That's probably why Darren is so mad,' Cian said.

'It's part of it. He's even attacked him. Last week, he was waiting at the house and the Gardai were called by a taximan.'

'That's terrible. He just can't get away with that.'

'Anyway, I've moved in with Carlos. He lives in Sutton, so Darren hasn't any suspicions that I'm there which is such a relief.'

'That's nice that you have someone else in your life, because Darren appears to be some sort of madman,' remarked Cian. 'You can do without him.'

'But he's connected with Julie and that family. I thought I said to you not to get too involved there,' muttered David.

'David, you can't tell Alva what to do with her life,' Cian exploded.

'And you can't control things like that, it certainly wasn't something I planned.'

David said no more.

'And she's an adult, David, so we certainly can't tell her what to do. I hope that you will be very happy with him,' Cian hugged her.

They continued going through their Dad's things.

'Cian and I have brought most of the stuff down here,' she explained to David. 'Those boxes over there are art and photos. His clothes are in the sitting room, and there might be things you would like, David, you're much the same build as Dad. Suits, shirts, etc., he had good taste and a lot of the brands are expensive.'

'If Sarah sees me bring any more shirts home, she'll kill me,' David said.

'Some of them are brand new and still in their packets.'

'I'll have a look.'

'And see these cuff links and watches, they're amazing.' Cian held them up.

'You should take them,' suggested Alva. 'I'm sure a lot of them were gifts. I might have given them to him myself for birthdays, Christmas, that sort of thing.'

'I think I gave him a couple of watches over the years as well, he loved them,' David said.

'Fantastic brands too. Expensive,' Cian agreed.

'You two can have those, I'd hate to throw them away.'

They continued sorting through the contents of the house, and by the end of the evening they had really made a big inroad into the various boxes and items which had been gathered.

'I can't believe we've got through it,' she said, thinking the house had a gaunt hollow sound. And their footsteps on the wooden floors were so lonely she almost couldn't breathe knowing that other people were going to come into this house and take their places.

'Has Darren improved his behaviour,' asked David.

'Yes, the texts are not as bad.'

'Report him to the Gardai.'

'He deserves what he gets,' Cian said.

'I know you blame me,' David murmured.

'No, I don't.'

'There's no point in blame, we just have to get on with everything,' Cian said.

Alva called a taxi and went back to Carlos's apartment. He wasn't there but she was glad to have time to herself. He could often be home very late, and they each did their own thing if that was the case. He ate at the hospital, and she usually had her lunch in a restaurant and only made a snack in the evening if she was hungry. There was so much happening, she really couldn't have dealt with his protestations of love. She had no answer for him. But in spite of that he hadn't put her under any pressure.

But pressure still came from Darren. His texts had turned hateful again. He wanted her back. And made threats about what he was going to do to her. Over and over. She took a chance and texted him about meeting to discuss the amount of money she would give him. While she had said her solicitor would text him, she felt it would be better if she had a face to face discussion with him. Maybe the money wouldn't make any difference at all. He might even still decide to keep texting to her.

They met at a café in town. A quiet place which had that delicious aroma of roasted coffee beans drifting inside. She was there first and ordered a regular coffee. The table was at the end and she was able to see anyone coming in. She could feel her hands shake and wondered what she was going to say to him when he eventually arrived. But he was the one who spoke first.

'Hi, Alva, it's good to see you. He sat in front her. Unexpectedly friendly.

'Thanks for coming.'

She couldn't believe the change in him and was glad that there was some normal conversation between the two of them. Now he didn't seem to be so aggressive.

'Coffee?' she asked.

'Thanks,' he said.

She waved to the waitress and ordered one.

They waited in silence until the mug of coffee was placed in front of them.

'I wanted to tell you ...' she said slowly.

'That you still love me?' he grinned.

'Not any more, you've hurt me too much.'

'I told you it meant nothing, it was just sex, that's all.' He dismissed it.

'There's more than that. All these texts are so violent. I hate them. Anyway, I've moved on, Darren.'

'With that other guy?'

'Not necessarily. He's just a friend. But I really came to talk to you about finishing off things between us.'

'I don't want to hear about that.'

'It has to be done. I mentioned to you that I'd ask the solicitor to text you with the amount of money I'd like to give you, but I changed my mind, I want to explain face to face, not just by text.'

'You're going to pay me off, is that it?' His mouth twisted.

'Well, I'll be inheriting money from my father and I'm thinking of giving you one hundred thousand.'

'That doesn't sound like much, certainly I'm entitled to half the apartment which would be much more.' His eyes flared angrily.

'But there's a mortgage on the apartment. You might be better accepting the money from Dad's estate.'

'It's paltry. His house will fetch at least a million.'

'But there are three of us and Dad's wife as well.'

'Wife? Who's she?'

'Our mother lives in Spain.'

'You never talked about her.'

'I didn't know where she was.'

'I'm sure the lads aren't too pleased about that.'

'We haven't seen her since we were small children.'

'Well, there's still a lot of money there.'

'Anyway, in spite of what you've done, I feel you deserve something.'

'I want you back, not a few bob.'

'I'm not coming back to you, it's finished between us, so I'm just giving you this as a gift. Though you may have to pay tax on it, although I'll put it down as expenses.'

'Since I'm on the dole now I'll hardly be paying anything to the tax man.'

'Where are you living?'

'Never you mind.'

'But I'll need your address.'

'I'll be in touch with you, don't worry.'

'Have you seen your parents recently?' she asked, just wondering if he might be staying with them.

'No,' he seemed disinterested.

They were a very nice family and Alva had often visited them with Darren.

'How is your mother, she wasn't well earlier in the year.'

'She's all right I think.'

'I must give her a ring.'

'Don't tell her about us,' he said sharply.

'OK.'

'The less they know the better,' he grunted.

'I must go, Darren. I hope we can have a better relationship from now on. I'd much prefer that.'

'But you won't come back?'

'No.'

'That's me slapped in the face.'

'Don't take it like that.'

'I'll slap you in the face.' He leaned closer to her across the table. 'How would you feel then?'

'Don't be ridiculous.'

It was the end of their conversation. She couldn't continue.

Chapter Twenty-one

Alva felt like she had been given a slap in the face as well. She couldn't understand Darren. Surprisingly, compared to his aggression of recent times, he had been quite normal today. But she put him out of her mind for now. Praying that he would accept the money she offered him and eventually leave her alone.

She was meeting Carlos to go for a walk in Howth this evening and she looked forward to enjoying the fresh air.

'I've missed you, we hardly ever see each other,' he said when they met.

She didn't like to tell him that she was deliberately giving him space. Although it was pleasant to slowly walk along, just chatting about nothing in particular. But as ever, thoughts of Darren were in the back of her mind. A flurry of annoyance swept through her. Was this going to be her life from now on, she thought. Always watching for him?

Carlos gently took her hand and held it in his. 'We'll have to spend more time together.'

'I feel the same.'

'But I'm always busier before I take a vacation. I have many patients.' He kissed her. 'I've already booked the time off for going home, so I have to allow for that. And you'll have to give me your details so I can book our flights.'

'Just tell me what flight you are taking, and I'll book the same one.'

'No, let me do that, I'd like to.'

'You mean to pay for my flight?' She was shocked.

'Why not?'

'No, I can't allow that.' She was adamant.

'Alva, you are coming for the first time to my home, to meet my family, it's very important to me.'

'I'd rather not.'

'*Por favor*?' he smiled.

'You're trying to get around me now.'

'I am of course. I should have learned to do that by now.'

'But you're not succeeding, Carlos.'

'I beg you, let me.'

'No. I can't,' she giggled.

'I can be very persuasive,' he warned.

'Please, let me book my own flight.'

'I feel this whole thing is slipping away from me,' he said. She laughed at him.

'I had such plans about bringing you to Cadiz and Seville.'

'I'll still be there.'

'I want to show you how much my home means to me.'

'It's just I'd prefer to pay for my own flight,' she insisted.

'I want to show you how beautiful the place is.'

'You'll have plenty of chances to do that,' she smiled.

'Please, just once, let me do this thing for you.'

'All right then,' she sighed and gave in.

'I'll show you the atmosphere of Spain as I know it.'

'It sounds fantastic. I'm really looking forward to it. I've been in Spain before, as you know, but they were short breaks which won't be as personal as visiting your home.'

She had received an email this morning from Julie who had said she was really looking forward to seeing her, and Cian, but that she was disappointed David couldn't come as well.

'Does Julie know that I'm staying in your apartment?' Alva asked hesitantly.

'I didn't mention it.'

'Just as well,' she agreed.

'Although I have said we have been out occasionally.'

'How do you think she will feel to know you and I …?'

'She hasn't made any negative comment so far. She's a very private person and doesn't interfere in our lives to any extent, not these days at least. When we were young it was different.'

Alva was worried that she would have to behave differently when she went to Spain. It would be hard not to show how fond she was of Carlos, and he was becoming more and more loving as time went by.

The evening darkened, and they walked back to Sutton. At his apartment, she poured two glasses of red wine and sat down on the sofa beside him. She was glad to do something for him, and she often did some housework before he arrived home, just to pull her weight since he had allowed her to stay here with him. But that night she mentioned something which had been on her mind.

'Carlos, I've been thinking about this for a while and I wanted to offer to share the costs of the apartment with you. Let's work out something.'

He looked at her in amazement. 'I invited you to stay here with me, and I'm certainly not asking for payment,' he laughed out loud.

'But …'

'No thank you, there is absolutely no need. And, I love having you with me, you know that. Say no more.' He pressed his finger against her lips. 'Also, I noticed you're doing some housework so that in itself is great. Although I usually just do it on a Sunday, and I have a woman who comes in to do the heavy work every so often.'

'You're too generous, and you don't know what it means to me to be here. It's so relaxing and there is no chance of Darren breaking in thank God,' she said.

'He is very violent,' Carlos mused. 'I will not allow him to hurt you, always remember that. I would kill him first.' He put his arm around her shoulders, pulled her close to him and kissed her forehead.

'It's not worth doing that.'

'Probably not, but I can't let him away with it. He is a madman.' He leaned over her and pressed his lips on hers. 'Always remember I love you and will do anything for you.'

She responded to his touch and he drew even closer to her, his smooth skin brushing, and she was sinking into the cushions on the couch without even being aware of it, every nerve ending so sensitive her body screamed for satisfaction.

'*Te amo, te amo*,' he whispered over and over. His fingers opened the buttons on her blouse. Kissing her pale skinned breasts in her lace bra, and with his lips he brushed her nipples which rose in response to his tenderness as he touched their softness and explored the very depths of her. Alva pushed her body into his and let him know that she wanted him as much as he wanted her. Her hands searched for him too. He began to take off her clothes until she found herself lying naked on the rug in front of him. Letting him see every detail of her body. All those imperfections that she thought she had. It was like a confession. This is me. Take me as I am.

'You are so beautiful,' he whispered. Slowly she reached to remove his clothes as well until they lay skin to skin. Now she came to life when he touched her and she clasped him close until he was deep inside her. Telling her how much he loved her. *Te amo*. I love you. In Spanish. In English. It didn't matter to her.

It was their first time together. And she knew then that she loved him. There was no doubt any longer. All that uncertainty which had dogged her lately had disappeared and any thoughts of what feelings she might have had for Darren had gone with it.

She wanted a champion. Someone who would fight for her. And she had found one. A person who would put himself on the line. Stand up and refuse to give in to a violent aggressor. He pushed his fingers through her shoulder length dark hair, and it floated. She loved the feeling it gave her. It was unearthly. Like a drifting spirit.

Their orgasm was amazing. The reason for their being together explained by that. And she told him then. For the first time. 'I love you.'

He took her into his bedroom, and they slept together in the wide bed that night. Bodies close. Arms around each other. Her head tucked underneath his shoulder. His lips touched her forehead. Her hands stroked his dark sallow skin. Softly. Gently. And he fondled her. And told her again how much he loved her.

They made love once more at dawn, and their union was even more satisfying as the light from the east drifted in through the high glass windows of the penthouse bedroom.

'What a way to start the day,' she murmured, her arms clinging to him.

'And every day from now on,' he said. 'That's the way I want it to be. I sometimes go out to Howth Head and watch the sunrise. It's quite exquisite. Maybe we'll do that some morning, the sun rises about six now, although it will get later as time passes.'

'I'd love to do that.' She was immediately enthused. To see the sunrise at dawn with Carlos somehow meant a great deal to her. It was so far away from anything she would have done with Darren.

'I hate leaving you.' She kissed him passionately, needing him to understand how intensely their night and morning of love had affected her.

'So do I, but unfortunately, our lives are calling us,' he smiled.

'I'd give anything to spend today with you. It would be like a dream, just the two of us, from morning to night,' she said.

'I hope there will be many days like that. For the rest of our lives. Am I being too forward?' He looked anxious for a moment.

'No, of course not.'

'Then I can ask you to marry me?' His large dark eyes were wide and gazed right through her, demanding a reply.

She was taken aback. She couldn't deny it. And tried to hide the element of surprise on her face which must have been obvious to him.

'As usual I am too forward.' His voice was dull, disappointment etched on his features.

'I have not thought of marriage with you, I would not have dared since we only know each other a very short time, and because I have so recently separated from Darren it would have seemed like it was on the rebound. And it would be unfair on you,' she tried to explain her thoughts.

'Were you going to marry him?' he asked.

'We had talked of it but somehow we had never got around to it.'

'Do you regret that you didn't marry him?'

'No,' she said vehemently. 'Now that I know what he is really like.'

'I would have been afraid for you if you had decided to marry him.'

'So would I.'

'I'm glad to know that, even if you do not want to marry me.'

'Can I think about your proposal. It is such a surprise to me I can't even say yes or no. I do love you but ...'

'Of course, my love, naturally you will have to do that. I can understand it is a big thing and mustn't be rushed without thought. And although I wanted you to say you would marry me immediately, I suppose I was being rather selfish.' He hugged her close.

'It is a compliment that you have proposed to me. I am astonished. It's the first time any man ever asked me to share my life with him. And I want to say thank you. It is so very special to me,' she murmured.

'Surely Darren did?' he seemed surprised.

'Not in so many words, we just drifted, which was thankfully why it never happened.'

'So there is still a chance for us, at least you have not refused me,' he said. 'Now let us have a shower and then I'll make you breakfast,' he said, putting his arms around her and helping her out of the large bed, and into the en-suite bathroom where he switched on the rain shower and drew her inside. Gathering her in his arms, the two of them stood there under the softly falling misty water. He took some shower gel and gently massaged it into her skin and his own.

'I want to make love again with you,' he kissed her. Their bodies pressed closer together, and feelings began to run away with them. But time did not allow. 'We will have to wait until this evening,' he whispered in her ear and drew slowly away from her.

Alva immediately wanted to hold on to him, but didn't. He turned off the shower, slid open the door and put his hand outside to pick up a white towel from the warm rail. Then he wrapped her in it, drying her gently. 'Now put on my robe.'

'Thank you.'

She felt cherished and pampered and couldn't quite believe what was happening.

Chapter Twenty-two

As Alva climbed out of the taxi, she didn't see Darren at first, but he had driven behind and waited until the taxi had pulled off and he drove into the space and jumped out of his car.

'Alva?' he yelled.

She ignored him, turned the key in the front door lock and pushed it open, but wasn't quick enough to keep Darren outside and he caught her arm.

'I want to talk to you.'

'No, Darren.' She pulled away from him.

'You haven't got your boyfriend around, where is he today? I don't see him.'

'I'll call the Gardai if you don't let go of me. This is a public street don't you realise that? I'm going to shout for help.'

'I'm your partner, no one is going to intervene.'

Suddenly Cian appeared in the reception area and came out. She tried to escape Darren's tight grip.

'Darren, you're hurting my sister,' Cian shouted.

'She's my partner, and she's coming with me.'

'You can't force her to go with you,' Cian said.

'She's mine.'

'She doesn't want to go. Can't you get that?'

'Shut-up you,' he yelled.

'Go away, Darren.' She was begging now.

'You're never going to escape me, Alva.'

'Please Darren, please?'

Cian ushered her into reception and closed the door on him.

Alva looked out through the glass window, searching for Darren, but all she could see were the pedestrians walking past outside. There was no sign of him, he had disappeared.

'Idiot,' Cian said, shocked.

'I can't bear it, Cian.' Tears flooded her eyes.

'God, I could kill him,' Cian said furiously.

'My life is destroyed. I can't go anywhere. He's following me all the time. I haven't used my car in ages, I have to take taxis everywhere. What am I going to do?' Alva was frantic.

'Come upstairs, I'll make you a cup of something and you can relax. He's gone off now anyway and hopefully we won't see him again.' He took her up in the lift.

But almost immediately the texts from Darren began to come through on her new phone. Even more hateful than before. Threatening her with every possible evil he could obviously think of. She didn't know how he had managed to find her new number, and was furious about that. Now she would have to go through the hassle of informing everyone on her contacts list that she had had to get another new number. What a pain. She thought. It really was too much.

The texts continued. Even worse than before. She didn't look at them and never answered any of them. Day after day. Hundreds of them came through. So much so, she just didn't know what to do. A couple of weeks later they stopped abruptly. But one morning Cian came into her office, carrying a very large bundle of letters.

'These were sitting on the reception desk, and I'm sure they're from the nutcase.'

'You're probably right.' She picked up one of the envelopes and opened it.

These days, most of her post was electronic and to see this large bundle of letters was a surprise, a complete shock. Darren had typed a letter which described in great detail what he would do to her if she didn't allow him back into her life.

You cannot get away from me. I will always follow you. And watch you. Waiting until you appear and are at your most vulnerable. And then I will strike. My hands around your neck. Twisting so tight you won't be able to breathe. And tighter and tighter. Until you choke. And that will be the end of you. And then there will be no chance to be together again. And you will have lost my love for ever. This is my promise to you.

She couldn't read any more, her pulse racing, a terrible sense of fear within her.

'I'm going to shred these into pieces,' she was enraged.

'No, you'll have to keep them to show the Gardai, he's threatening your life.'

'I couldn't bear to go through that now. There will be so many questions asked. I'll wait until I come back from Spain, I'll be better able to deal with it then.' She pushed the bundle of letters into a press.

During the day, she tried hard to put the vision of those letters out of her head. Afraid even to go outside the building on her own, she had to ask Cian to walk around with her to the phone shop which was nearby. Watching out all the time for Darren, and terrified that she would meet him. She bought another phone, chose a new number, and then contacted everyone on her existing contacts list and gave them the new one.

But to her dismay, the following day an even larger bundle of envelopes appeared. This time, she didn't even open one and just put them away in the press with the others, her sense of anger growing and growing.

She waited over the next few days in the hope that he might give up, but that didn't happen, and by the end of the week the pile of envelopes had grown even larger and she had begun to despair.

Then to her surprise. Darren's letters suddenly stopped arriving. Each day she waited for the post with bated breath. When a whole week passed she began to think he had given up and the feeling that someone was constantly watching her drifted away to some extent. It gave her confidence now to think of going home. She would need clothes for the holiday in Spain and her passport and other bits and pieces. So she decided to take a chance and go back to her apartment.

She ordered a taxi as usual and the car dropped her off outside. It was dark now and she stood at the gateway examining the cars in the carpark and was glad Darren's car wasn't there. She opened the door, and hurried to the lift. But it had gone up to the top floor and she had to wait until it returned before she could go up to her floor. She pressed the button and the doors slid open. Then she stepped inside and it took her up. She walked out on to the carpeted corridor and opened the door into the apartment, but before she could go inside, something hard was pushed into her back and she stiffened with fright as she felt it.

'Who's there?' she gasped.

'Get inside,' Darren growled.

'What are you doing?' she burst out, very angry now.

The thing pressing into her back dug harder.

'Darren ...stop. You're hurting me.'

'Go into the bedroom.'

'What for?'

'Because I want you there.'

She swallowed the fear which rose within her.

'Give me your phone.' He put his hand around her, palm up.
'What do you want it for?'
'Don't ask stupid questions.'
She took the phone from her pocket and put it in his hand.
Then she could see him switch it off.
He pushed her into the room and banged the door closed.
She immediately turned back and tried to push it open.
But she could hear him drag over the hall table outside.
'Darren, she shouted. 'Let me out.'
'You can stay in there now until I choose to let you out,' he shouted. 'And I've got the key as well, so don't think you can escape.'

Alva could hear his footsteps on the wooden hall floor and pushed against the door. But couldn't open it. He must have found the key in the hall table. She looked around the bedroom to see if there was any way of getting out. There were glass doors which led out on to the balcony which ran around the whole length of that side of the apartment. But all of them were locked and she couldn't see any way of escaping. She sat on the bed and wondered if Carlos had rung her and received no reply. He sometimes rang if he had a minute to spare. Now she longed for him to call her but she couldn't answer because Darren had turned off her phone.

It was only then she realised that she was sitting on the bed where that bitch had been with Darren and immediately she stood up, feeling contaminated. She went over to the door and banged on it. 'Darren, let me out of here,' she shouted. 'I'm going to bang on the neighbour's wall now and they'll call the Gardai. Someone will hear me.'

There was no response for a while and she kept shouting. Then she heard his footsteps and the key was turned and the door burst open.

'Shut-up you stupid bitch. Stop that shouting.' He came towards her brandishing a long-bladed knife. You know what is ahead of you if you don't.'

Her voice faded and she stared at the knife with a sense of shock. So that was what he had pushed into her back.

'Now, you're going to shut up.' He pulled a roll of tape from his pocket and put down the knife on a low table near where he stood. Then he came towards her. 'Don't move. If you do, I'll cut you to pieces.' He pulled a length of the tape and tearing it, lunged towards her and strapped the tape across her mouth.

She protested, almost falling back because of Darren's strength, and struggled against him in an effort to push him off with her hands. But then he grabbed the knife from the table and as she tried to defend herself, he slashed at her hands and arms which began to bleed profusely. She couldn't speak now at all and only mumbled incoherently.

His next move was to drag her two arms behind her and strap a length of tape around her wrists. 'That will keep you quiet,' he muttered, and roughly shoved her on to the bed and left her there. 'I don't know how you live in this place, there isn't a scrap of food in the fridge. I'm sending out for a take away.' He left the room, and she could hear the key turn in the lock.

She lay there on her side, her mind going around in circles trying to think of some way of escaping Darren's clutches. But without her phone there didn't seem to be any chance of that unless Carlos wondered why she had not arrived at his apartment. She prayed that he would and might guess where she was.

Sometime later, Darren came in again. 'That was a tasty meal,' he said with a grin. 'And I found a nice wine to go with it.' He took a slug from the neck of the bottle of red wine he carried.

She was very thirsty but couldn't ask him for water, and she just rolled back and forward trying to indicate she wanted him to remove the tape. But he just laughed at her and held the knife towards her. She stopped moving. He grabbed her and forced her around to lie on her back. She stared at him, terrified now. He brought the knife closer and slipped the shining blade under the narrow shoulder band of the pink and purple dress she wore. He put pressure on it and cut straight through the fabric. And did the same on the other side. 'See how easy this is?' he smirked.

The top of the dress eased downwards slowly and he did the same with the straps of her white bra, and pulled it down completely, until her breasts became visible and he was able to move the point of the blade across them.

She squealed, really scared of him now.

He cut the rest of the dress downwards and ripped it off with his other hand revealing her panties, which were also cut through with the blade and pulled down.

'Haven't seen you like that in a while. Of course, your other man probably thinks he has got you to himself all the time now but he won't have you any longer. You're mine now.' He pulled off her purple sandals and flung them on the floor. She was completely naked now, and at his mercy. She was terrified.

She tried to roll across the bed to get away from him, but every time she reached the edge, he pushed her back into the middle. Then he knelt over her. A knee each side. She kicked up with her legs but he leaned down on top of her and it was easy for him to prevent her moving at all.

'I'm going to have you whenever I want. You're going to stay in this room and be available to me. We'll be back to the way we were before. You can forget about work. Forget about going out. Forget about your man, whoever he is. You'll be a prisoner here. For my use only.'

She tried to scream. But all that came out of her mouth were garbled noises. Certain words repeated in her head over and over, particularly the word *prisoner*. That frightened the life out of her. Was Darren actually sane?

He leaned down on top of her. Holding the knife blade across her neck. She could feel something hot dribble down her skin on to her chest. She stopped moving. Maybe she was causing the sharp blade to cut through her skin by doing that.

She forced herself to lie still. Shaking.

'That's better,' he said. 'Using your head.' He leaned down on top of her, fumbling with his trousers, and she forgot about the knife and struggled against him. An instinctive move. Anything to prevent him continuing with his plan.

Suddenly, there was a bang on the door. Someone was calling her name.

'Alva, Alva, *estás bien*, are you all right?' She could hear Carlos calling her.

'This is the Gardai, open up.' Another voice shouted.

She couldn't believe that Carlos was there, and the Gardai as well.

'Fuck off,' Darren muttered. His trousers almost pushed completely down now, his body lying on top of her heavily.

The banging continued.

Darren moved up and down. Trying to force his way into her.

Noise came from the window. The jangled resonance of glass smashing as some implement was thrown against it.

'Fuck off,' Darren yelled again.

Glass shattered on to the floor. And then the Gardai and Carlos burst in. He immediately rushed over to Alva, as Darren was seized by the Gardai and pulled off her. Carlos gently tugged the tape off her mouth and held her close to him. Speaking in Spanish as he covered her with the duvet.

A Garda came over. 'I'm sorry sir, but we must check for forensics.'

He didn't want to let her go, but the woman insisted, and two medical people came over, and began to examine Alva. Carefully, removing the tape and releasing her wrists. Carlos stood back and let them do their work.

Alva was taken to hospital, and Carlos went with her. Darren was arrested.

They kept her there for a couple of nights but by then she had recovered and was very glad to leave. All the cuts had begun to heal and Carlos looked after her, managing to take some time off so that he would be at home. Under his care, the shock of the whole experience lessened and she began to recover.

'I am so glad that we are going to Cadiz soon, it will do you good to have a break,' he said. 'And if I have you with me, I promise that you will be safe.' He kissed her.

She was back at work within a few days after that, and was able to make sure her work was up to date and that she would be able to go away without undue hassle. Cian and Natalie were only going to Cadiz for a long weekend so he would be able to hold the fort at the office in her absence, as he wanted her to spend much longer in Spain. But even still, she was worried about Darren. He had been allowed out on bail, although she had no idea who had put up the bail for him. But he had to have some money in his own bank account, even though he wasn't receiving a salary on a regular basis. When he had resigned, he had received a lump sum, including holiday pay and commission which he was due, so he may well have been able to put up bail for himself.

The Gardai involved had told her that he had had to give up his passport and must report at the Garda Station once a week. Her solicitor applied for a barring order against him although she didn't really believe he would take the slightest notice of that.

But for Alva it wasn't enough. She continued to feel she had to look over her shoulder every time she went out and wondered when Darren's case would come up in court. It could be six months to a year at least before that would happen. And would she be able to live a normal life until then, she asked herself. She wasn't sure. Also, her solicitor told her that he had pleaded not-guilty in the court, even though he had been caught in the act by the Gardai, and unless he changed his plea by the time of the court case, she would have to appear and give evidence. She dreaded the thought of that. Knowing that she would be cross-examined by the prosecution and defence. Asking her questions about every aspect of what had happened on the night Darren had attacked her. Every detail of it. The way he cut off her clothes. The feeling of the blood as it dribbled down her skin after he had slashed her. How he tied the tape across her mouth. And around her wrists. And kept her immobile on that bed. How could she explain to them about that bed. And what it meant. She couldn't imagine doing that. And they would ask her question after question. She had heard about that and how awful it was. Would she have to endure that?

But for now, at least the letters had stopped. And the texts too. And she prayed that he wouldn't start sending them again and that would be the end of it.

Chapter Twenty-three

Carlos and Alva took a taxi to the airport. Cian and Natalie would arrive on the following day. It was only when that door in the aircraft was closed that she felt a sense of relief, and only then knew that Darren couldn't cause her any further hassle. He was unable to travel out of Ireland without his passport. She sat in the seat and put on the seat belt. Now she was able to breathe normally and was delighted there was no-one else sitting on the third seat on the aisle.

'My love, how are you feeling?' Carlos put his hand on hers and squeezed.

'So much better,' she smiled.

'You can leave it all behind you. Forget about Darren. He isn't worth it.'

'Darren seems to have changed so much since the early days. I thought I knew him. But he's crazy now. All that stuff at the apartment was like a film script. Something he saw on the screen.' She stared out the window. At the bright blue sky. And below a bank of white cloud. She relaxed back in the seat looking forward to being away with Carlos.

'Don't be nervous,' Carlos said softly.

'You see through me,' she laughed.

'I like to think I know you.'

'You do.'

'But I want to think that you will get to know me equally well. That's very important to me.' He kissed her.

It was strange, but up at thirty-thousand feet, she felt she did know him at last. There was no interference from anyone else. Nothing going on.

'I love you,' he said.

She smiled and moved closer to him.

'Will you stay with me when we get back?' he asked.

She nodded.

'Although my greatest wish is that you would be my wife, I am asking again I know but ...' he hesitated. 'You can tell me that I am like a broken record if you wish,' he laughed.

She hadn't expected that he would ask her to marry him again quite so soon, particularly when she had put him off the first time, but now she was so glad that he had and put her arm through his to let him know that he had her agreement and murmured shyly. 'I think I'd like to get married.'

'Then we might announce our engagement when we meet the family?'

'What will they think?'

'I don't know. We're adults. We're entitled to make our own decisions. I won't accept any opposition. I don't know why we're even discussing this,' he laughed.

'Your father might be the person who would have something to say.'

'It's possible. He is of the old school.'

'I've heard that Spanish families are very conservative.'

'You're right, but he is going to love you.'

'I hope. What do you think about Julie? Will she ...'

'She is very happy. I've already told her how I feel about you,' Carlos smiled.

'She never mentioned anything to me in her emails.'

'No, I didn't want her to say anything. Not before I'd asked you myself. I don't think you'd have appreciated that,' he smiled.

'No, I wouldn't,' she giggled.

'But we'll announce it anyway. We'll choose the best time. And celebrate. We're going to be very happy, my love. And we'll take no notice of the family. So I don't want you to worry. Nothing will happen to upset our plans. I'm going to marry you regardless.'

The steward arrived to take orders for drinks, and Carlos ordered champagne.

He poured the bubbly liquid into the plastic cups, and touched it against hers. 'To us, my love.' They sipped.

'When we arrive, we will have really good cava, and crystal glasses to celebrate the happiest time of my life.'

'And mine too.'

'But these little bottles of champagne mean just as much, even if the glasses are plastic. These are the happiest moments in both of our lives.'

It was very hot in Seville, and she could feel the heat pressing on top of her head as they walked down the steps from the plane. A black limousine with a uniformed chauffeur waited for them outside the airport, and it was only then that Alva realised the status of Carlos's family. They were obviously wealthy, and she began to feel intimidated. While she had met her mother, Julie, and they had got on very well, the other members of the family were strangers and she didn't know how they were going to accept her.

'We'll stay a night in Seville, and then join the others at Cadiz tomorrow. Would you like that?' he asked, his arm around her as they sat in the back seat of the car.

'Sure, that's fine.'

'I want you to myself for a night, is that too much to ask?'

'No, course not.' She was relieved in some way not to have to meet all the family this evening.

'We'll relax for a while and then have dinner at a really good

221

restaurant. You'll enjoy it.'

The limousine drove through high wrought-iron gates and above she could see the name of the stud farm, *Caballos Rodriguez*, in gold lettering on black metal. The house came into view, it was very large and built in the typical Andalusian style with magnificent gardens.

The car drew up at the entrance and the chauffeur came around and opened the door. She stepped out, and Carlos took her hand and led the way to the front door of the house which was open. They went through into an amazing indoor courtyard which had a looping roof covering above to keep the heat of the day from penetrating.

'This is beautiful,' Alva murmured, taken aback by the curved archways around the area, and white pillars between them. The floors were terracotta tiles, and dark wooden beamed ceilings could be seen beneath the archways. Fountains sparkled in the sunlight, and she could see through the pale blue water to the ancient tiles in the floor below.

'It reminds me of the Alhambra.' Alva gazed around her at the beautiful courtyard.

'A lot smaller,' Carlos laughed. 'Many of the older Spanish houses were built around the same design.'

A maid appeared and threw her arms around Carlos in welcome, speaking rapidly in Spanish.

Carlos responded and Alva could see how fond the woman was of him.

'Anna this is Alva,' Carlos introduced them in English.

The woman kissed Alva as well, a big smile on her face.

'Could you make us some coffee, Anna, we'd appreciate that,' Carlos asked her.

'Of course, un momento.' She nodded.

'Thank you,' Alva added.

'I'll bring you up to your room, Alva, and you can freshen up.'

He took her case and they went upstairs to a gallery which had a balcony overlooking the courtyard below, and he brought her into a large bedroom. 'It's wonderful to have you here.' He put down the case and embraced her. 'I love you.'

'And I love you.' She responded as they kissed and stood holding each other.

'I wish I could take you to bed now,' he murmured. 'It is too tempting.' He moved towards the big four poster bed.

She laughed. 'Anna will have the coffee ready.'

He grimaced. 'Come down soon.'

'I'll just take a quick shower.'

'The bathroom is over there.' He pointed. 'I'll wait for you in the courtyard.' He kissed her again.

The shower was refreshing and because of the humidity she changed into loose blue linen trousers with a matching shirt and felt the better of it. She combed her hair, and refreshed her lipstick and then hurried on to the gallery, glancing over the edge to take a glimpse of the pool below and saw Carlos sitting at a small table.

'Sorry, I've probably taken too much time, but I needed to change.'

'I've changed also, it's the humidity.'

'The warmth of the evening is wonderful.'

'In Seville it's always very hot at this time of the year. A lot of people escape to the coast, as we do ourselves. Although my father comes back and forth, he can't bear to be away from his horses.'

'Where are the stables?'

'I'll take you there tomorrow before we leave. Do you ride?'

'I used to, but then I was thrown and lost my nerve.'

'Were you hurt?'

'No, but the horse was a thoroughbred and something spooked

him and he raced off at a mad pace until he stopped suddenly and I went over his head. After that I couldn't even canter, a trot was all I could manage,' she laughed, feeling foolish. Obviously, this family were all very good riders and she couldn't see herself fitting in easily.

'I'll choose a gentle horse for you if you like? There are plenty.'

'And I'll make a complete fool of myself up on that horse,' she giggled.

'I'm sure you won't, riding is like cycling a bicycle, you never forget.'

'I have to say I loved it. I used to go riding once a week and I would forget everything when I was on a horse. But I stopped going after my fall,' Alva explained.

Anna came out carrying a tray with a coffee pot, milk jug, cups, saucers and put them down on the table.

'I have café solo when I'm home which is just expresso,' said Carlos lifting the coffee pot. 'But you might prefer café con leche with some warm milk?'

'That would be fine for me, thanks.'

He poured both coffee and milk together for her, and just a small amount of café solo for himself. They sat together as the evening darkened, and Carlos talked about his life here in Spain. Alva really enjoyed listening to him, until suddenly her phone rang.

Immediately, her heart started to thump as anxiety swept through her. Could this be Darren? Had he found out her latest phone number? She nearly fainted at the thought as she rooted for the phone in her bag. 'I'm sorry, I'm not expecting a call, would you mind?' She rose, shaking, and looked at the phone, but relief flooded through her as she saw that it was Julie and she was delighted to hear from her.

'Hi Mum?' she smiled at Carlos.

'I was just wondering if you had a safe trip and have arrived?'

'We're sitting in the courtyard.'

'Can't wait until I see you tomorrow.' Julie sounded excited.

'I'm looking forward to seeing you too, it's been too long since we met.'

'We have some friends in this evening and that is why I wasn't at the airport to greet you. They are important business contacts of Pedro so I had to do my hostess thing,' she laughed.

'I hope you enjoy the evening.'

'I would prefer to be with you,' Julie murmured, her voice low.

Alva didn't know what to say as she was sitting beside Carlos.

'I'm looking forward to tomorrow,' Julie said. 'Do you know what time Carlos and you will arrive?'

'I'm not sure, let me ask Carlos. What time will we arrive tomorrow?'

'I want to take you over to the stables in the morning so it will be sometime later in the day.'

'I heard that,' Julie said. 'Love you.'

'See you, Mum,' Carlos added.

'Love you too,' Alva said.

'Don't let him keep you away from me for too long,' Julie said.

'I won't,' she smiled at Carlos. 'Bye.'

'*Adios,*' he said.

'I will have to make the very most of our time now. No possibility of staying an extra day somewhere,' said Carlos with a rueful expression. 'I am disappointed, I was hoping to get away on our own.'

'At least we have tonight and part of tomorrow to ourselves.'

'And I am so glad about that.' He reached across the table and kissed her. 'I have booked a table at the restaurant for nine, is that time all right for you.'

'Perfect. It won't take me long to get ready.' They went upstairs.

'You always look beautiful to me,' Carlos said.

'I'd prefer to change into something more formal if we're going out to dinner.'

She wore a black dress. It was just a simple design but she felt it would suit the occasion. She didn't know where they were going but didn't think Carlos would take her to some casual outdoor bar. Somehow, she couldn't see that it would be his style.

The limousine was waiting outside the house for them and the chauffeur held the door and then closed it after they had sat in.

'I want to enjoy some cava with you this evening, because we're celebrating,' Carlos said. 'And if I drive myself then I won't be able to do that.'

They made themselves comfortable and sat close together, his hand holding hers.

She was right. It was a very upmarket restaurant, and it was a relief to walk into the cool air-conditioned interior from the heat outside. The manager rushed over to welcome them as soon as he saw them come in the door, and ushered them to a window table overlooking an ancient courtyard.

'This is a lovely restaurant, and I hope you will enjoy the food. It is typical Andalusian fare.'

The wine waiter came over with the wine list, but Carlos didn't bother to look at it, and just ordered a bottle of cava that he obviously knew well. The waiter was back in a few moments and placed it in an ice bucket and proceeded to give Carlos a small amount to taste. He gave Alva a glass to taste as well, and she agreed that it was very good. Then produced another bottle, popped the cork and poured.

'*Salud* to us,' Carlos said. 'We are celebrating our engagement properly now.'

She smiled.

'That makes me feel very happy.'

'I love you, Carlos. It's not every day I agree to marry someone, and I want to spend the rest of my life with you,' she assured him.

'Thank you,' he said. 'I am honoured.'

He raised his glass and they clinked.

'Sláinte,' she said.

'Salud.'

The waiter brought the menus then, and there was a set selection of various small dishes which meant she didn't have to spend a lot of time trying to decide what she might like. It was a gourmet restaurant, and the chef came over later to enquire as to how they were enjoying the dishes which were served up. Carlos obviously knew him and introduced Alva, assuring him that they were really enjoying their meal. If she had any doubt about the exact ingredients, then Carlos was able to tell her what they were.

'You really enjoy the dishes?' Carlos asked.

'Yes, they are delicious, the flavours are amazing. And they are very different to anything I've ever tasted.'

'I'm glad.'

'Is this one of those restaurants where you have to book a year in advance?' she asked.

'Usually.'

'But you had no trouble getting a table,' she smiled at him.

'We know the owner, so it's a little advantage.'

After finishing their meal they left the restaurant, and the chauffeur drove them back to the house. They sat at the table in the courtyard, and listened to the trickling sound of the fountains, and the crickets chirping. There was something so tranquil about this place, Alva felt she had left all the stress in her life behind and couldn't believe that she had almost forgotten about Darren.

Carlos put his arm around her and they sat there in silence for a while.

Then he took her hand and they walked up to the gallery and

into the bedroom. She was like someone in a dream as they took off their clothes and he gently lay her on the bed and put his arms around her. She clung to him. Knowing now that she wanted this man to be hers for ever.

He kissed her over and over, and she did the same. On every part of their bodies. Lips damp on their skin, aware of the aroma of each other. His fingers were gentle, and his tongue moved down across her stomach and further, letting her know that this was what he wanted. And then suddenly pushing to reach a climax together, the highlight of their need. They embraced each other and sighed deeply as they both let go and lay down again, until eventually sleep overcame.

Chapter Twenty-four

Alva opened her eyes just a little. For a few seconds she didn't know where she was but then as she looked upwards, she could see the elaborate ceiling above, and knew then. Carlos had his arm across her and she twisted around until their faces were close together and kissed his lips softly. It was only then his dark brown eyes opened and he responded to her touch with a smile.

'Good morning, my love,' she whispered.

'*Buenos dias, amor*,' he murmured.

They moved closer to each other, and immediately their need for each other burst into being and they clung to each other, only wanting one thing now. This time it was wild. And they rolled around in the bed, their legs entangled, boisterous, until their passion took them to new heights of satisfaction.

'I want to begin every day with you like this,' she said.

'Such promise takes me to a place of wonder.' He cupped her face with his fingers and kissed her eyes, her lips, her forehead. 'You are mine, dear Alva. Mine alone. Let no-one take you away from me.'

'I'll never leave you.'

It was early and she was glad of that. Wanting to spend every second of this day with him. 'I'll take you to the stables while it is cool so if we stay in bed all day we'll never get there,' he laughed. 'And it will be too hot.' He looked at his watch on the bedside table. 'It's seven thirty now, and the sun has just come up,' he said. 'Let us have a swim in the pool and we will be ready for the day.'

She found a bikini in her suitcase, and was glad the scars of Darren's attack were not still visible on her arms any longer.

The pool was really big. 'This must be almost Olympic size is it?'

'It is. Do you dive?' Carlos asked climbing up on the diving board.

'Maybe not so high as that.' She looked up at him.

'Come on,' he encouraged.

She climbed up, and they stood on the edge of the board.

He grinned at her.

'OK. Let's.' She put out her arms. 'Into the deep end.' She took a deep breath.

'Right. Who's first?'

'I'll go.' She stepped forward, and took a deep breath, leaping off the board and crashing through the surface of the water, her hands pointed, and going down and down into the blue until she surfaced again.

'Well done,' Carlos yelled. And then he dived. Up and arching high, zipping through the water and disappearing until he surfaced again near Alva.

'You are wonderful.' He put his arms around her, and then they swam through the water together slowly.

'Let's race,' she suggested.

'*Si.*'

She was glad she could swim. As her riding ability wasn't great, at least she could do something well.

They kicked against the pool wall, and forged through the water, both doing overarm stroke. But she knew that she couldn't compete with Carlos. He was already ahead but then slowed down and allowed her time to catch up and they arrived at the end of the pool in much the same time.

'Thanks for giving me a chance. I don't swim as well as you,' she laughed.

'I'll give you a better chance next time.'

'Thanks. I'll need it.'

They continued swimming lazily for a few minutes and then climbed out of the pool. The day was already heating up, but she felt refreshed, and went back to the bedroom and changed for the day. Then she met Carlos on the patio, and they went into the breakfast room where it was beautifully cool with air conditioning on.

'What would you like for breakfast?' he asked, standing at the large sideboard.

'Just something simple, perhaps a croissant and coffee please.'

'Anna has put out the usual, cheeses, meats, bread rolls, churros, croissants, a wide selection of food.'

'I couldn't eat that much in the morning.'

'Help yourself. I'll get your coffee.' He poured *café con leche* for her and brought it over.

'Thank you.' she sat down. Suddenly wondering if any other family members would appear. She hoped not. But it was only the two of them and she was very glad that no one else happened to appear.

'Well, I'm going to start the day well.' He helped himself to a plate of mixed meats, cheeses, and as usual black coffee.

'Would you like to change into riding gear?' he asked as soon as they were finished breakfast.

'I don't have any with me.'

'There is plenty at the stables.'

'I'm not sure if I want to ride,' suddenly she was uncertain.

'If I find you a nice quiet pony?'

'Don't expect me to go any faster than a trot on this pony,' she

231

warned.

'I'm not stupid. I don't want you falling off and hurting yourself. Then you'd never trust me again, and I couldn't bear that.'

'You're right,' she laughed.

'Is this all your land?' she asked, as they drove away from the house.

'Yes, many acres. Originally owned by my great- grandfather.'

'It's beautiful. I can see the horses out training.' She pointed to the group which galloped in the distance.

'You'll always see them in the morning. And there are the stables.' He pointed.

'How many horses have you?'

'I suppose there's a few hundred. It varies.'

'Amazing.'

'We breed them, so there are always young foals being born.'

They drove closer to the buildings. There were a lot of workers there. Carlos pulled up the jeep, and they got out and he introduced Alva to various people. Some of them could speak English, others only Spanish.

'Come on, I'll find you a quiet pony.' Carlos led the way into the stables.

Alva was enthralled to see the horses. Stopping to stroke their faces as they walked past.

'Which is your own horse?'

He came to a stable where a beautiful black stallion immediately pushed his head out to touch Carlos.

'He's fabulous. So beautiful. And I love the white diamond on his forehead. What do you call him?'

'Galaxia.'

'What does it mean?'

'Well, Galaxy – for the stars. But it also means very fast.'

'He's wonderful. Are you going to ride him today?'

'If you would like to ride the pony I have for you?' he grinned.

'All right, let me see him.' She took a deep breath, praying that she wouldn't make a complete fool of herself.

'He's in the next stable block with the younger horses.'

He took her hand and they walked over to that area.

'Now, see the ponies here. He's the lovely brown coloured pony with a black mane and tail.

'What's his name?'

'His pet name is Tonto. He's very gentle, and that's why I'm giving him to you because he is suitable for younger riders.'

'I'm only a child,' she laughed.

'I hope you're not insulted,' he laughed too.

'He's perfect for me.'

'If you're happy riding him, then there are other horses which will suit better and be more of a challenge, so you can try them later.'

'I wonder if I'll ever get to that stage.'

He squeezed her hand. 'Course you will. I'll give you confidence.'

'I hope so.'

'In the changing rooms there are jodhpurs, jackets and boots which should fit you, and a helmet as well. They are all new so don't worry about that.' He pushed open a door, and there were wardrobes with various clothes hanging inside. Soon he had her togged out in everything and she was ready to go.

'I have my own here,' he said, and changed.

'When they came out, one of the stable hands had both the stallion and the pony harnessed and saddled. Carlos thanked the man, and he led the two horses out.

'We'll ride this way, and see how you get on.' The man held Carlos's horse, and Carlos brought Alva over to meet Tonto.

She rubbed his neck and back, and tried to get him used to the sound of her voice, murmuring soft words.

'Can you mount?' Carlos asked.

'I think so.' She put her foot into the stirrup and swung herself on to Tonto's back. He stood there, quiet, without a move as she settled herself.

'Comfortable?' Carlos patted her hand.

'Yes, I'm fine thank you.' She took a deep breath and prayed that the horse wouldn't move too quickly.

Carlos mounted up and his horse was a bit skittish, moving back and forward as he tried to find control. But it only took him a short time to do that and the horse calmed down and did exactly what he wanted.

'Sorry, Galaxia can be a bit excited, so let's go.' He rode ahead of her, and she followed behind on Tonto, who didn't do anything very fast, and only when she kicked his sides did he break into a slow trot. Carlos waited for her and together they rode along a track.

'Sorry, I'm a bit slow,' she said.

'You're fine. You certainly know how to ride, your hold on the reins is excellent.'

She kicked, and Tonto went a bit faster, and she felt more confident as she trotted beside Carlos.

'Fancy a canter?' he grinned at her.

She kicked again, and Tonto cantered and she felt she was back again in those days before she was thrown. Maybe she should have ridden again and not waited so long. She cantered along the track and laughed at Carlos. And then she encouraged Tonto to gallop and he did exactly as she wanted. And she could feel the air whirr past her, and loved every minute. Carlos galloped beside her and together they covered the length of the track, until eventually it wound around in a wide circle and quite a while later brought them back to the stables once again.

'You've done very well,' he said, dismounting from his stallion.

'You gave me confidence.'

He put up his hand and helped her down. She patted Tonto

and put her arm around his neck. 'He's a great horse, and knew exactly what I wanted. I know he's for children, but I don't care about that, I'd ride him any time,' she laughed.

'There are other horses at Cadiz so you'll have more opportunities to ride there.'

'I'm looking forward to it now.' At least she wouldn't look so stupid, she thought. She had been quite a good rider before she had been thrown, so hopefully she still had what it took to ride a horse with some degree of expertise.

'Let's head back, it's getting very warm now.' Carlos passed the reins of the two horses to a stable man who took the horses away. She changed again, but Carlos told her to keep the riding gear, she would need it in Cadiz.

'Thank you.' She climbed up into the jeep, and he drove back to the house.

'Would you like to have something to eat?'

'After all that exercise, I could eat a horse,' she laughed. 'Literally. Thank you for this morning, I loved the ride on Tonto.'

'Someone at the stables will bring our horses over to Cadiz later today but you can choose another one if you like. You are a much better rider than you admitted.'

'I suppose it is all about confidence.'

'And you have plenty of that, my love. Fancy a swim before lunch?' Carlos asked.

'Sure, I'd love that, it's so warm.'

They enjoyed the swim which cooled them down, and afterwards they had a light lunch which had been prepared by the maid, Anna.

'We must leave for Cadiz soon. I promised Julie that we'd be there in the afternoon. But in the meantime, we'll go upstairs, can't drive on a full stomach,' he laughed. He took her hand and they walked upstairs to the gallery and into the bedroom. 'Let's just rest for a while.' The shutters were closed and the room was in shadow at this, the height of the day, and when he closed the door, he pulled her close to him, and the *rest* turned into a mad romp which did delay their departure somewhat. But eventually, they set off in the jeep and arrived at the family estate on the outskirts of Cadiz about an hour and a half later.

'I'm nervous about meeting everyone,' Alva murmured, as high gates opened slowly.

'Don't be,' he leaned across and kissed her.

'Will they feel awkward about meeting me do you think?' She felt stupid even asking such a question.

'Course not. You're part of the family now. And we're going to tell them in a very short time,' he smiled, as he drove up the long driveway.

The house was a large sprawling building, even bigger than the one in Seville, and much more modern. She stared out the window and wondered how she would manage to fit into this family as Carlos seemed to think she would.

'Here we are.' He drove around the back of the house and into one of a number of garages. Immediately, a woman ran out of the house towards them.

'Alva, Carlos?' Her voice rang out. Alva went towards her. 'How are you, Mum, it's wonderful to see you.' She threw her arms around her mother and they hugged tight and Julie kissed her.

'I thought you'd never get here, I didn't even bother with siesta, although everyone else is still asleep. But that gives us some time to ourselves.' She put her arm around Alva and together they walked on to the wide veranda. 'You can use a room here, although yourself, Cian and his partner, Natalie, will be staying in that villa over there. It gives you some privacy and if you just want to do your own thing then you're free to come and go without having to fall over all of us.'

Carlos followed and put his arm around Alva.

'Are you hungry,' Julie asked.

'No, actually we had lunch before we left Seville.'

'And I suppose it was really hot, it's such an oven at this time of the year.' Julie sighed.

'It is much cooler here,' Alva said, 'and lovely to see the sea.'

'There's always a breeze in Cadiz, that's why we are lucky to be able to escape from Seville in August and September. But we come back and forth during the year from time to time as well.'

'We could swim if you like, the pool is over there, or walk on the beach, it isn't very far,' suggested Carlos.

'When the others are up, they'll all want to meet you.'

'Sit down now, and I'll get some drinks.' Julie disappeared into the house.

'I love to be here.' Carlos was enthusiastic.

'Yes, it's beautiful.'

'You did very well today,' he reached and took her hand.

'I'll probably be stiff as a poker tomorrow it's been so long since I was up on a horse.'

'That will ease out,' he laughed. 'By the time you go home you'll be in fine form, and we can go somewhere to ride in Dublin.'

'I don't know how you'll have time. The hours you work are even worse than mine.'

'A lot of the hours I work, particularly at weekends, are voluntary, and I could leave a lot of it to my team. But, being a rather solitary person, I like to keep an eye on the progress of my patients and there hasn't been a reason for me to be at home up to now, but with you in my life, Alva, everything will change.' He leaned towards her and their lips met and softly touched each other. 'I love you, Alva.'

She was just about to say the same when Julie arrived back with a tray. They moved a little apart.

'Can I help you?' Alva asked.

237

'Not at all. Here we have staff, but I prefer to do some of the work around the house myself,' she laughed. 'Now what would you like, white wine or apple or orange juice.'

'Apple juice would be nice, thank you.'

'Carlos?'

'The same for me.'

'And myself.' She poured and handed them glasses. 'I'm so looking forward to seeing Cian and Natalie, they'll be here about six.'

Carlos took Alva's hand underneath the table and held it tight tickling the centre of her palm with his finger. She found it hard not to giggle.

'But I wonder about David and Sarah, and the children, is there any chance of seeing them?' Julie asked.

'Not this year, he has a lot going on. He's setting up a new company.'

Purtell Vintners' financial situation was now normal, since the money in the British Virgin Islands accounts had been returned. They were solvent again. But David's attitude towards Julie because of the past was worrying, and Alva said a silent prayer that he would change, as she was certain he would regret it in the future.

'Hola,' a tall man, who had a look of Carlos, appeared and with a big smile he held out his hand to Alva, and kissed her on both cheeks. 'Welcome to our home, dear Alva, it is wonderful to meet you at last.'

'It is my pleasure, Pedro,' she said, smiling.

'Carlos, how are you? Glad you could come home this year. We've missed you.' He threw his arms around his son and kissed him too.

'Because of Covid I didn't get home for nearly three years,' Carlos explained to Alva.

'Hola,' two smiling young women walked out to the patio.

'This is Nuria, and Pacqui,' Julie introduced them.

They both kissed her, and she returned their embraces, and then they sat down around the table.

'I see your likeness to Julie,' Pedro said.

'It is wonderful, isn't it Pedro, to meet my daughter after all these years?' Julie took his hand.

'Yes, indeed it is.'

'A glass of wine?' She poured it for him.

'Thank you.'

'You studied in Dublin, Nuria?' Alva asked.

'Yes, at Trinity, and I'm still in contact with the friends I made when I was there. I love Dublin. I'm like Carlos, he loves Dublin as well and might never come home. It's something in the blood of Mama which has come through to us.'

'And Pacqui, you work with the horses?' Alva asked.

'It is what I love.'

'Carlos took me riding this morning,' she explained.

'And she is an excellent rider and even surprised herself,' Carlos smiled.

'Then you'll fit into this family, we all ride,' Pacqui laughed. 'What horse did you take out?'

'A pony called Tonto. He was perfect for me.' Alva had to admit.

'That was a good choice,' Julie said.

'Then she showed me what she could do, cantering, and galloping too, I don't know how she managed to get him going so fast.'

'He was a nice pony,' she smiled.

'We'll find you another here, although we've brought Tonto over if you still want to ride him,' Carlos smiled at her.

'I'm looking forward to it.'

'There is something I want to say,' Julie spoke quietly. 'Now that we are all together.'

The others looked at her and waited.

Alva wondered too.

'As you all know, because of the death of my husband, in Irish law I am entitled to a portion of his estate,' she said slowly.

They listened.

'But I have decided to invest this money into the company when probate is complete,' Julie said.

Alva was astonished. While the company was solvent again now because of the return of the money which had been stolen, it was still amazing for Julie to decide to do this.

'I think that is a very good decision,' Pedro said.

'I hope you agree with this?' Julie asked Alva.

'You've taken my breath away. I can't believe it.'

'We will discuss it in more detail at a later stage. And now I must go and talk to the cook about dinner this evening, so please excuse me.' Julie stood up, kissed Alva again, and hurried inside.

'I'll take you over to the villa, Alva,' Carlos said. 'And you can settle in. We'll see you all later.'

'Drinks as usual at nine,' Pedro reminded.

They drove over to the villa which was somewhat smaller than the main house, but had its own swimming pool as well. Carlos brought her inside and showed her around the rooms, and she admired the luxurious décor.

'This whole place is amazing,' she said. The family were very affluent. Goodness knows how much land and property they owned, she thought. Carlos had given her no impression of such wealth when first she met him in Dublin, and neither had Julie.

'I'll take you up to the bedroom.' He stepped into a lift which whizzed them up to the upper floor.

He opened the door, and she walked into a very big room, immediately taken aback by the stunning view of the beach and blue sea through the large windows.

Standing behind Carlos put his arms around her and drew her

240

close to him.

She giggled.

He kissed her cheek and walked her over to a door which led out on to the balcony, where they sat on soft cushioned chairs.

'I was going to make our announcement this evening, would you like that?' he asked.

She smiled. 'Yes, thank you.'

'So you're happy to become one of the clan.'

'Yes Carlos. I am privileged to be invited.'

'And I am grateful that you have accepted me.' He stood up. 'I'll go down to the jeep and bring up our bags.'

'You're staying as well?' she asked in surprise.

'You think I'm going to leave you alone at night? No way,' he laughed.

Chapter Twenty-five

Cian and Natalie arrived in the limousine, and Alva was delighted to see them and Carlos was very welcoming to them as well.

'This is a fantastic house, Carlos,' Cian said. 'Thanks so much for inviting us to stay.'

'There will only be Alva and myself here, so you can do whatever you like.'

'Thank you.'

'I'll bring up your bags,' Carlos offered.

'Not at all, I'll take them up,' Cian said.

'You are the guest, I am the host,' he smiled. 'Welcome to our home.'

Alva chose what she would wear that evening very carefully. A light pale grey dress and jacket with matching stilettos was the final choice.

'You look beautiful,' Carlos said in admiration. Handsome in cream trousers, matching shirt, and navy blazer.

She smiled. 'Thank you.'

'And I have something for you.' he handed her a small black velvet box.

'Thank you,' she stared at it, excited.

'Look inside,' he urged.

He stood watching. 'You're like a child, eyes wide with wonder,' he smiled.

'I'm always excited when someone gives me a present,' she

admitted. 'And this looks amazing.'

'It's only a box,' he laughed.

She opened it. Stunned into silence when she saw the contents. It was a ring. An amazing ring. With a large square diamond in the centre of the gold band, surrounded by smaller diamonds of the same shape. It was simple. But exquisite. She stared at it, unable to believe he had given it to her.

'Let me.' He picked up the ring from its blue satin bed in the box and took her left hand. Then he slid it along her third finger where it sat, glittering.

'Do you like it?' he asked softly.

'I love it, I can't even think of a word to describe my engagement ring.'

'We are now betrothed,' he whispered. 'And you will be Senora Rodriguez, but you can keep your own name also if you wish.'

'Senora Rodriguez,' she repeated. 'I am just amazed.' She was entranced at the thought. 'And the ring fits perfectly,' she gasped. 'How did you know my size?'

'I took the size of the other ring you wear on your right hand and just hoped. This is actually my mother's ring. My father gave it to me some years ago. He told me my mother wanted my wife to have it.'

'That makes it so very special,' Alva said. Tears drifted down her cheeks.

Carlos lifted her chin with his fingers and wiped the tears away.

'Sorry, I'm just so emotional.' She looked at the ring sparkling on her finger. 'My ring is so beautiful. I love it. Thank you for giving it to me.'

'And you are happy?'

'You can't believe how happy I am,' she smiled at him through her tears.

'And I can say the same, my love.' He held her very close and kissed her.

Even with Cian and Natalie here, Alva still felt shy when they arrived at the main house, holding the ring against her dress afraid someone in the family would see it before Carlos mentioned they were engaged. But she needn't have worried, as he took hold of her left hand and the ring was hidden when they walked into the drawing room where everyone waited. Julie and Pedro, Nuria and Pacqui welcomed her effusively, everyone was kissed. This time she was introduced to Carlos's grandmother, Abuela, who was an elderly woman who welcomed her warmly as well. They all spoke English, and she regretted that she hadn't more words of Spanish which she could have used.

Then a butler came in with a tray carrying an ice bucket with a bottle of cava in it. The glasses were already on the table and he poured cava for each of them and handed the glasses around.

'This is a special occasion,' Pedro said, standing up, and we want to raise a toast to Alva, Cian and Natalie who are now part of our family. And David, Sarah and their children too, whom we hope to meet soon. *Salud.*' They all raised their glasses and toasted them both.

Then Carlos stood up. 'I have a few words to say as well,' he said. They waited.

Alva sat there with bated breath, trying hard to calm herself knowing this was the moment. He turned to Alva, took her hand and she stood up beside him.

'I have just asked Alva to marry me, and she has accepted my proposal,' Carlos announced to the assembled family with a broad smile.

There was an explosion of excited voices. Everyone stood up, and there was much kissing and hugging and many congratulations. Carlos turned and kissed Alva, and then took her hand and showed them the beautiful diamond ring he had just put on her finger.

244

There was delight then, as everyone knew that it was his mother's ring.

'I am so happy for you, Alva.' Julie hugged her. 'And congratulations Carlos, you have certainly chosen a very wonderful woman to share your life.'

'Carlos, and Alva, congratulations to you both, *estamos muy contentos.*' Pedro kissed her and Carlos and seemed delighted at the news.

'Hey, you kept that a very tightly guarded secret,' Cian hugged her, as did Natalie.

'It was a surprise to me as well,' she admitted. 'And only happened recently.'

'I'm delighted for you.' Cian hugged her.

'Your ring is really beautiful,' Natalie admired it.

'Carlos only gave it to me this evening.'

'It's time for dinner,' Julie announced, and they moved into the dining-room, and sat around the table, still chatting and talking about Alva and Carlos's plans for the future.

'So when are you getting married, have you set a date?' Pedro asked.

'Not yet,' Carlos smiled at Alva.

'As soon as we can,' she said.

Carlos took her hand and kissed it.

'Let it be here, we would love that,' Julie said.

'What do you think, Alva?' Carlos asked.

'At least we would probably have good weather. In Ireland we can't rely on it.'

'I just want to be with you, Alva, whatever the weather.' Carlos seemed quite happy.

'I can't believe this, Alva. You have agreed to marry me.' Carlos kissed her that night in bed.

'Tonight was wonderful, everyone was so glad for us.'

'We'll get married as soon as we can,' he murmured.

She couldn't believe it had happened either. She glanced at the black velvet box on the bedside table. It was a sign of their love, and Carlos's pledge to her of a life which would be spent together, hopefully over many years. But as usual Darren came into her mind.

The strange individual he had become was still a danger to her and she really couldn't see that she would ever return to her apartment with any degree of safety when she went back to Dublin. Not that it mattered if she was getting married and would probably stay living with Carlos until then. But neither could she drive her car, and must continue to use taxis. It took the gloss from the happiness she felt with Carlos. Would they be able to live a normal life, she wondered.

And if Darren continued to plead *not-guilty,* she would have to give evidence and be cross examined by the prosecution and defence, and the thought of that frightened her. And that led her on to think that if he was not convicted and was set free, would their lives be in danger then? And she had heard that very often the victims of violence were not told when the perpetrator was released so would they have to look over their shoulders every day of their lives if Darren found out where they were living?

She felt guilty then. Thinking that she had brought Carlos into this web of intrigue which had nothing to do with him.

Perhaps she should have thought more about it. Agreeing to marry Carlos was like being on an emotional rollercoaster. She truly loved him, but prayed that he would not be affected by her connection with Darren.

She opened her eyes and looked at Carlos. He slept holding her close with his arm around her, a look of peace and contentment on his face. But would he look like that in the future if Darren was free to walk the streets and be a danger to them both. She hadn't been sleeping well in recent months and it was only now since she had been with Carlos that her sleep pattern had improved and particularly since they had come to Spain. She tried to put the whole thing out of her mind. It was destroying her happiness with Carlos and she wasn't going to allow Darren do that. She turned in the big bed, put her arm around Carlos, closed her eyes and drifted off.

The following day, they spent time by the pool for a while, and then Carlos and Julie took Cian, Natalie and herself in to visit the city of Cadiz. There they spent some time walking through the narrow streets and later they went to a restaurant which overlooked the sea and had lunch, while Carlos and Julie chatted about the history of Cadiz. It was fascinating to listen to them.

'I love spending time with you and Cian and Natalie, it's been wonderful to get to know you better, it's been too long since I had a chance to love you. All those years lost have been cruel. I've really missed you all.' There were tears in Julie's eyes. She took Alva's hand and clasped it tight. 'I want to have all that time back. Those precious years. Do you think you can give it to me?'

'Of course, we can,' Alva said, and kissed her. As did Cian.

'And maybe I'll be able to meet David as well, please persuade him if you can. I want to meet his wife and my grandchildren. I long for that.'

'We'll talk to him, see what we can arrange,' Cian said, looking at Alva.

'Thank you.' Julie was grateful.

They could see her emotion. It was quite obvious.

'Don't worry, he will be able to meet you soon, it's just the circumstances at the moment.'

'I hope that's all it is, I couldn't bear it if he didn't want to meet me? Is there any particular reason, do you know?' She seemed very concerned.

'Not as far as we know,' Cian shook his head.

Alva didn't know what to say.

247

'I'm sure he'll be over to see you soon,' Carlos said, smiling. His pleasant attitude smoothed over the awkward moment.

'I hope so,' she said softly.

After lunch, they went back to the house for siesta, and everyone rested for a couple of hours including Alva and Carlos. The night before had been very late and she felt she needed the rest. She was trying to get used to the Spanish traditions and it was lovely to be with Carlos during the day.

When she awoke she went out on to the balcony and sent an email to David. She wanted to tell him about her engagement, and didn't want him to hear from Cian when he had gone back. She told him about Carlos, emphasising that she was very much in love and hoped they were happy for her. When she had sent it off, she felt a certain sense of relief. She would have hated to exclude him from her life because of his resignation from the company.

Checking her inbox she saw an email from their estate agent about the sale of their father's house, and was delighted to see that he had received a very good firm offer and wished to know if they would accept it. She replied saying that she would discuss it with her brothers and get back to him.

Later she talked with Cian.

'What do you think?'

'It's a good offer.'

'I'll call David and see what he thinks,' she said.

'Hope he agrees with us.'

She phoned there and then and told him. To their surprise he agreed immediately. 'Yeah, go ahead and accept. We must get the house sold as soon as possible. And I just see your email there, congratulations on your engagement. Hope you'll both be very happy.' He actually sounded glad for her and she was surprised at that. And then Sarah spoke. 'Congrats Alva, it's wonderful news. When's the big day?'

'We don't know yet, soon I hope.'

'A chance to wear the hat then, I'll have to dust it off,' she laughed.

'We look forward to seeing you when we get back.'

'See you soon.'

'I'll email the estate agent and tell him to go ahead.'
She said to David.

'Yes,' he said

Alva and Cian looked at each other with a sense of relief.

'Thank God,' she whispered. Although the feeling that suddenly things were moving at last was uncomfortable. She didn't want her old home sold, but there was no alternative.

Chapter Twenty-six

Julie and Carlos arranged trips for them to take while they were staying in Cadiz and the following day, they drove to see Ronda, a most beautiful town in the mountains.

'At this time of the year, almost every town in Andalusia has a traditional festival or féria,' Carlos explained. 'The place itself is amazing and the old town is split by a gorge. One half is fifteenth century and the other half is Moorish. The Puento Nuevo is a stone bridge which spans the towns. We'll have a chance to see the most incredible views all over the valley below.'

'Look up,' Julie pointed, and they were all astonished to see the ancient white town clinging atop the precipitous mountain peaks.

There was already a festive atmosphere and the cafés and restaurants were packed with people enjoying themselves.

'The striped tents selling drinks along the streets are called casetas,' Carlos told them.

Alva was enthralled to hear the sound of music and see people dancing traditional flamenco, clapping, and twirling in time to the rhythm.

'We should have worn our flamenco dresses,' said Julie.

'I don't have a flamenco dress unfortunately,' laughed Alva.

'We'll dress up when we go to Jerez, the Wine Festival is on there. We have lots of dresses at home you can have,' Julie said.

Alva smiled, really enjoying herself. 'Look over there.' She pointed to a group of women gathered around a bar, all wearing frilled flamenco dresses in a myriad of gorgeous colours, and dancing to the music of a band playing in the bar.

Julie clapped her hands, and twirled around joining with the women. 'Come on, girls, dance.'

Alva felt self-conscious, not sure that she could follow any of the steps, but Natalie immediately made an effort, Cian and Carlos clapping.

Alva felt rather awkward, but then Julie danced towards her, and slowly she managed to follow her steps. They all enjoyed themselves, and when the music stopped, there was a round of applause from the Spanish women.

'We always appreciate when people make an effort,' said Carlos. 'That was Sevillianas, a folk dance of Seville, and it's popular at férias. And you both did very well.' He hugged Alva and Natalie. They ordered drinks from the caseta and continued walking through the town. Every now and then joining spontaneously in the dancing which was happening in the casetas. And every age group took part. Men and women. Grandmothers. Grandfathers. And children too. All dressed up in flamenco outfits.

'It's wonderful,' Alva said.

'Great fun,' Natalie laughed. 'We'll have to persuade Cian to shake the light fantastic at the next caseta.'

'Not me, thank you very much,' he laughed. 'I've always had two left feet you know that.'

'Never too late to change. Doesn't the music get you moving?' Natalie teased.

'I love the music,' Cian laughed. 'But the feet won't follow the rhythm.'

'There are lots of men dancing, you can do it too if you make an effort,' smiled Natalie.

'They've probably been doing it all their lives, it's like us with Irish dancing.'

They laughed.

Carlos and Cian stood outside while the girls stopped at a shop, and walked in, looking at the items on the shelves. Mostly it was ceramic, and there were many pieces on sale. They all bought souvenirs and continued to wander along the narrow streets. Next was a jewellery shop, and they spent time admiring the fabulous earrings and bracelets inside. Suddenly, Alva noticed some gold cuff links and asked the man to take them out of the display. Quickly, she chose an oblong pair which had an engraving of a stallion on each of them. They were exquisite. She asked the price, and then just handed her credit card to the man. He spoke English and told her that they were 18 ct. gold. She nodded and prayed that Carlos wouldn't come in and see her buying them. She wanted to give him a surprise at Christmas.

They continued on and passed the afternoon, finally sitting down to eat delicious paella at a restaurant on the square as the night began to close in. The lights of the lanterns which hung above were bright and joyful and they could still hear the music echoing.

'This will go on until the small hours,' Carlos said.

'Pity we can't stay,' Alva smiled.

'We'll catch another féria,' he said. 'The Jerez Wine Festival is on now as well. It coincides with the beginning of the grape harvest and is a great celebration.'

'That would be nice, I didn't stay long enough when I was there and missed seeing the city itself,' admitted Alva with regret.

'And we could also visit the Royal Equestrian School, and see some amazing horse riding,' he suggested.

For the festival in Jerez, the girls were loaned flamenco outfits by Nuria and Pacqui. Alva was given a pretty red and white flounced dress, which to her amazement fitted her perfectly. 'This is fantastic.' She twirled in the dress.

'It's beautiful on you.' Julie was delighted.

'Let's see what suits you, Natalie.' She searched in the wardrobe and took out a pink dress and held it up against her. 'I think it's a bit long.'

'Just a little.'

Julie examined it.

'It would be ruined if it dragged on the ground,' Natalie said.

'I'll ask Anna to take it up a little,' said Julie.

'Would she be able to do that?'

'Oh yes, Anna is a very good seamstress and can do anything in that line.'

She asked her and when she came into the room, she immediately agreed, measuring Natalie, and noting the amount she would have to take up the dress so that it would be perfect.

Julie herself wore a yellow dress, Pacqui blue, and Nuria Green.

Cian wasn't as tall as Carlos, but they found a jacket which fitted him, and he looked very handsome wearing a broad brimmed hat, and a red scarf around his neck. Carlos and Pedro wore black, over a white shirt, and Carlos had a red cummerbund around his waist, and Pedro a red fringed sash. All wore black hats.

'Cian, you'll just have to learn to dance flamenco, you look a million dollars. I'm falling in love with you all over again,' Natalie said, smiling.

'I'll drive the carriage,' he grinned.

'Definitely.'

They hugged each other.

Alva posed. 'What do you think?' She raised her arm in the air and clicked her fingers.

'You look great.' They clapped.

'When they were dressed, they each tied up their hair, and held it with a coloured comb, and tucked a flower in it.

'I think we really look the part,' Alva laughed.

'And so we do.' Julie put an arm around her and held her close.

'I'm really looking forward to seeing the féria in Jerez,' Alva said.

'We'll travel in the cars, but the carriages and horses will have already gone on ahead.'

There were two carriages, and the paintwork on both was a shining black, the wheels painted red. The carriage lamps were bright brass, as were other accoutrements. The drivers' clothes matched the colours of the carriage cushions, and there were two grey horses drawing each carriage with colourful red and yellow tassels around their necks, and pom poms hung in the horses' manes and tails. They sat into the carriages, and as the horses drew them along in the procession they were really excited.

They loved the experience. Taking photos of the people in the audience who were watching, and themselves as well. There were casetas here too and lots of music with people celebrating and carrying large baskets of grapes. Groups of men and women trampled in vats of grapes barefoot, the traditional way to release the grape juices and begin fermentation.

In the competitions, there was a prize for the best carriage and Caballos Rodriguez won First and Pedro and Carlos were delighted with the win, it was very prestigious.

On the following day, they took it easy. Alva, Carlos and Julie went riding along the beach. The horse Carlos had given her was a bit more sprightly than Tonto, but she was getting used to riding again and didn't feel quite so awkward when she saw how adept Julie and Carlos were on the back of a horse. It seemed they were naturals.

They rode out on to the long white beach which seemed to go on for miles, glimmering under a cloudless blue sky. The waves curled on to the deserted sandy beach and the horses enjoyed galloping along in the shallows, the water splashing up against them. Alva felt exhilarated as she rode along. This was something else. But then Julie took the lead and the pace of her horse suddenly increased and he raced ahead of Carlos and Alva. It seemed Julie was well in control, Alva thought, and was amazed at how she could manage the animal. Then he took the bit and galloped even faster. Carlos followed, although Alva stayed behind, unable to believe how fast Julie's horse was travelling. She watched Carlos put on speed, but he couldn't catch her. Then unexpectedly, the horse stopped and Julie was thrown over his head and with horror Alva saw the horse's hooves trample on Julie as she lay on the sand. Very worried she pushed her own horse faster, but could see that Carlos had reached her by how. He dismounted and bent down to check on her. Alva reached them and she dismounted as well and held both Carlos's horse and her own by the reins. Julie's horse was calmly chewing on some grass at the beginning of the sand dunes nearby and seemed unaffected by his mad run along the sand.

Carlos was talking on his phone to someone, but he was speaking rapidly in Spanish and she couldn't understand, although he was probably calling for an ambulance. As far as she could see Julie was unconscious and he looked desperately worried. There was a glaze of perspiration on her skin, and her lips were purple. All of them were only wearing light clothes and she regretted that she had nothing to cover Julie to counteract the shock of her fall.

Alva didn't speak to Carlos, feeling that she would be in the way, and concentrated on holding the reins of the horses. The area they were in was very desolate and she could see there were no houses nearby so no help could be expected from anyone. She prayed that help would come quickly, but then didn't even know if a vehicle could make its way along the beach at this point, and how long it would take. And time seemed to crawl as they waited there, Carlos crouched over Julie.

Eventually, she was drawn to look up in the sky when she heard the noise of a helicopter engine in the distance, and could see it fly towards them.

'Alva, can you keep the horses away from the helicopter, they'll be very frightened by the noise,' Carlos asked urgently.

She nodded, and prayed she could control the animals. Then she led their two horses across the beach to join Julie's horse, and took the three of them over the dunes out of sight of the rapidly approaching helicopter.

Alva whispered the Our Father and Hail Mary, and she repeated the prayers over and over. It was only now that shock affected her. Tears drifted down her cheeks, and she couldn't stop crying, beginning to shake as she thought of what had just happened. She had only found her mother, and to know that she might lose her again suddenly was just too much.

Eventually, the helicopter rose into the sky again, flew towards the city and disappeared. She found a narrow pathway at the back of the dunes and walked along holding the horse's leads, and couldn't believe how quiet they were. Her phone rang, but she couldn't take it out of her pocket, but knew it was probably Carlos. A group of riders came towards her, and she stopped so that she wouldn't be in their way. But they stopped as well, and she recognised Pedro.

'Are you all right, Alva?'

'Yes, I'm fine, but Julie …' she was in tears again.

'Carlos called me from the helicopter, and we're praying she will be all right. We'll take the horses back,' he said. 'Do you feel like riding?'

'Yes.' She put her foot in the stirrup and mounted the horse, returning to the stables with Pedro and the men who lead the two stallions.

It was only then she was able to talk to Carlos.

'How is Julie?'

'She's in theatre at the moment.'

'Will she be all right?' Alva asked breathlessly.

'I hope so.'

'I must call Cian,' she said, dreading the thought.

'I told him what happened, he's on his way to the hospital, I tried to call you.'

'I couldn't take a call because I was leading the horses. Anyway, I'll go in to you as well, I want to be with Julie.'

'Pedro is coming in, he'll bring you.'

'See you soon.'

They left for the hospital immediately after they arrived at the stables. Alva sat beside Pedro. She felt so shocked, she couldn't imagine something like this happening to Julie.

'He was galloping so fast, he was like a wild thing,' she murmured after a while.

'He had got the bit between his teeth and nothing was going to stop him.'

'It's tragic.'

'We've all fallen from time to time, but none of us have been injured seriously. The doctors are doing various scans now so we should have some information soon.'

She sat outside Intensive Care with Carlos, Nuria, Pacqui and other members of the family. They were all silent. Waiting for hours to know how Julie was. But receiving very little factual information. Julie had been put into an induced coma now and Pedro was the only one who was allowed in to see her. He sat by her bedside but he didn't know how Julie was either as the results of all the scans were not fully available yet.

Later that evening, a doctor appeared with Pedro, and Carlos stood up and walked towards him.

'We have results of the scans,' the doctor said.

'It isn't good,' said Pedro.

'Give me the details,' Carlos asked the doctor.

They stood together, listening.

'She has kidney failure as a result of her injuries,' Carlos translated.

'My God,' Alva was horrified, and she put her arm around Cian. 'What does that mean, exactly?' she asked.

'They don't know yet, but it could mean transplantation.'

Alva was desperately worried.

Already she had decided to stay here in Spain until Julie was well. She could work remotely. If she was staying here, then her brothers could handle the sale of their old home and she could go back for a couple of days to sign documents, and finish off clearing it out.

It was the following morning when she returned to the house with Carlos. She was exhausted after spending all night at the hospital.

Cian and Natalie had deferred their flight home. And Alva took a chance and called David. Whether he would be concerned was another thing, but she had to tell him.

'I'm calling …' She hesitated for a few seconds, but continued on. 'To tell you that Julie has had an accident and is in hospital.'

'Oh …'

As she expected he didn't seem very interested. But she went on to tell him the details of what had happened, and mentioned transplantation as well. She ended the conversation after that and said she would let him know how Julie was recovering. She turned off the phone, disappointed.

Over the days, they took it in turns to sit with Julie, and slowly the doctors brought her out of the coma. They had done a lot of tests and then she was put on dialysis. But because both of her kidneys were failing due to the injury, she would never survive without transplantation.

Chapter Twenty-seven

'We might have to delay our wedding, *mi amor*,' Carlos kissed Alva softly.

'We haven't set the date yet.'

'No, but I was hoping that it would be soon.'

'I don't mind a delay. We will be together in the meantime and that's all that matters.' She leaned closer to him in the bed, wanting him to know how she felt. Every nuance of her love. 'But it's all about Julie now. I couldn't go ahead until she's better. I have found my mother and I want her to give me away which is very important to me,' Alva said. 'Let us hope that a kidney will become available. Julie might not survive on dialysis only, and a transplant may be the only option.'

'But you must keep in mind that transplant is not always guaranteed to work. You would have to face the emotional consequences of that.' He cupped her face in his hand and kissed her. 'I worry about you, and Cian too. This has been a terrible tragedy for all of us.'

As they spent day after day at the hospital, the time ate up their holidays. But for Cian and Natalie, they had overstayed their original long weekend, and now rather than stay on, Cian offered to go back to the office and leave Alva here to work remotely, so that she could watch over Julie. Natalie went with Cian and Carlos to Dublin, and Nuria to Madrid.

'Thank you for doing that, Cian, I can work from here for the moment,' she said, very grateful to her brother. Carlos had a lot of appointments in his clinic with patients who needed his attention and he couldn't cancel the list.

'I'm going to miss you, Carlos.' She hated the thought of being here without him.

'Father and Pacqui will be back in Seville, so I think you should stay there with them,' he said.

'Do you close up the houses here?'

'Not completely, the family come out occasionally during the year.'

'I'll have to see Julie every day,' she insisted.

'Jose will drive you out, but as Julie is on the list for transplant, she will be moved to a Barcelona hospital which specialises in transplantation. We hope that she will receive a kidney soon,' Carlos explained.

'But she will be all alone. I think I should be with her. I'm sure your father won't be able to spend a lot of time there, he has to run his business, and probably can only travel back and forth to see her.'

'That's true. But it would be very lonely for you in Barcelona.'

'I don't care about that. I'll get a hotel for the length of time she will be in hospital, and I can work from there.'

'You're very generous to do that.'

'She is my mother,' she said softly.

'We can certainly organise a hotel for you. That's no problem.'

'Thank you.'

Jose the chauffeur drove them to the airport the following day, and it was very emotional for Alva to say goodbye to Carlos. He was last to go through, as Cian and Natalie went on ahead and it gave Alva and Carlos a few minutes to themselves.

'Look after yourself, Alva, I will be thinking about you all the time.' He put his arms around her and held her close. 'At least you will be safe here from Darren. He won't know where you are.'

'That is a relief.'

'I will call you as soon as I get back.'

'Please, I'll be waiting.'

'I must go,' he kissed her again before he walked through with a quick wave, and disappeared.

She stood there for a while, but eventually she left the airport and went back to where Jose was waiting for her in the car. She was silent as they drove back to Cadiz. Her fingers covering her engagement ring as if she was holding Carlos's hand. While the driver could speak English as did the rest of the family, she couldn't even think of saying anything to the man, her heart beating rapidly as she thought about Carlos, and wondering when she would see him again.

Julie was transferred to the hospital in Barcelona, and Alva travelled with her in the helicopter. She was booked into a hotel within walking distance. Then it was just herself and Julie. Although Pedro and Pacqui visited a couple of times a week. Alva talked when Julie had energy, although it wasn't often. The rest of the time, Alva spent on her laptop working. Sending emails back and forth to the Dublin office. Before she had come out to Spain on holiday, there had been some personnel changes because of the resignation of Hugh, David and Darren. They had promoted the Assistant Accountant into Hugh's position as Chief Accountant. A Sales Manager for Ireland to replace Darren, and David's replacement was now working in France. They had been lucky to find a young woman who spoke both French and Spanish so she could deal with clients in both countries if necessary. Presently, as Alva was in Spain, she could deal with the clients here. And already she had been on to Bodega Los Vinos, and was glad to be in a position to place an order for those sherries she had chosen when she met Antonio Sanchez in Jerez earlier in the year. She had also made a decision to try to learn the language and felt that this time gave her the opportunity she needed. When she chatted with Julie, they sometimes used her limited Spanish, and it helped her absorb the basics of the language.

Carlos texted or called as often as he could, but it was usually when he had finished work at night that they had the best chance to see one another on WhatsApp. But it meant he was very much at a distance, and the physical side of their relationship was on hold. But the following weekend, he flew out on Saturday. She was thrilled, although it was only for twenty-four hours, but still it re-ignited their love, and Julie was very happy to see him as were the rest of the family. They all relied on Carlos.

On the way to the hospital she told him that the doctors were waiting there with Pedro to discuss the possibility of transplant for Julie. He met them in the foyer.

'It's good you're here,' Pedro said.

'Have they talked to Julie about it?'

'Not yet, they only called me a short while ago, so it's good timing. You can ask all the right questions and explain what the doctors are saying exactly, and in Spanish and English if necessary.'

They walked towards the medical suite, and found the medical team gathered there.

The most senior man there shook their hands, and asked them to sit down. He went on to explain that Julie's condition had worsened and she was in need of a transplant urgently and there wasn't much chance of a donor becoming available on the Spanish register.

Carlos asked some medical questions which Alva didn't really follow. But with her minimal Spanish she understood a certain amount of what they said.

'They're talking about a living donor,' Carlos explained. 'And a family member would be the best possibility.'

'I could be that person,' she offered immediately.

'You would?' Pedro asked.

'Of course, Julie is my mother.'

'I don't know why I am surprised. You are the most obvious person.'

'Please arrange for me to be tested immediately.'

'Thank you so much Alva,' Pedro kissed her.

Carlos spoke to the doctors, and they agreed with whatever he said, and smiled at Alva. Nodding with satisfaction.

There was more discussion then, and it seemed to Alva that the pace had accelerated.

'The medical people want to go ahead with tests as soon as possible, will that be all right with you,' Carlos asked her. 'They'll begin today, they don't want to waste any time.'

'Of course it will, and I hope that I'll be compatible.'

'I hope so too.'

Alva was admitted to the department and the team of doctors who would oversee the tests which would be carried out on her. Among these were blood tests, tissue type, tests for any illnesses which might be in her system. Ultrasound. Angiogram. Scans. She was kept in overnight, and the following morning they allowed Carlos in to see her, although, as many of the tests were carried out in different areas of the hospital, and he was a doctor, he still wasn't admitted while they were being carried out. Eventually, she didn't see him anymore and knew that by then he had left for the airport. All the time she prayed that her kidney would be compatible with Julie and that she could help save her life.

It took a few days for the results to be analysed and become available, and it was frustrating to wait. She didn't discuss the possibility that she would be a living donor with Julie. They had decided that because of the uncertainty of the result, they wouldn't mention what was happening to Julie as it would only upset her if Alva wasn't compatible.

Carlos flew back on Saturday much to Alva's joy, but to their disappointment the results of the tests revealed that Alva wasn't compatible, and she would be unable to donate one of her kidneys to Julie. Alva was very upset, and when Carlos and herself were told the sad news, she immediately burst into tears. Carlos put his arm around her, and together they left the office.

Now it was Cian who was approached. Alva called and asked him if he would be willing to be tested. He immediately agreed and flew out. But sadly, he was not compatible either.

They were faced with a problem. There was only one person left and that was David and his attitude towards Julie so far had been hostile.

'One of us has to approach David. Should it be you Cian or me?' Alva asked him.

'I don't know.'

'David is very resentful towards me, Cian. He blames me for the fact that he had to resign from the company. Maybe it might be better for you to talk to him?'

'Perhaps,' Cian agreed.

'Hopefully, you will be able to persuade him to agree. You heard me talk to him on the phone, and when I told him about Mum's accident, he didn't say anything at all. Nothing.'

Cian shook his head.

'I've been thinking, I'll fly home with you for a few days and we can go through the rest of Dad's things before the sale of the house goes through, then there will be two of us to try and persuade David to agree to be tested,' Alva suggested. 'I'll ask our solicitor, John, to have any documents ready for signing and we can do both.'

Chapter Twenty-eight

Ostensibly, Alva flew back to Dublin to sign documents for the sale of the house, although she was very reluctant to leave Julie. But Pedro and Pacqui flew up to Barcelona to see her more often so Alva didn't feel so bad leaving her mother.

She took a taxi from the airport and went straight to Carlos's apartment. Although he couldn't meet her at the airport because of his commitments, there was a bottle of champagne on ice, with a beautiful bouquet of red roses waiting for her with a lovely note assuring her of his love.

Still using a taxi, she went into the office and was delighted to meet some of the newer members of staff. Cian filled her in on what had been going on in her absence and she held a meeting with the more senior members of staff as well. They gave her a lovely round of applause after her few words which made her feel she might have been missed by some of them at least.

Then the temp on reception called her and said Darren was waiting to see her. She didn't know what to say, shocked that he had the nerve to disobey the barring order.

'Has he come in before?' she enquired.

'No, he phoned today and asked if you were here, and I said you were,' the girl said. 'So he's here now.'

Alva realised that as she was only a temp, she wouldn't know that Darren had worked here before, or that they had any connection with each other. She didn't know what to do, but called Cian and told him.

'I'll go down.'

'I will too. There hasn't been any further texts lately or letters, so maybe he has accepted the situation.'

They went down together to see Darren sitting comfortably in one of the armchairs reading a newspaper.

'Hi Darren …' she said, trying to force herself to be friendly.

'Darren …' Cian murmured.

'You're looking very well Alva with that nice suntan. You must have been away, have you?'

'No, but the weather has been good,' she wasn't going to tell him anymore than that.

'Sit down,' he waved to the other armchairs. 'Let's have a chat.'

'We haven't much time,' she told him. 'We're very busy.'

'Come on, we haven't seen each other in a long time, why don't we catch up? But maybe on second thoughts why don't we go into one of the offices where we can have some privacy?'

'What do you want, Darren?' she said, beginning to be irritated by his attitude.

'As I said, a catch up.'

'You're not supposed to be in here. There's a barring order against you,' Cian said.

'Have you got your measuring tape?'

'If we call the Gardai you'll be in more trouble.'

'Stop calling the Gardai every time you see me, Alva. All I want to ask is for you to tell them I'm not guilty of anything, and they'll let me off. You've pressed charges against me.'

'But you are guilty of a whole lot of things.'

'If you don't press charges then I'll be free.'

'I'm not pressing charges, the Gardai are taking a case against you, so it doesn't matter what I do.'

'They won't take a case if you don't support it. You can just tell them you have no evidence, and the whole thing will collapse.'

'I can't do that.'

'I could make you,' he hissed, his face contorted.

'Go away, Darren.' She just waved at him.

'What's that on your finger?' he asked, standing up.

She suddenly realised he had seen her engagement ring, and she was furious with herself that she hadn't thought of taking it off.

'Darren, come on, we told you we're busy.' Cian moved closer to him.

'Fuck off you.'

'Darren, we've no more time to waste,' Alva intervened.

'So, you're getting married, are you?' he sneered sarcastically.

'Yes, I am.'

'Probably to your security man no doubt.'

'Please Darren,' Alva said, and moved towards the lift.

'Bitch,' he snarled. 'I'll catch up with you. Don't think you'll ever escape me.' He came towards her but Cian put out his arm and pushed him away.

Darren took a swing at Cian, and caught him on the chin. Cian almost fell but grabbed a table, and steadied himself.

'I'll ring the Gardai,' said Alva, and pressed in the digits on her phone and talked to the person who answered. Luckily, the lift was still at ground level and they were able to get inside and close the doors, and pressed the button to go up.

'Are you all right?' she asked Cian.

'Come back here, you two, don't think you can escape me.'

They could hear Darren's voice in the distance.

'He's going up the stairs.'

'We can't get out of the lift now.' Alva looked at Cian.

'Better go down. Hopefully, the Gardai will come quickly.' She pressed the button for the lift which went to the ground floor still able to hear Darren who was shouting somewhere on one of the other floors.

To their relief, as they stepped out of the lift a Garda car appeared outside, and two Gardai came in.

'He went upstairs. Listen to him shouting,' Alva said.

The Gardai took the stairs two at a time.

Cian followed them.

And after a few minutes they dragged a protesting Darren downstairs.

'It's not me you want,' he shouted. 'It's them.' He pointed at Alva and Cian.

'He's broken a barring order,' Alva explained to the Garda. 'And he's threatening us.'

'Right. Down to the station with you.'

One Garda arrested Darren and brought him out to the car, and the other one took their details.

Alva rang her solicitor, John, and told him what had happened. He said he would go to court for her if necessary, although for Darren there could be a prison term for breaking a barring order and a fine, but that it may be just added to another sentence. He said he would check what had happened with Darren in the meantime and let her know.

Cian drove Alva over to their family home, and for the first time she felt a little more relaxed because Darren was in police custody now and she wasn't in danger. Cian had called David and asked him to come over to the house as well to look through the last of their Dad's belongings before the sale was completed.

They let themselves in, and Alva took off her camel jacket, and blue cashmere scarf, and put them hanging over the end of the bannisters. To her, it looked like she was still living here in her old home.

'Cian, would you check the kitchen window please, Carlos arranged for it to be repaired?' she asked him.

'Yeah, sure.'

All of the furniture had already been auctioned or given to charity shops and the house looked bare and empty except for an odd piece. She wandered upstairs. Softly touching the doors and walls with her fingers, reminded of how it was when she was a child. Then she went into her father's bedroom, sat on the window seat and stared into the room which had played such a major part in her life.

'Dad,' she whispered. Suddenly anxious to talk to him. 'Dad, are you there? I hate leaving because you are here. And I'll be so lonely without you knowing that someone else will be living in this house. Sleeping in this room. Eating in the dining-room. Doing all those precious things that you did, and we did as a family. Give me an answer Dad, just let me hear your voice, a whisper, a murmur, anything so I know it's you.' Tears welled up and trickled down her cheeks. She wiped her eyes as she heard the front door open downstairs, stood up, and walked out on to the landing. She leaned over the bannisters and waved at David who stood looking up at her. Then she hurried down.

'Congratulations on your engagement,' David walked towards her with a broad smile and she was amazed that his mood seemed to have improved so much. He held out his arms and hugged her. Then he caught sight of her ring and admired it immediately. 'That's a beautiful ring.'

'Thank you.'

He kissed her. 'Sorry I've been such a creep since we had to resign. You were only doing your job and it wasn't really your fault.'

The back door opened and Cian appeared. 'How are you, David?' he asked with a smile.

'Ok.' He shrugged. 'Although it's probably one of our last days here in our old home.' He actually seemed quite emotional which was very surprising to Alva.

'It's sad,' Cian agreed.

They stood in the hall for a few minutes, silent, staring around their old home.

Even though David said nothing about Julie, Alva decided to go ahead and mention her regardless.

'Julie is still very ill,' she said. 'Both Cian and I were tested to see if we could be living kidney donors but we were incompatible. She has been moved to a specialist hospital in Barcelona and we're just waiting now for a donor, but she isn't at all well and needs it very quickly.'

David said nothing, and there was an awkward silence.

'Do you know what we've forgotten,' Cian said suddenly.

'What?' asked David.

'The safe,' he said.

'Imagine forgetting that,' they laughed.

'I hate looking into it somehow, Dad probably kept all of his personal stuff there,' Alva said as she led the way upstairs to the bedroom.

'It does seem intrusive,' David said. 'Maybe that's why we forgot.'

They walked over to the wardrobes which spanned the width of the room.

'Do we have the password? I've forgotten where it is?' Cian asked.

'It's written on the back of a section of the wardrobe,' said Alva.

'With a whole lot of other numbers mixed in with it.' David opened the door, shifted the section and turned it over. 'See there, he used chalk.'

'Every third number backwards,' added Alva.

'Wonder would any burglar be able to work that out,' Cian laughed.

'Don't think so.'

They opened a false door at the back, and could see the safe which had been secured to the wall. Then they tapped in the password and the safe door sprang open. They stared into the aperture. 'There isn't much in there. Just a big envelope.' Alva put her hand in, removed it and looked inside. 'And there are smaller envelopes inside.'

'Are they letters?'

Alva took one of them out and examined it. 'Yes.'

'Should we read them, do you think, they could be very private?'

'They're all addressed to Dad.'

'Are there dates on them?' Cian asked.

'Let's read one and see,' Alva decided. 'Some of them have already been opened, so Dad has read them.'

They sat on the window seat and opened the letter.

'The date is 1993.'

'Who is it from?'

'It's from Julie,' Alva said in astonishment.

They stared at the letter, shocked.

'Her handwriting is beautiful, so precise.'

'What does the letter say?' Cian asked eagerly.

'I'll read it.' Alva straightened out the single page, which still had the fold marks imprinted into it.

Dear Frank, I hope that you are well and that the children are too. I'm glad you have a nurse to look after David and Alva, and I really miss both of them terribly and you too, and want to say to you that I'm doing really well here. The doctor has said that with more therapy I can hopefully return home before too long although he hasn't given me a date yet. But there will have to be more sessions, individually and group, which will help me I am sure.

I want to be a good wife to you and mother to my darling children, and I will make a supreme effort to be the person you

want me to be. It is all I want.
Your loving Julie, xxx.
'My God,' David said.
'Read another,' urged Cian.
Alva unfolded one. 'This is dated 1997.'
David and Cian looked over her shoulder.

My dear Frank, I am very sad that you do not want me to
come home. I have been longing to see Alva and David, and
particularly baby Cian. He needs his mother, and I do not know
how you can prevent me from seeing him and allow another
person to look after him instead of me. It must be very hard on
him and the other children. Now the doctors have discharged me
and say that I can manage to live normally without any support.
So I want you to come to see me and take me home. Please do
that as soon as you can, I beg you. And please do not cut me off
when I phone you. It is most upsetting.
I love you very much. Your Julie. xxx

'Dad wouldn't bring her home, I can't believe that.' Alva was
shocked.
'And she had managed to quit drinking after being in hospital,'
Cian said angrily.
They read more of the letters. One in particular was so
heartrending, Alva was reduced to tears.

My dear Frank, it is two years now since I have written to you,
and called on the phone, but you do not answer my letters or
speak to me. When I was discharged from the clinic, I managed
to rent a room in a house not far from home, and I found a part-
time job in an office in the city.
Sometimes I watch the children going to and from their different
schools. It is very hard for me to see them growing so big now, and

particularly little Cian who wouldn't know me at all, although I wonder if Alva and David would recognise me either. It is very hard for me to be so close to them, but yet not even be able to say hallo. The person who takes them to the different schools watches them like a hawk, and even though one day I walked into the playground and waved to Alva when she came out, she looked at me blankly. The teacher was there as well and asked me what I was doing. I told her that Alva was my daughter, but she immediately took her back into the building, and refused to let me talk to her. The woman who takes them to school drove up in the jeep a few moments later, and I followed her in hoping to talk to her.

'But she told me that she would call the Gardai if I didn't leave. I demanded to see Alva. But the teacher took her into another room. Obviously, you have told the school that I am not allowed to see my children. And as I have no money other than my paltry wages, I cannot fight you for custody as I have nothing to offer them.

I pray you will let me come home. My heart is broken.

Your Julie. I love you and my children. xxx

'Here's another,' Cian opened one and read.

My dear Frank, I have almost given up hope that you will write to me. Since you do not want me anymore, with the money I have saved from my job, I have decided to move to Seville, Spain. It is somewhere we enjoyed spending time together on holidays and loved. I hope to find a job there and make a new life. I will continue to write to you in case you ever change your mind.

Your Julie. I will always love you and my darling children, Alva, David and Cian. xxx

'That is so awful. I can't believe that Dad would treat her so cruelly,' Alva exploded.

'Look at the rest of the letters,' Cian took another bundle out. 'They haven't even been opened.'

'He never read them?'

Alva's eyes were full of tears.

'What is the date on that one?' She chose one out of the pile and read the postmark. This is 1999. And here's another dated 2005.'

'So Julie kept writing.'

'And this is 2000.'

'And most of them are from Spain.'

'God help her.'

David stood looking out the window, but he said nothing.

'What will we do with the letters?' Alva asked.

'Maybe we should give them back to her. They're not ours.' David suggested, turning to look at them.

'Yes, I agree with that,' Cian said.

They gathered them up and put them back in the big envelope. There was nothing else left in the safe. It was empty.

'Will we remove the safe? Why should we leave it for the new owners?'

'I could use it,' Cian said. 'I'll come back tomorrow and get it. And it was Dad's after all.'

'I'll look around the rest of the house and see if everything has been removed,' Alva said.

'Do you want to do a check as well?' she asked Cian.

He nodded.

'Have we cleared the attic?'

'I think so.'

'Maybe you'd look up there, David?'

'I will.'

She looked around the bedrooms, and lastly, in her own bedroom, she was assailed by emotion again. Remembering those years mentioned by Julie in her letters. She tried to pinpoint a day when her mother came to her school as she described in her letter. But sadly she had no recollection of it. Although her Dad had mentioned that Julie had left them when Alva was five or six.

Now she could see herself lying in her bed as a child, arms cuddled around her favourite brown teddy, and with her collection of dolls smiling at her from the shelves around the room. All those childish things had been given away when she moved out of home, and now she was sorry she hadn't kept even one of those sentimental things, as slowly she closed the door on the past.

They said a final goodbye to their old home. Cian helped Alva on with her jacket, and scarf, and she locked the door, and they hugged each other.

'Will I take the letters back to Julie? I'll be heading to Spain in a day or so,' Alva offered.

'Of course, you should do that,' Cian said. 'Will we see you before you go back?' he asked.

'Come to us for dinner tomorrow night?' offered David. 'And bring Carlos.'

Alva asked Cian to take her to the apartment to get her winter clothes, jewellery and other bits and pieces. She checked on the broken window but was glad to see that it had been properly repaired. But she didn't stay long, and found being in the bedroom very uncomfortable. She didn't think she would ever want to live here again.

Dinner with David and Sarah was very enjoyable. Sarah was an excellent cook, and served up a delicious dinner. Luckily, Carlos managed to get there reasonably early and it was a very pleasant evening.

'I was very sorry to hear about Julie,' David said to Carlos, quite suddenly.

Alva was surprised.

'How is she doing now?' he asked.

'She has weakened unfortunately, but we hope that a kidney can be donated soon,' Carlos explained.

'I must send her a card,' Sarah said. 'But in the meantime, tell her we were thinking of her.'

Again, Alva was very taken aback by this change of attitude.

As they left, David came out to the car with them, and as she hugged him, he murmured a few words to her.

'I might go out to Spain to see Julie in a few days, can you text me the name of the hospital in Barcelona and her room number?'

Chapter Twenty-nine

Alva flew back to Barcelona where she found Julie much weaker then when she had left. It was a shock because she had only been gone for a few days. While Carlos had prepared her somewhat, she shouldn't have been so surprised, but she was.

She texted David and Cian then, letting them know how their mother was now. Wanting particularly to tell David. She had already given him the name of the hospital and waited anxiously to know when he was coming out to see Julie. When he finally texted her on his arrival at the airport, she was delighted, and was waiting for him in the front foyer of the hospital when his taxi drew up.

'Thank you so much for coming.' She was in tears now.

'I should have been here sooner,' he murmured.

'Would you like anything? Coffee or …' she asked.

'No thanks, I'd just like to meet Julie.'

'Sure, we'll go up.' She went to the lift, and pressed the button. There was no-one else with Julie now and Alva was glad of that. They arrived at her room.

'I'll let you go in,' she said.

'Will she know me?' he asked hesitantly.

'Yes, she will.'

'Did you tell her?'

'No, there was no need.'

She stood outside the room, staring through the wide glass windows which took her eyes over the city. She was so glad David had decided to make peace with his mother. If she didn't receive a transplant in time to save her life then at least she had met all of her children, and that was most important to her. To hold the hands of her children and tell them she loved them. That she had always loved them and always wanted them.

'Alva?' David called her.

She went with him into the room where Julie lay on the bed. Their mother smiled and held both of their hands, tears in her eyes. Alva kissed her and sat close.

'It's so wonderful to have you here with me, David, at last,' she whispered.

'Cian is coming out soon,' Alva said.

'You're my darlings. This is my dream come true at last. I have my children back.'

David sat on a chair, still holding his mother's hand. 'There's something I want to say ...' he said slowly. 'Mum, I would like to give you one of my kidneys if we are compatible.'

Julie burst into a wild sob, as did Alva.

'You are wonderful,' Julie murmured, her thin arms reaching for him.

Alva and David hugged each other as well. They were overjoyed.

'Thank you for giving me a chance at life. I can't thank you enough.'

'It's the least I can do, you gave us everything,' David said gently.

Events moved very quickly after that. The doctors set up the tests for David, and then there was that endless wait. Each morning and afternoon, as only one by one the vital results came through. The week passed. And it was only when the last antibody match and tissue match were available that the medical team called them together for a meeting and were able to announce to them that David was successfully compatible with Julie and a kidney transplant between the two of them could go ahead.

They were all really happy that Julie now had a chance to live, and Alva found herself spending time in a nearby church every day. She had to admit to herself that she was brought up a Roman Catholic but these days wasn't a religious person, although she did believe in a God, and if there was a God then she was going to pray to this entity for Julie. Please give my mother another chance at life. She deserves it. She murmured as she knelt at the back of the dark silent church, her head bent, and her face hidden in her hands. Lighting a candle for her mother each day.

When they were told the approximate date the transplant would be done everyone was extremely nervous. Pedro insisted that Sarah and the children should be flown out to be here with David. Cian and Natalie arrived before the operation although Carlos wasn't free to come out until closer to the time. They didn't see either David or Julie for a few days after that. They were in quarantine and kept apart from anyone in case of infection and that made it more difficult, as they had to wish them all the best on that last day and leave their loved ones in the hands of the medical teams.

They went home to Seville as they waited. Travelling by the fast train so that Jon and Sisi would enjoy the trip. At the stud farm, the children were very excited to see all the horses, and newly born little foals, and took their first horse riding lessons on the small ponies they had there. They were thrilled, as was Sarah who had never ridden before. It made the waiting for the operation just that much easier, and for the children they could forget all about it. Although for the adults, every moment their minds were in Barcelona with Julie and David. Then the medical teams were in touch again and they told them the operations would take place in two days' time. Tension spread among them, and there was a flurry to arrange travel back.

Again, it was a waiting game. And during that time counsellors came to see them and talked them through the emotional consequences if the transplant was not successful. To Alva's joy, Carlos arrived, and they were all so glad to see him. He could always understand what the medical people were saying and would translate the details afterwards to the Irish contingent, which was such a relief to them.

On the day of the surgeries, they gathered in the waiting room. It was expected that the time it would take to remove the kidney from David and transplant it to Julie would be from three to five hours or even longer, and it certainly seemed to be far longer than that. Someone from the medical team would come in and out to let them know how things were progressing and that helped. But it was tough, and no-one knew what to say to the other, and they sat in silence, the anxiety between them palpable.

Finally, in the afternoon, the medical team came in, wide smiles on their faces. They spoke in Spanish, although Carlos translated immediately for those who couldn't speak the language.

'The transplant has been very successful, both Julie and David are recovering well.'

Alva actually understood enough with her limited Spanish, and particularly by the expression on the team's faces. And they screamed then, hugging each other, a wild emotional response from them. Alva held on tight to Carlos and then Cian and Sarah, but she wasn't able to say very much, totally overcome with emotion, just so glad that her mother and brother had got through the operation without any problems. Pedro was the only one allowed into Intensive Care to see Julie for a few minutes, and Sarah to see David. But that meant everything to them. Alva and Cian were able to see them for a short time the following day.

David and Julie made good progress and Julie felt so well she didn't even need to use the morphine pump in the first days.

'I feel so normal, the way I did before my fall. When my kidneys failed, I was always cold, and now I can actually feel the blood pumping through my body, touch my hands,' she reached out to hold Alva's, and she could immediately notice a difference.

'They're so warm, it's astonishing.'

'And it is the same in my feet and all over my body,' she smiled.

'We are all so happy for you.' Alva kissed her. 'And you are looking so well.'

'But tell me how David is?' asked Julie.

'He is very well and recovering too. Sarah is in with him now.'

'I wish I could see him,' Julie said.

'I'm sure they'll arrange that as soon as both of you are recovered sufficiently.'

'I pray he will recover. He is such a generous person with his whole life ahead of him, and with a lovely family as well. To do this for me is an extraordinary thing. When you see him will you tell him how much I love him?'

'Of course I will, I know he loves you as well,' Alva assured.

In a matter of weeks both Julie and David had made amazing recoveries from those life-changing surgeries, and Julie was well on the way to living a normal life again after her fall from the horse.

David got to know Pedro and all the family while he was recuperating from the surgery in Barcelona. And he was very grateful to Pedro for paying all of his expenses in coming out to Barcelona with Sarah and the children, and of course, all the hospital expenses as well.

For Pedro, he told David that by donating a kidney to Julie he felt that David had given the Rodriguez family a new lease of life and would have given him anything he wanted by way of thanks.

As both Julie and David were recuperating so well, Alva was able to go home with Carlos, although she missed Julie and the family, having got so used to being with them. Leading up to Christmas was always a very busy time in the wine business and it was the same for Carlos at the hospital.

To her relief there was no contact at all from Darren. John, her solicitor, told her that he had received another sentence for his behaviour that last time, and it could be added to the overall sentence when his court case would finally be heard next year.

Carlos and Alva flew out to Seville for Christmas and she was glad to have a couple of days at least to spend with the family, and would return on the twenty-seventh with Carlos. It was wonderful to see Julie, who was doing really well after her transplant surgery so much so, Alva felt her mother had completely returned to normal life. David had also recovered well.

In Seville, they celebrated with dinner on Christmas Eve, and went to Midnight Mass after that in the little local church in the village close by. On Christmas Day they took out their horses and went on their traditional ride in the morning. Julie wasn't riding yet but was looking forward to the New Year when she could get back on her horse. They called to see friends who lived on a neighbouring stud farm some distance away and returned home before siesta.

Christmas Dinner was a big affair with the extended family visiting and it was very enjoyable with grandmother Abuela there as well. Alva would have liked to stay on longer but Carlos and herself had to leave, and she had to face back to Dublin and possibly Darren. The thought of him never really left her. And she dreaded hearing from the Gardai about the court case which should happen sometime the following year.

Chapter Thirty

'How do I look?' Alva twirled in front of the full-length mirror. The off-white satin sleeveless dress with the lace overlay was exquisite.

'Wonderful,' Naomi smiled.

Alva and Carlos had a mix of Irish and Spanish traditions at their wedding. As there was no best man or bridesmaid, she particularly wanted her best friend Naomi as well as Nuria and Pacqui to be her bridesmaids. Their dresses were all the same colour as Alva's but in different designs.

Naomi now moved closer, holding the flower arrangement with the fine veil in her hands and preparing to position it with pearl combs on to Alva's hair. 'There, what do you think?'

'Thank you, it's lovely.'

Alva's phone rang.

'Probably the groom,' Naomi giggled.

Alva smiled and picked up her phone from the dressing-table and answered it.

She shook her head at Naomi as it wasn't Carlos. Although her heart dropped as she heard the voice of her solicitor. Why John had to call now, on this very day, she didn't know. She had tried so hard to put Darren out of her head this last while and now he had jumped back in again, reminding her of everything that had happened.

'Hi?' she replied.

'Hope I'm not ringing at a bad time, I know you're in Spain

now.'

'Just getting ready to leave for the church,' she said with a smile.

'Oh my God, forgive me, will I call you on another day?' he asked. She could tell he was flustered by hearing that.

'No, there's enough time and you may as well tell me whatever it is,' she assured.

'Well, it's good news and that was why I wanted to let you know as soon as possible.'

She waited, her pulse racing. Her hand gripping the phone tight.

'Darren has changed his plea to *guilty*.'

She couldn't believe what she was hearing as all this time he had insisted on pleading *not guilty* which she felt was crazy since he had been caught in the act of attempted rape, and she had all the proof of the huge number of texts he had sent, and all those letters too.

'So that means you don't have to appear in court, and obviously he will be sentenced but it's all up to the judge after that.'

'Thank God.' The breath eased out of her. 'And thank you, John. You've no idea what this means to me and Carlos.'

'I think I do,' he said. 'And I wish you every happiness on your wedding day, this is my present to you. Have a wonderful life.'

'Thank you, John,' she whispered.

The door opened and Julie appeared followed by Pacqui and Nuria. Mother of the bride, she had made an amazing recovery and was now back to normal life.

Alva turned to Julie and embraced her. 'You're looking so well,' She kissed her. 'And that colour of turquoise really suits you.'

'I have never seen you look so beautiful, your dress is magnificent,' Julie said emotionally.

Then Sarah appeared with the two children who were also dressed in off-white, Alva's flower girl and page boy. It was to be a very big wedding here in Seville. The ceremony held in the tiny village church, and the main reception in the house with marquees set up for the drinks reception, music and dancing afterwards.

When everyone else had gone on to the church, Alva and Julie stood together.

'I'm so glad you are able to give me away,' Alva put her arms around her mother. 'To know you at last means everything to me.'

'And for me too, I never thought we would be together again after all these years.' Julie held her close.

'There is something else I want to give you, I have it quite some time but I wanted to wait for the right moment,' Alva said, going across to a drawer in the bureau. Taking a parcel from it, she went back to Julie and handed it to her.

'What is this?' her mother looked puzzled.

'When we were clearing out my father's house, we found these in the safe. They are your letters which you wrote to Frank over the years.'

'Oh my God,' Julie's eyes widened with shock. 'Thank you.'

'We wanted you to have them, they are yours.'

'I can't believe Frank kept them, although I don't know whether I could read them now.' She held them close in her arms.

'Maybe you should never read them again, just burn them perhaps,' suggested Alva.

'I suppose I would not want to upset Pedro. He never knew I wrote to Frank.'

'I could take them home and burn them for you if it would be difficult to do here.'

'Yes, please do that for me.' There were tears in her eyes.

'I will. It is history now,' said Alva, putting them back in the drawer of the bureau.

'Let us go to the church.' Julie took her hand.

Alva smiled and they walked downstairs together, around the courtyard, and out through the heavy doors to where the family carriage and four white horses stood waiting. The grooms held the horses, and the coachman opened the doors and helped them climb in. Julie arranged Alva's dress in the carriage, and when they were ready, they set off the short distance to the nearby church.

Alva felt nervous now as she stared at the crowd of people there. Everyone had not been invited to the ceremony, many more people would arrive later for the reception and the dancing. At the church, the music was provided by two guitarists, and when Alva and Julie arrived in the vestibule they began to play. Naomi handed Alva her bouquet of flowers, and her niece, Sisi, the little flower girl walked ahead of Alva and Julie, carrying a velvet cushion with the two gold rings. Her nephew, Jon, the pageboy carried a velvet cushion with thirteen coins on it. This Spanish tradition was known as *arras* (or unity coins) and signified the bride and groom's commitment to share everything they have.

Arm in arm, Alva and Julie walked slowly along after the children and were followed by the bridesmaids, Naomi, Pacqui and Nuria. When they reached the altar, the children put their cushions on a small table. Julie gave Alva's hand to Carlos, and he took it and smiled at her, murmuring the words *te amo* as she stood beside him, and she said *I love you* to him.

The wedding ceremony of Alva to Carlos was conducted in both Spanish and English.

It was a very simple form they had decided on themselves, which was beautiful and reflected how deeply they loved each other.

The priest said the opening prayers, and then spoke to Carlos.

Carlos, aceptas a Alva como tu legítima esposa para tenerla y conservarla desde hoy, en lo bueno y en lo malo, en la riqueza y en la pobreza, en la salud y en la enfermedad hasta que la muerte os separe?

Smiling, Carlos said, 'Lo hago.'

Then the priest spoke to Alva.

Alva, do you take Carlos for your lawful husband, to have and to hold, from this day forward, for better, for worse, for richer, for poorer, in sickness and in health until death do you part?

Smiling too, Alva said. '*I do.'*

After that Carlos picked up her gold wedding ring from the cushion and put it on the third finger of her right hand. And she picked up his wedding ring and slid it on his finger.

The priest spoke again.

Ya sois marido y mujer.
You are now husband and wife.

Carlos leaned close to Alva and kissed her tenderly.

They were married at last.
And utterly happy to be together as one

TO MAKE A DONATION TO
LAURALYNN HOUSE

Children's Sunshine Home/LauraLynn Account
AIB Bank, Sandyford Business Centre,
Foxrock, Dublin 18.

Account No. 32130009
Sort Code: 93-35-70

www.lauralynnhospice.com

Acknowledgements

As always, our very special thanks to Jane and Brendan, knowing you both has changed our lives.

Many thanks to both my family and Arthur's family, our friends and clients, who continue to support our efforts to raise funds for LauraLynn House. And all those generous people who help in various ways but are too numerous to mention. You know who you are and that we appreciate everything you do.

Thanks to all at LauraLynn Children's Hospice.

Grateful thanks to all my friends in The Wednesday Group, who give me such valuable critique.

Special thanks to Vivien Hughes who proofed the manuscript. We really appreciate your generosity.

Special thanks to Martone Design & Print – Brian, Dave, and Kate. Couldn't do it without you.

Special thanks to Workspace Interiors.

Grateful thanks to Transland Group.

Thanks to CPI Group.

Thanks to Power Home Products Ltd., for their generosity in supplying product for LauraLynn House.

Special thanks to Cyclone Couriers and Southside Storage.

Grateful thanks also to Permanent TSB. Supervalu.

Many thanks to Elephant Bean Bags – Furniture – Outdoor.

Special thanks to CarveOn Leather – Custom Engraved Leather Goods.

And in Nenagh, our grateful thanks to Tom Gleeson of Irish Computers who very generously service our website free of charge. Nick Long, Website Designer. Walsh Packaging, Nenagh

Chamber of Commerce, McLoughlin's Hardware, Cinnamon Alley Restaurant, Ger Gavin House of Gifts, and Caseys in Toomevara.

Many thanks to Ree Ward Callan and Michael Feeney Callan.

And much love to my darling husband, Arthur, without whose love and support this wouldn't be possible.

MARTONE DESIGN & PRINT

Martone Design & Print was established in 1983
and has become one of the country's most pre-eminent
printing and graphic arts companies.

The Martone team provide high-end design
and print work to some of the country's top companies.
They provide a wide range of services including
design creation/development, spec verification,
creative approval, project management, printing, logistics,
shipping, materials tracking and posting verification.

They are the leading innovative all-inclusive solutions
provider, bringing print excellence to every market.

The Martone sales team can be contacted at
(01) 628 1809 or sales@martonepress.com

CYCLONE COURIERS

Cyclone Couriers – who support LauraLynn Children's Hospice – are the leading supplier of local, national and international courier services in Dublin. Cyclone also supply confidential mobile on-site document shredding and recycling services and secure document storage & records management services through their Cyclone Shredding and Cyclone Archive Division.

Cyclone Couriers – The fleet of pushbikes, motorbikes, and vans, can cater for all your urgent local and national courier requirements.

Cyclone International – Overnight, next day, timed and weekend door-to-door deliveries to destinations within the thirty-two counties of Ireland.

Delivery options to the UK, mainland Europe, USA, and the rest of the world. A variety of services to all destinations across the globe.

Cyclone Shredding – On-site confidential document and product shredding & recycling service. Destruction and recycling of computers, hard drives, monitors and office electronic equipment.

Cyclone Archive – Secure document and data storage and records management. Hard copy document storage and tracking – data storage fireproof media safe – document scanning and upload of document images.

Cyclone Couriers operate from
Pleasants House, Pleasants Lane, Dublin 8.
Cyclone Archive, International and Shredding, operate from
11 North Park, Finglas, Dublin 11.
www.cyclone.ie. Email: sales@cyclone.ie Tel: 01-475 7000

SOUTHSIDE STORAGE
Murphystown Road, Sandyford, Dublin 18.

FACILITIES

Individually lit, self-contained, off-ground metal and concrete
units that are fireproof and waterproof.

Sizes of units : 300 sq.ft. 150 sq.ft. 100 sq.ft. 70 sq.ft.

Flexible hours of access and 24 hour alarm monitored security.

Storage for home
Commercial storage
Documents and Archives
Packaging supplies and materials
Extra office space
Sports equipment
Musical instruments
And much much more ....

Contact us to discuss your requirements:

01 294 0517   -   087 640 7448
Email: info@southsidestorage.ie

Location: Southside Storage is located on
Murphystown Road, Sandyford, Dublin 18
close to Exit 13 on the M50

ELEPHANT BEAN BAGS

Designed with love in Co. Mayo, Ireland, Elephant products have been especially designed to provide optimum support and comfort without compromising on stylish, contemporary design.

Available in a variety of cool designs, models and sizes, our entire range has been designed to accommodate every member of your family, including your dog - adding a new lounging and seating dimension to your home.

Both versatile and practical, our forward thinking Elephant range of inviting bean bags and homewares are available in a wealth of vivid colours, muted tones and bold vibrant prints, that bring to life both indoor and outdoor spaces.

Perfect for sitting, lounging, lying and even sharing, sinking into an Elephant Bean Bag will not only open your eyes to superior comfort, but it will also allow you to experience a sense of unrivalled contentment that is completely unique to the Elephant range.

www.elephantliving.com

THE MARRIED WOMAN

Fran O'Brien

Marriage is for ever ...

In their busy lives, Kate and Dermot rush along on parallel lines, seldom coming together to exchange a word or a kiss. To rekindle the love they once knew, Kate struggles to lose weight, has a make-over, buys new clothes, and arranges a romantic trip to Spain with Dermot.

For the third time he cancels and she goes alone.

In Andalucia she meets the artist Jack Linley. He takes her with him into a new world of emotion and for the first time in years she feels like a desirable beautiful woman.

Will life ever be the same again?

Available now online
McGuinness Books
www.franobrien.net

THE LIBERATED WOMAN

Fran O'Brien

At last, Kate has made it!

She has ditched her obnoxious husband Dermot and is
reunited with her lover, Jack.

Her interior design business goes international and TV
appearances bring instant success.

But Dermot hasn't gone away and his problems encroach.

Her brother Pat and family come home from Boston
and move in on a supposedly temporary basis.

Her manipulative stepmother Irene is getting married
again and Kate is dragged into the extravaganza.

When a secret from the past is revealed Kate has
to review her choices ...

Available now online
McGuinness Books
www.franobrien.net

THE PASSIONATE WOMAN

Fran O'Brien

A chance meeting with ex-lover Jack throws Kate into a spin.
She cannot forgive him and concentrates all her passions on
her interior design business, and television work.

Jack still loves Kate and as time passes
without reconciliation he feels more and more frustrated.

Estranged husband Dermot has a
change of fortunes, and wants her back.

Stepmother, Irene, is as wacky as ever
and is being chased by the paparazzi.

Best friend, Carol, is searching for a man on the internet,
and persuades Kate to come along as chaperone on a date.

ARE THESE PATHS TO KATE'S NEW LIFE OR
ROUNDABOUTS TO HER OLD ONE?

Available now online
McGuinness Books
www.franobrien.net

ODDS ON LOVE

Fran O'Brien

Bel and Tom seem to be the perfect couple with successful careers, a beautiful home and all the trappings. But underneath the facade cracks appear and damage the basis of their marriage and the deep love they have shared since that first night they met.

Her longing to have a baby creates problems for Tom, who can't deal with the possibility that her failure to conceive may be his fault. His masculinity is questioned and in attempting to deal with his insecurities he is swept up into something far more insidious and dangerous than he could ever have imagined.

Then against all the odds, Bel is thrilled to find out she is pregnant. But she is unable to tell Tom the wonderful news as he doesn't come home that night and disappears mysteriously out of her life leaving her to deal with the fall out.

Available now online
McGuinness Books
www.franobrien.net

WHO IS FAYE?

Fran O'Brien

Can the past ever be buried?

Jenny should be fulfilled. She has a successful career,
and shares a comfortable life with her husband, Michael,
at Ballymoragh Stud.

But increasingly unwelcome memories
surface and keep her awake at night.

Is it too late to go back to the source
of those fears and confront them?

Available now online
McGuinness Books
www.franobrien.net

THE RED CARPET

Fran O'Brien

Lights, Camera, Action.

Amy is raised in the glitzy facade that is Hollywood.
Her mother, Maxine, is an Oscar winning actress, and
her father, John, a famous film producer. When
Amy is eight years old, Maxine is tragically killed.

A grown woman, Amy becomes the focus of John's
obsession for her to star in his movies and be as
successful as her mother. But Amy's insistence
on following her heart, and moving permanently to
Ireland, causes a rift between them.

As her daughter, Emma, approaches her eighth
birthday, Amy is haunted by the nightmare of
what happened on her own eighth birthday.

She determines to find answers to her questions.

Available now online
McGuinness Books
www.franobrien.net

FAIRFIELDS

1907 QUEENSTOWN CORK

Fran O'Brien

Set against the backdrop of a family feud and prejudice
Anna and Royal Naval Officer, Mike, fall in love.
They meet secretly at an old cottage
on the shores of the lake at Fairfields.

During that spring and summer their feelings for each
other deepen. Blissfully happy, Anna accepts Mike's
proposal of marriage, unaware that her family have a
different future arranged for her.

**Is their love strong enough to withstand
the turmoil that lies ahead?**

Available now online
McGuinness Books
www.franobrien.net

THE PACT

THE POINT OF THE KNIFE
PRESSES INTO SOFT SKIN ...

Fran O'Brien

Inspector Grace McKenzie investigates the
trafficking of women into Ireland and is
drawn under cover into that sinister world.

She is deeply affected by the suffering of one
particular woman and her quest for justice
re-awakens an unspeakable trauma in her own life.

CAN SHE EVER ESCAPE FROM ITS
INFLUENCE AND BE FREE TO LOVE?

Available now online
McGuinness Books
www.franobrien.net

1916

Fran O'Brien

On Easter Monday, 24th April, 1916, against the
backdrop of the First World War, a group of
Irishmen and Irishwomen rise up against Britain.
What follows has far-reaching consequences.

We witness the impact of the Rising on four families,
as passion, fear and love permeate a week of
insurrection which reduces the centre of Dublin to ashes.

This is a story of divided loyalties, friendships,
death, and a conflict between an Empire
and a people fighting for independence.

Available now online
McGuinness Books
www.franobrien.net

LOVE OF HER LIFE

Fran O'Brien

A man can look into a woman's eyes
and remind her of how it used to be
between them …once upon a time.

Photographer Liz is running a successful business.
Her family and career are all she cares about since
her husband died, until an unexpected encounter
brings Scott back into her life.

**IS THIS SECOND CHANCE FOR LOVE DESTINED
TO BE OVERCOME BY THE WHIMS OF FATE?**

Available now online
McGuinness Books
www.franobrien.net

ROSE COTTAGE YEARS

Fran O'Brien

The house in the stable yard is an empty shell
and Fanny's footsteps resound on her polished floors,
the rich gold of wood shining.

Three generations of women, each leaving the home they loved.
Their lives drift through the turmoil of the First World War,
the 1916 Rising, and the establishment of the Irish Free State,
knowing both happiness and heartache in those years.

Bina closes the door gently behind her.
The click of the lock has such finality about it.
At the gate she looks back through a mist of tears, just once.

Available now online
McGuinness Books
www.franobrien.net

BALLYSTRAND

Fran O'Brien

The future is bleak for Matt Sutherland when he is released from prison after being convicted of murder. He faces life in a changing world and rehabilitation begins in a homeless shelter.

His sisters, Zoe and Gail, anticipate his return with trepidation and are worried that their father will react badly.
When Matt calls to see them on Christmas Eve, this visit precipitates events which change their lives.

A letter is found. A secret is revealed. An unexpected meeting causes Matt to reach the limit of his endurance.

WILL IT TAKE ANOTHER DEATH TO
RIGHT THE WRONGS OF THE PAST?

Available now online
McGuinness Books
www.franobrien.net

VORLANE HALL

Fran O'Brien

TWO WOMEN LIVE OVER
TWO HUNDRED YEARS APART.

STRANGELY THEIR LIVES SEEM
TO MIRROR EACH OTHER.

Beth Harwood, passionate about history, is invited by
Lord Vorlane to research his family archive at Vorlane Hall
in Kildare, where against her better judgment
she is attracted to his eldest son, Nick.

In 1795, Martha Emilie Vorlane lived with her husband
on his sugar plantation in the British Virgin Islands.
In her journal she described her love affair with an
army captain and the pain and loss she suffered.

Reading Martha Emilie's journal captures
Beth's imagination and leads her into a situation
which changes her life dramatically.

Available now online
McGuinness Books
www.franobrien.net

THE BIG RED VELVET COUCH

Fran O'Brien

Claire allows ex-husband, Alan, to take their son, Neil, to visit his Chinese grandparents in Beijing. Alan doesn't bring his son home after the holiday and tells him that his mother doesn't want him anymore. Neil blames himself for doing something to upset his Mum.

Claire is heartbroken and travels to Beijing, but Alan refuses to reveal where Neil is, only allowing her to speak to him on the phone. If she takes legal action, he threatens to disappear with Neil and she will never see him again.

Back at work in Dublin, Claire rents two rooms in her house to help pay the mortgage and finance her trips to Beijing. But the family still refuse to allow her see or talk to Neil. She meets Jim. They fall deeply in love. But until her son comes home, Claire cannot share her life with anyone.

In a twist of fate, a pandemic overwhelms the world. Will Claire and Neil ever find happiness together again?

Available now online
McGuinness Books
www.franobrien.net

CUIMHNÍ CINN

Memoirs of the Uprising

Liam Ó Briain

(Reprint in the Irish language originally published in 1951)

(English translation by Michael McMechan)

Liam Ó Briain was a member of the Volunteers of Ireland
from 1914 and he fought with the Citizen Army of Ireland
in the College of Surgeons during Easter Week.

This is a clear lively account of the events of that time.
An account in which there is truth, humanity and, more
than any other thing, humour. It will endure as literature.

When this book was first published in Irish in 1951,
it was hoped it would be read by the young people of Ireland.
To remember more often the hardships endured
by our forebears for the sake of our freedom
we might the better validate Pearse's vision.

Available now online
McGuinness Books
www.franobrien.net